# *The Lady [illegible] the Champ*

**PAT BOOTH**

SPHERE BOOKS LIMITED
30/32 Gray's Inn Road, London WC1X 8JL

First published in Great Britain by Sphere Books Ltd 1980


*All characters in this book are fictitious, and any resemblance between them and any person, living or dead, is wholly coincidental.*

TRADE
MARK

Set in Monotype Baskerville

Printed in Great Britain by
William Collins Sons & Co Ltd
Glasgow

For Me Mates:–

*ANOUSKA*
*CATHY*
*NORMA*

and my love always to

*GARTH*

# The Lady and the Champ

# Chapter One

With serpent silence the waiter was at the table. Reverently, like a priest at High Mass, he poured the cognac into the two large balloon glasses. He placed the bottle between them and, with a hint of a bow, disappeared like an apparition through the blue haze of cigar smoke.

The two men at the table did not acknowledge his existence by so much as a flicker of an eyelid. Lew Klein slid his fingers under the bowl of his glass and gently swirled the cognac. He sniffed once, twice, at the contents and then sipped gently, feeling the luxurious fire touch his throat. Klein's fingers were soft, well-manicured, almost delicate. It was hard to believe those fingers had taken the fingers of other men and broken them, quickly and efficiently, causing the maximum pain and damage.

Sir Peregrine Hamilton, on the other hand, entertained no such ritual with the glass before him. He grabbed it as though it were a teacup without a handle and swallowed half the contents at one gulp. He belched theatrically. The point was not lost on Klein. The Sir Peregrines of this world wrote their own rules of etiquette.

Klein dominated people physically. If they crossed him, he hurt them or arranged to have them hurt. In extreme cases, men who crossed him died. Sir Peregrine Hamilton ruled the lives of others in a different but no less drastic way. He granted them favours, or withheld them. He spoke in hushed whispers to quiet old men in deep leather chairs in slumbering London clubs. And other men made fortunes or lost them. Men knew it and took care not to cross him any more than they would cross Klein. They had often wondered, the Knight of the Realm and the East End gangster, just which of them was the most ruthless.

Klein broke the silence, his words sending out blue clouds like smoke signals across the table. The two Havana cigars burned slowly on the two ashtrays at their side.

It was one of the better London clubs. A place of deep leather armchairs, good claret and impeccable service. The world outside may have rushed into the third quarter of the twentieth century but here Edwardian values prevailed. Entrance was not something money alone could buy: many had tried and proved the point. Membership was limited, available only on recommendation and subject to the severest vetting. Sir Peregrine's family had been members for generations. He loved the carefully polished antique furniture, the mosaic tiles, and above all the small dining room with its limited but excellent menu. The service that never varied in its discretion. The word privilege was bandied about so often by the popular press, but when Sir Peregrine looked around Blake's Club he savoured the word as though it were fine wine.

'He's good, Perry. Very good. I wouldn't waste my time or yours if he wasn't. As you know,' Klein waved a pink hand to take in the restaurant, 'I'm not one for the fleshpots.'

Sir Peregrine emptied the remainder of his cognac, swallowed quickly, placed the glass on the table and waited with interest to see if Klein would refill it. Klein did not move and after a few seconds Sir Peregrine refilled his own glass. He took a long pull from his cigar.

'Lewis, you're a dear chap, but you puzzle me sometimes. You know I trust your judgement in matters of boxing, but you know as well as I do that if I had a pound for every time I had heard someone say, "He's very good Perry, he's very good", I'd be a rich man by now.'

Klein laughed, a genuine laugh, and played his expected line, his arms across the table in mock surprise: 'But you *are* a rich man Perry.' Sir Peregrine laughed too, but his mirth ended as abruptly as a tropical rainstorm. The face read business.

'Lew, he's still an amateur and you've got him as the next

heavyweight champion of the world. Why, Lew? Don't you think you're rushing things a bit?'

'Not the next champion, Perry, a future one. Two, maybe three years.'

'Details, Lewis, give me details, not dreams.' Sir Peregrine relit the cigar.

'Firstly, he's not turned pro because we've not let him. He doesn't need the money, that's taken care of. We don't want him knocking over stray niggers down at Bethnal Green Baths or having some punch-drunk idiot stamping on his toes in front of thirty people. He's bigger than that. He is red-hot. Red-hot. He's had thirty-two amateur fights, lost one on points when the judges were all pissed, and k.o.'d sixteen blokes. He's never hit the canvas himself and he's unmarked. If he was still amateur in three years – which he won't be – he'd take a gold in Moscow.' Klein paused for breath and poured himself another cognac. He poured a little into Sir Peregrine's glass as well. He had made his point earlier.

'Yes Lewis, I know, but there are many good amateurs. They don't make good professionals, all of them, let alone world champions.'

'This boy,' said Klein, 'is quite simply the best. Next month he wins the A.B.A. title. He wins it, no question. Then he turns pro. A year; two, five, six, maybe eight fights. Good ones. Ones we pick. Not pushovers or old men, he doesn't need them. After that a shot at the title.' Klein's face was flushed now and it wasn't the Chateau Margaux or the cognac. He leaned forward and stabbed the empty air with his forefinger. 'Thirty years I've been around boxers, Perry, thirty years, and I tell you, he's the best I've seen with the exception of Ali, and I've seen 'em all. Marciano, Patterson, Liston, Frazier, Cooper, Mildenburger – Tommy could take 'em all with a few pro fights under his belt. He's got everything, physique, speed, deadly punch and the ability to take one. He's got a brain, knows what he's doing, where he's going.' Klein tapped his right forefinger against the side of his head.

Sir Peregrine feigned boredom. 'He's not the only clever

fighter in the world, Lew. Tell me more.'

Klein shook his head slowly as he struggled for the right words. 'It's not that he's clever, it's just something in there. Some instinct. Something that tells him what to do. And he's got the motivation. You know the old cliché about the hungry boxer?' Klein laughed, 'Well, thanks to our wonderful Labour government the Welfare State saw an end to that. But he's got something like that, something that drives him. He wants to be world champ. He told me. Can you imagine a kid of nineteen telling you that? And you know what, Perry, he didn't say, "Mr Klein, I want to be world champ", he said, "Mr Klein I'm *going to be* world champ". He believes it, totally. And so do I.' Klein sipped his cognac, swallowed, and cleared his throat noisily.

'I'm still listening, Lewis.'

'Well, Perry, believe me, outside the ring he's the nicest kid you could ever wish to meet. East End story book. He loves his mum and dad, helps his kid brothers and sisters with their homework, doesn't drink, polite to the local bobby. I'm not even sure he screws his girlfriend. But get him in the ring and he's something else. His eyes go cold, like he's switched something off behind them. You give him advice and you can see it sinking in. But it's the way he takes his opponents apart. It's as though he doesn't want to be involved with them, just cuts 'em down as soon as he can. I'm telling you he demolishes. He was up against this Nigerian idiot last month, legs like Spiderman he had, and he was hanging over Tommy like he was a drunk on his way home. Second round it was as though Tommy got fed up. He jabbed him twice – one, two, side of the head. I think the lad was on his way down, but Tommy made sure. An uppercut, so help me, and you don't see many of them today. Came from his waist and the guy went down like the lights were out. He was out for five minutes flat; Tommy was frightened in case he'd killed him.'

'Why Lewis, I haven't seen you so excited since the day Robert Mark left our gallant Metropolitan Police.'

Klein ignored him. 'So I said to Tommy, "You hit him a

bit hard, didn't you?" His eyes went all cold again. Know what he said? "He was in my way", not "He got in my way", no, he was in his way. I tell you, he knows what he wants. He wants to be the heavyweight champion of the world. And he's not doing it for Britain or Stepney or his mum or me or dear old Maxie.' Klein jabbed his own chest. 'He's doing it for Number One. Tommy Booth. He's not going to be just a good fighter, he's going to be a great one; the great white hope that no spade from Detroit is going to knock over.'

Sir Peregrine said, 'Don't let Monique hear you talk like that. I imagine she'd cut off your supplies for a month.'

Klein laughed. 'Year more like. What do you think, Perry? Do you want a slice of the action? I'm heavily committed at the moment or I wouldn't be doing you this favour. Do you want a part of a future heavyweight champion of the world?'

Sir Peregrine refilled Klein's glass. He felt a little drunk now. 'Yes, Lewis, I do. I've seen him and he's good. The right training, the right fights,' he gave a slight shrug, 'it could happen.'

Klein looked at him in amazement. 'You've seen him, when?'

'Wembley, last year. I just went for the bill, I didn't even know who he was, but I remember him. A very good looking boy. I was impressed, and you've confirmed it. What do you want, Lew?'

Klein pulled a small piece of paper from his inside pocket and handed it to Sir Peregrine. 'It's all there.'

Sir Peregrine read it and put it carelessly aside. 'I see no problems. There is one condition though. He wins the A.B.A. first. A fighter who can't win that can't think in terms of serious fighting.'

'It's won,' said Klein calmly.

'Lew,' said Sir Peregrine evenly, 'we'll be there, myself and others, so everything will have to be ship-shape and Bristol fashion. After that we can talk percentages.'

Klein spread his arms wide. 'Perry, I could fix the Commissioner before the A.B.A. finals? Do me a favour. Anyway, it may mean a hundred grand or more by the time we're through, but it'll be gilt-edged.'

Sir Peregrine scribbled a hieroglyphic on the discreetly folded bill placed wordlessly before him by another silent waiter, took a ten pound note from his wallet and handed it to the man. The transaction took place without a word being exchanged.

'And of course, Lewis, in time, this could even mean a trip to the Palace for you. Manager of Britain's first heavyweight champion of the world, a captain of industry, giver of charity, popular local man. Sir Lewis Klein, that would be nice, wouldn't it?'

Klein smiled a tight, professional smile. A knighthood. Sir Lewis Klein. The final accolade. A curtain to a mean childhood of bread, margarine and tea, air raids and beatings, and a life backed up by his fists. The sword blade on his shoulder. He closed his eyes in anticipation. He wanted it with an almost sexual desire. And then, thought Klein. And then he had plans for Sir Peregrine Hamilton. He wanted to see the shiny, well-fed aristocratic face squeal in terror. See that blue blood spilt. Klein smiled warmly. 'Perry, my old love, you flatter me. A knighthood is the last thing on my mind. Why, I'd never get a drink in my local again.'

Both men looked at each other, long and hard. And each decided that, after all, the other was far more ruthless.

Tommy Booth lay immobile on the hard, wooden bench. Every muscle was relaxed, his eyes were closed, his breathing regular. Some people spent small fortunes trying to learn what Tommy did naturally. Relaxing, clearing the mind of the accumulated trivia. If anyone had told him that men and women threw down handfuls of pills, lay for hours on psychiatrists' couches, and made frantic forays into fringe religions to learn this art, he would have chuckled in disbelief. He could not remember a moment of his life when he had not been able to slow down his mind and body like a switched-off dynamo, and drift into dreamless, controlled sleep.

He was, without qualification, a magnificent figure of a man. Six feet two inches tall in his bare feet. His body rippled with firm, carefully developed muscle, but lacked the obscene exaggeration of the professional body-builder. The shoulders were broad but without the extra inch that would have made him look like some heavy in a Chicago gangster film. The stomach was flat and hard. It could take repeated blows from a heavy medicine ball, hurled at him with all the force his trainer and mentor, Maxie Wellington, could muster. The arms and legs were muscled and hard from long hours of gym training and road work, and were in a proportion to his body that would have pleased Michelangelo. The back was straight but supple.

An enthusiastic sports writer on an East London newspaper, flushed with lunchtime beer and his own prose, had once described Tommy as having the face of a Greek god. The man was no judge. True, the hair was blonde and given to curls, the face firm and chiselled. But there was none of the hint of weakness, the femininity, that one detected in Greek statues and the modern depictions of them. The face was too irregular. The nose just that fine fraction of a degree off centre. The mouth just that shade too wide.

Tommy Booth was what he looked. A man, and a man's man too. He would not willingly step on a cockroach and would cross the road to avoid a street brawl. But he could whip a man with his fists. Humble him, bring him to the canvas for all the weight and power of his opponent. Tommy was a super-fit athlete, a man with a man's tastes, and an ambitious fighter.

'Tommy.'

Maxie Wellington, his trainer, touched the boxer gently on the arm.

Tommy's eyelids opened and the ice-blue eyes, instantly alert, swivelled to meet Maxie's.

'Time to bandage you up, Tommy. You okay?'

'I'm fine, Maxie.'

The boxer lifted himself up from the prone position and put his legs down to the floor. Like a dog begging for biscuits, he put out his hands in front of him while Maxie took out several rolls of bandage from the battered leather doctor's bag he carried.

Tommy's eyes gazed past Maxie as his trainer cum mentor began to unroll the bandage and wrap it round the boxer's fingers, taking care to keep it firm, but not too tight. Occasionally Maxie looked up from his work, as he fixed the bandage in place with strips of sticking plaster, to see Tommy's eyes far away in some distant world.

What a lad, thought Maxie. If only I could have had a son like that. Instead, his boy was a chartered accountant in Toronto with a wife, two overweight kids, a house in the suburbs and a station wagon. If only he could have been like Tommy, the fighter I never was. The fighter I should have been. Painfully, Maxie thought of his fights. He'd been good at first, sure. Fast, a good punch, quick on his feet for a heavyweight. But things had been different in those days after he got out of the Marines. Times were hard and if the boss said fight, you fought. They could've wheeled in King Kong wearing gloves and you would still have had to climb in the ring. He'd taken some beatings, cruel beatings, from men way out of his class.

He winced involuntarily as he thought of the Joey Baldero fight. The Albert Hall, August 16, 1952. His manager, Danny Robinson, had said it was his big break. 'Win this one Maxie and you're a contender.' Baldero from Sacramento was ranked tenth and Maxie should never have been in the same country with him, let alone in the boxing ring. He lasted four agonising rounds, his face a mask of blood, his whole body a receptacle of pain.

In the first round the American came out cautiously. He'd been told there'd be no trouble with this guy. Just another bum of the month to be put away, then a train ride to Southampton for the boat back. But he wasn't taking risks. He tried a few jabs and caught Maxie cold. Maxie tried to rush him but the Negro dodged sideways and punished Maxie with head punches as he came in. In the second, the

American decided he might even catch the night train. He butted Maxie quickly and skilfully during a clinch, with the referee unsighted. Maxie felt his twice-broken nose go again. The American was scoring at will and the referee was watching only one man – Maxie. In the third round Maxie couldn't breathe at all through his nose, and he took searing lungfuls of air quickly through his mouth. Blood was in his eyes and at the end of the round his seconds pleaded with him to let them throw in the towel. But Maxie was game, wasn't he? Good old Maxie. Never-say-die Maxie. The battling Green Beret. Maxie was the boy who gave the crowd their money's worth. Out he went into that small and private hell. Baldero clobbered him from the bell, working him over street style. Go down you sonofabitch. Maxie began to see double, his defence was gone. He lifted a glove to wipe the blood from his right eye and the American hit him with a piledriver to the ribs. Maxie's guts churned even now at the thought of the pain. He went down on one knee hoping for a brief respite. But the American was from the tough school. He barnstormed in and unleashed a flurry of punches to Maxie's head. The East Ender hit the canvas face down.

He lifted his head, vainly, hopelessly. He couldn't feel his legs. He saw a blur of double faces at the ringside. They swam in and out of focus, a double nightmare. He saw his manager Danny Robinson and another Danny Robinson. They were whispering into the ears of two identical blonde girls, and then all four laughed. Maxie remembered nothing until he woke up, his career over.

He wished to God he had had a manager like Tommy's. Someone to nurse a fighter until he was ready to go pro. Then pick his fights. This for experience, that for prestige. Proper training, proper diet and financial security.

What had he ever given Marjorie? At the end, as she lay, white-faced and drugged, the unrelenting claws of the cancer still cutting through the painkillers, she had laid a hand like a fragile autumn leaf on his and said, 'You've been good to me, Maxie. I've been very happy.'

But Maxie knew it was the sweet, all-forgiving lie of the

deathbed. He'd given her a life of hard work and misery. Of humiliation at his defeats and unspoken agony at his pain.

He finished the bandaging and looked up at Tommy. 'There you are lad, right as rain.'

Tommy wouldn't be like that. Maxie, stupid old Maxie, and Lewis Klein the winner would see to that. Tommy would be one of the new breed, TV interviews, Rolls Royces, grand houses with swimming pools, and a wife with an automatic dishwasher and an au pair to take the drudgery out of life. Klein was a tow-rag, a villain, a crook. Maxie knew that. But Klein looked after his boxers so that when they finished they still had a brain fit to let them read a newspaper without mouthing the words. No Klein fighters ended up emptying slops in spit and sawdust pubs.

We'll look after you lad. Me and Klein. We'll see you right. Fuck the others.

The dark green Daimler turned off the road lined with expensive cars in the heart of London's fashionable Belgravia and purred into the quiet mews. A coach lamp came on in the porch of the end house as Sir Dudley Creighton, Member of Parliament, Privy Counsellor and Leader of Her Majesty's Opposition applied the handbrake and switched off the engine. Grabbing his leather attaché case from the passenger seat he eased himself out of the car.

Margot was standing in the doorway in a long, pale blue, silk nightdress. It plunged at the divide between her breasts and Dudley could see a glimpse of them, soft and full. The damp night left a halo round the lamp and, framed in the doorway as she was, his wife reminded him of some advertisement he had seen in a glossy magazine. He made a futile, irrelevant mental note to find out which one.

She was a stunningly attractive woman. Her soft, dark brown hair was expensively cut, framing a strong but not stern face, deep brown eyes, straight nose and wide, inviting mouth. When her lips parted the teeth were white, even and strong. She was tall for a woman – almost five feet ten – but her body showed no hint of the masculinity which can befall tall women. Her breasts were firm, but with a hint of softness; her hips were not too large and her bottom, while clearly a woman's, was not too rounded. Her skin was vibrant, almost translucent, and cared for as the prize asset it was.

Margot Creighton, Lady Margot Creighton, exuded power and its handmaiden – sexual appeal. There was a confidence about her, a sense of ease and purpose. This was one of the world's deciders, not followers. Boredom would never put its deathly pallor on her skin. Margot chose to do something and did it. To Margot, life was good wine to drink to the full, savour when the mood took, but to take with gusto and not too much respect.

Her family had been casualties of the changing Britain of the second half of the twentieth century; aristocrats who could trace their lineage back to Charles I, a family tree littered with famous names, famous campaigns, follies and political adventure. Stately homes, as the popular press always called them, had been their natural resting place. But democracy and a fair day's work for a fair day's pay being the order of the day, death duties and taxes ate insidiously into the family name and led to its decline. The estate in Wiltshire had gone when she was a child. The lake where she'd swum as a young girl now echoed to the screams of day-trippers in brightly-painted canoes. There was a cafeteria in the splendid long room where her father had given banquets, and a miniature fairground where she'd grazed her pony.

Margot took each turn of the family wheel of fortune with the same nonchalance. At nineteen, Margot Houndsworth-Smith gave the newspapers a field day by abandoning the bright lights of the night to become a model. In a few months, months of hard work and stubborn persistence, she was *Vogue*'s principal model. She was dubbed 'the modelling deb', but Margot didn't care. She worked hard. The old days were over. Her parents went to the South of France. There was no son and the line of the Houndsworth-Smiths was over. She didn't shed a tear for it. The past had never existed, the future only as long as she breathed.

There was a much publicised affair with an American pop

star. She was convinced the media's main interest was because he was black. It had never occurred to her. Racial prejudice and racial interest were to Margot equal nonsenses. Like all the other girls at her public school with its dormitories and repressed sex she had had 'pashes' on older girls and even on teachers, but she had never felt the need, as some of her fellow pupils had, to lie next to the warm body of a schoolchum and suffer the furtive fumblings in the dark. But at twenty-one – with that coolness of decision which was her trade mark – Margot accepted an invitation to homosexual lovemaking from the model with whom she shared an apartment in Kensington.

It had been interesting, novel and an intense experience both sexually and intellectually.

For three weeks that had seemed like a year, Margot believed it possible to be in love with someone of her own sex. One morning she awoke to find – almost as though a fever had left her – that she wanted none of it. It had been an excursion, an adventure, and it was over. She wanted honest, heterosexual love, in marriage, to a man whom she could love and who loved her.

She found it in The Honourable Dudley Creighton.

She had met him at a garden party. He was widowed, handsome and an aspiring politician. For four months he took her to dinner, the ballet, the races and even a jaunt by private plane to Antibes, without the word sex even being mentioned. The night they went to bed together Dudley proposed and Margot accepted. Without apology, she loved her husband totally.

But now, after five years of marriage, Margot, honest, realistic Margot, could realise, without self-pity, that something was leaving their marriage as surely as sand trickles through an egg-timer. Perhaps her husband was having an affair, it occurred to her. Or maybe ambition was elbowing out in its bullying fashion the qualities of love, tenderness, passion.

She looked at him in the damp light which softened the ravaged lines of his face. She had read somewhere that politics was a mistress, leading, demanding, pulling, twisting.

Dudley Creighton had made no bones about his ambition as they had lain together and spoken quietly in the small hours. He wished to be Prime Minister of the United Kingdom. To join that famous line of men – Disraeli, Lloyd George, Churchill. He wanted to walk with the powerful, stand at that famous, much-photographed front door. Greet leaders from the Soviet Union, from the United States, although he knew he would not have a hundredth of their power. That was what Dudley wanted and he knew that Margot was his major asset. She was young, beautiful, and she had a way with people. The lesson of Jackie Kennedy was not lost on him.

It was Presidential politics now, like it or not. It was about presence, charisma, the ability to sell yourself. Policies could be changed, doctored, discarded to the whims of foreign bankers or domestic changes. But a First Lady was always there. And Margot fitted the bill. He had honestly forgotten now whether he loved her or simply needed her. The definition was too blurred for him, but he couldn't let her go. Despite Emily.

Emily with her mousy hair, boyish figure. Her absurd enthusiasm for the meat and drink of politics. Emily who raced off at every spare minute to sky dive out of aeroplanes for all the world like Superman. Emily with her ability to enjoy sex for what it was, and with that dynamo power of mind. Yes, despite Emily he couldn't let Margot go.

He looked at her across the few yards that separated them. She was, he thought, with all the aesthetic appreciation of a man admiring an oil painting in a musty gallery, a most beautiful woman. But desire lay dead in him like the ashes of a morning camp fire.

'Darling, you're late.'

He put his right arm, the free one, around her waist and kissed her neutrally on the cheek. 'Emergency committee dear, last minute thing, just couldn't dodge it.'

She smiled, easily. 'I cooked dinner myself. We were going

to have some of that rather good champagne Harry sent over. Perks of the trade I suppose you'd call it.'

'Sorry dear, it couldn't be helped, really. We've got them on the run and we've got to keep pressing. Number Ten would suit you, you know.'

'What's Number Ten, darling, a new perfume? Come on, let's go to bed. I'll open the champagne and you can tell me all about your day.'

The brown eyes, warm, large and almost liquid in the half-light, stared up at him. He knew what was coming. He'd known all the way home, and tried, hopelessly as always, to think of some way of staving off the inevitable. He tried to disengage his arm, which was still awkwardly around her waist, but she held it with her own. He felt like a captured animal in the first entangling snare of the thrown net.

Christ! Why don't I want to make love to her?

She whispered in his ear. There was no one to hear as they entered the hallway, but it was all part of the game. He tried to mouth a reply, an impossible reply for there were no words to follow her promise. But nonetheless he tried and the words would not come. She led him to the stairs, and meekly he let himself be led. Like a condemned man, numb with horror, who cannot find the phrase to make them stop all this nonsense.

With Emily it was simple. An affair with one's secretary. It was so silly, so simple, so obvious as to be almost a cliché. She wasn't even attractive. A good brain, stout English country girl's body, a degree from Oxford and a bursting ambition to help him become Prime Minister. Yes, with Emily it was simple. Emily adored him, Emily was impressed by his position. Emily was happy with a curry at some Indian restaurant in West Kensington, poring over the files as they ate, no one suspecting. Just ambitious Creighton slumming it with his plain-Jane secretary in the horn-rimmed spectacles.

But afterwards, the bottle of wine at her apartment in Fulham, and then the half-awkward move, the fumbled kiss, the hand reaching for the light switch, and his hands kneading, squeezing her small breasts. They would move to the bedroom and undress quickly and in silence. Emily would lie down, her eyes closed, and he would enter her quickly and without preliminaries. She would moan slightly and that would be the only audible hint of their passion. Afterwards she would make them coffee and they would drink it in the dark and never speak of what they had done. And the next day she would take his telephone calls and type his letters and make his appointments, and never hint, with a word or a glance, that she had taken some secret thing from him.

It was clean and uncluttered, neat, organised. He could deal with it, cope with it. Put it away until it was necessary to take it out and re-use it. But Margot was a woman. Real, demanding, passionate, sexually versed, giving fully, openly and needing in return. It was too much for Dudley and he wondered how long Margot would take his excuses.

God in Heaven, he wanted to be Prime Minister, she'd never leave him then.

The bedroom was lit by a single bedside lamp. The counterpane was turned down to reveal white, hand-embroidered linen sheets. Margot unzipped his trousers and pulled them down and over his feet. He stepped from them, and as she brought her face up it brushed against his sleeping groin. He stood there, this feared politician, future Prime Minister, trouserless and helpless before a woman.

'I'm very tired,' he said hopelessly, 'we've had a lot of late night sittings.' She led him to the bed.

'Get in, darling, we won't bother with the champagne.'

He breathed a sigh of prayer for the darkness and slid between the sheets. The bedside lamp off, he watched as she slid the nightdress from her shoulders, bathed in a pool of moonlight, and walked naked to the bed.

At last, he felt physical desire stirring in him, reacting to some stimulus removed from his thinking process. She slid in next to him and he felt the slightly cold flesh against him and her scent powerful in his throat. Patiently, methodically he went through the foreplay, working with the meticulousness for which his committee work was renowned. He said 'I love you', twice, at decent intervals, and kissed his wife softly on the neck as he entered her. He knew from habit when she was reaching orgasm and when he felt he had done his duty withdrew and lay panting slightly, his head on the pillow. Then her lips were tracing a soft, wet path down his chest and stomach as she pushed back the sheets. His reward. He felt her mouth close on him and saw the silky hair in the moonlight, waving slightly on her shoulders.

Before his climax he thought, strangely – and with an absurdity that almost made him giggle – of Emily. She would, he concluded, be quite shocked at what was going on here.

Archie Taylor pushed at the brass handle and eased himself into the lunchtime crush of El Vino's. As he threaded his way through the crowded bar he rubbed shoulders, literally, with the famous of Fleet Street, the High Court and the Old Bailey. He saw the *Mirror* man drinking with two crime beat buddies from the *Express*. Richards, a barrister currently making a name for himself up at the Bailey defending a bent copper, was demolishing a bottle of claret with a small, dark woman Archie recognised as being number two on the women's page of a top-selling tits and bums tabloid. He made a mental note of the liaison. It could just be casual; a feature on a new glamour boy lawyer. It could also be a bit on the side for Richards. He had looks like something off an after-shave ad, and rumour had it the ex-Bunny who now rejoiced in the title of Mrs Richards, and kept a feather duster flying on their house at Godalming, had ceased to occupy quite the place she had in Richards's sexual Top Ten.

He saw Dennison, editor of a left-wing political weekly, chatting amiably with the deputy editor of one of Fleet Street's leading right-wing newspapers. Dennison was the one who looked like the nineteenth-century coal owner. Heavy three-piece suit, watch chain, and a thick cigar clamped between his teeth. Simons looked like a downtrodden little Marxist. Shabby suit, tiny, wire-rimmed spectacles and a permanent hang-dog expression. Between them they were making serious inroads into Britain's annual champagne import.

Archie'd heard whispers old Dennison was changing political colour just a wee bit and wouldn't hold his job very long. He kept warning too often of the dangers of the Soviet arms build-up for the trendies of Hampstead, who liked their Russians big and butch but peaceful; and too often for the advertisers, who offered 'friendship' tours to the 'socialist' countries. Simon's paper would just love a defector who they could commission to write pieces with a 'I was one of them but then I learned' bent.

Not bad for thirty seconds on my own doorstep, thought Archie. Wish it was always so easy. At the end of the bar he spotted Mike Daniels caressing a bottle of Veuve Cliquot. Daniels was guarding an extra seat by the simple expedient of putting his leg across it.

'Mike. How've you been?'

Daniels took his leg off the seat and poured champagne into the empty glass, then topped up his own. 'Couldn't be better, Archie. You?'

'Marvellous, tip-top.' Archie sipped at the champagne and felt the delightful effervescence prick at his nostrils. He eased himself back in the chair. 'How's the antique business, made your fortune yet?'

Daniels laughed. 'Slowly; slowly but surely.'

Archie knew not to rush him. He was there for a reason but he didn't like being interrogated. He wasn't the kind of contact who just spewed it, said 'How much?' and then gave you his name and address. They were narks and knew it. Daniels? Well, Daniels thought he was doing the world a favour ratting on all his old school chums. Archie didn't care much. They all had their motives but it amounted to the same thing in the end. They told you something you didn't know, and with Daniels, tips weren't that thick on the ground; three or four times a year, but when they came they were goodies.

'How's Veronica, made a decent woman of her yet? You were always threatening to marry her.'

Daniels shook his head with mock sorrow. 'Bloody fine

journalist you are. We sent you an invitation. Kensington Register Office last May.' He stabbed an accusing finger. 'And you, my dear fellow, didn't bother to show.'

Archie smacked a hand to his forehead. 'Oh Christ, I do remember. I went off to Monte Carlo or somewhere and I asked my secretary to give you a buzz. Didn't she?'

'Not a dickybird Archie, you should give her a bollocking.'

'Mike, I've had two since then. They come, get screwed, get married, have kids and leave. And not, I might add, always in that order.'

They lapsed into silence. Archie finished his glass and poured himself some more champagne. He raised the bottle to Daniels: 'We'll manage another, Mike, won't we? You don't have to rush back?'

Daniels shook his head. 'Half-day closing. It's the one day of the week Veronica allows me to get pissed.'

He took a dry biscuit from the small plate on the table, crunched it between his fingers and nibbled at the debris. Between bites he said: 'It's a belter, this one, Archie. I'm no journalist, of course, but something tells me it's a belter.'

Archie gave him the requisite compliment. 'You've never been out yet Mike, you seem to have a nose for it. If you ever pack in antiques I wouldn't mind having you on my diary if I could get you past those buggers in the National Union of Journalists.'

'Thanks Archie, I'll remember that.' He leaned across in the conspiratorial way he always did when imparting a tip. 'Heard of David Grenfell?'

'Jam people?'

'The same. Old man's worth about five million. David went through the whole bit the old man missed out on. Eton, Oxford, spell at Harvard. Nice lad, dream of a son, short haircuts, not into drugs, everyone who meets him thinks the world of him. Well last year he met some French count's daughter when he was down in the South of France. Her old man owns half the vineyards in France, ultra-respectable, very pro-British, ex-Resistance leader.'

Archie tensed. If Daniels had come to tell him this . . . the bloody thing had been in all the papers over a year ago. 'Mike,' he said, gently, 'that's not new, you know. We carried a fair spread on it ourselves. They gave that bloody great engagement party at his chateau with all the workers toasting their new master-to-be in champers.'

'Yes, yes,' said Daniels impatiently. 'Come on Archie, I don't flog you last year's stories. No, just hear me out. So David and Dominque, or whatever her name is, are all set for a July wedding. White veils, champagne and bliss all round. But . . . David only goes off to Barbados for a couple of weeks last month with some mates for a sort of pre-nuptial stag bash. And while he's there he only meets a bloody black go-go dancer by the name of Coco, doesn't he?' Daniels's face was close to Archie's; his right index finger was extended. 'And for the *pièce de resistance*, Archie, he didn't get a flight back. And do you know why? Of course you don't. But I do. Because he is only shacked up with the said black in her Bridgetown flat. And what is more, he has rung the old man to tell him he is not coming home. No Dominique, no July wedding, no extending the dynasty, unless Mr Raspberry Grenfell fancies a picaninny carrying on the line. The French lot are apoplectic. The girl's threatened to kill herself, the Count apparently wants pistols at dawn, and old Grenfell is on the point of needing intensive care.'

Archie gave a small, low-pitched whistle. The waitress, thinking it was for her and not liking the method by which her attention was drawn, bustled across.

'You don't,' she said with feeling, 'have to whistle. I am not a dog.'

I'm sorry,' said Archie with a grin, 'I wasn't whistling at you, but since you're here can you give us a bottle of the same and a couple of rounds of smoked salmon?' He turned to Daniels. 'You're sure this is all on the level?'

'Archie, when I get excited and lapse into the South London vernacular, with my "isn't he" and "didn't I", and "he only did this", and "he only did that", you can be sure I am more excited than if I'd just flogged a bit of old junk for a grand to one of our visiting Knights of Bushido. It's straight all right.'

He picked up his glass and realised it was empty.

'Bloody service in here doesn't improve. I don't have to, Archie, but I'll tell you. Old Grenfell is a friend of the family. My mother and he once had a bit of a pash, to be honest. Didn't come to anything, obviously. But they're still friends. After my father died Grenfell and his wife sort of looked after mum, made sure she was okay in the cash department, that sort of thing. Wasn't necessary but they also made sure she still got invited to dinner parties and the like. Mum told old man Grenfell about my shop and he and his wife popped in from time to time. He didn't spend much, a knick-knack here and there and that's all. But he came once a month or so and we got pretty friendly. Naturally when David was engaged he was full of it and told me how proud he was etcetera.'

The champagne and sandwiches arrived and Archie paid with a ten pound note. As an apology for the whistle he left a one pound note on the empty tray. Mike took the cold bottle and filled the two glasses. He drank half his and continued, grateful for Archie's silence. Some people never listened, but you couldn't say that about Archie. Maybe that was why he was so successful. Good listeners were thin on the ground.

'So. Last week he came into the shop to pick up an escritoire he'd asked for months before and I'd managed to get for him. He didn't seem any different, just a bit quiet, when suddenly he breaks down. Burst into tears, Archie, right in front of me. Veronica was out, the shop was empty, so I put up the 'Back in fifteen minutes' sign, took him in the back and gave him a cup of tea. He told me everything. He was distraught, I can tell you. You can imagine it, can't you? One minute he's got a clean-limbed heir about to cement an *entente cordiale* all his own, next thing he's off shacking up with some bloody West Indian go-go dancer. Heck of a story, I think you'll agree, Archie.'

Archie picked up a smoked salmon sandwich and popped

it into Daniels's half-open mouth. 'Michael, my friend, I would say it is, as you so rightly put it, a heck of a story.'

Daniels pulled in the sandwich like an ant-eater dealing with lunch. His face contorted as he tried to swallow the sandwich quarter in one go. He succeeded and said: 'The thing is, Archie, I'm sure you'll agree, it's a bit more than a diary para, isn't it? I mean, if I read your business right, if you get someone to talk to him in Barbados, and you do pictures of him and this black bird he's shacked up with, then it's a page, with pix and the lot. Am I right?'

Archie looked him up and down. Some informants you despised, some you just wondered about, but Daniels . . . Well, he quite liked Daniels. In his own naive, just out of school way, he was a shrewd man. He tried to remember never to buy anything from his Putney shop.

'Michael you are quite right. It's more than a diary para. If we can stand it up and particularly if the kid talks, then it's a cracker. I'll tell you what. Whatever happens I'll pay you a hundred. If we get it properly and give it a good show, it's five hundred. Suit you?'

Daniels nodded. 'Fine Archie. You've always been fair. One whatever, five if it makes a good show.'

He put out his right hand. Archie took it. They shook briefly and then set about the champagne and smoked salmon. The second bottle nearly empty and an acre of small talk between them, Archie leaned back reflectively. This was what he liked about Fleet Street. The silly, pointless decadence of it all. It didn't matter a damn, he'd convinced himself of that years ago. If he hadn't, he reckoned he'd have gone potty or gone off and been a missionary or something. No, it was all completely and utterly irrelevant. It had as much effect on the day-to-day world as a snowstorm up the Amazon. He looked across the seating area at the columnists, the leader writers, the editors, the lawyers, even the Fleet Street young bloods buying their way into the haven of the elders and betters for the shared price of a bottle of house claret. At three or later they'd all tumble back to their offices and write stirring stories about social security scroungers poncing an extra two quid a week off the state, or stirring leaders about the need for people to work harder and earn less. After kissing goodbye to their mistresses or temporary bits on the side they'd chase off with photographers to harass some politician or vicar discovered doing the same thing. Archie hated them, including himself, and yet loved them in the same breath. They were comic, gross, but because they were irrelevant they weren't harmful, he felt. Just silly pompous dinosaurs whom no one really took any notice of anyway. And himself? Well, he'd long ago ceased to dislike himself with any seriousness. That was a stage for any journalist to get through – like the inclination to follow fire engines or use words like 'scoop'. Now he felt he recognised the job for what it was. A decent living, a chance to do the things you like – drinking champagne for example – usually at someone else's expense.

And he liked the power. He'd come to terms with liking it, too. Everyone in the goddamned world, he reckoned to himself, had some sort of power, if only to stop you getting on a bus you wanted to catch, or to hand you a parking ticket. Show me, thought Archie, someone who doesn't want any power and I'll show you a bloody saint.

He liked seeing the blue bloods squirm. They had say over everything else. Their kids went to the best schools, they lived in the best houses, they got the best medical treatment. And when they said jump, people jumped. But publicity was one area they couldn't control. One area where a cheque book couldn't keep the hounds at bay. The old family secrets, indiscretions, embarrassments leaking out and being read by the kind of people they wouldn't normally give the time of day to.

At first they'd liked Archie, thought he was one of them. A foreigner, perhaps, but in, in the circle, part of the old set-up. When it was too late and they realised he wasn't, his spies were set up everywhere. He chuckled when he thought of it. Melodramatic that, spies. But it was true. He had a network now of reliable and trusted agents. All with their own motives – greed, revenge, bitchiness. Some reason that made them rat on their friends, leak out the little things the set thought best kept secret. Just like some little secret joy in telling someone something no one else knew – like kids in school who can't wait to rat on the sexual leanings of Jones Minor.

And Archie enjoyed it. Every minute of it. He loved going on TV chat shows and the discussion panels to which he was constantly invited. He shamelessly took their money and free drinks in the Green Room and gave them what for. Articulately he defended with a straight face an art he thought only funny. He enjoyed needling the churchmen, politicians, policemen and other 'heavier' journalists with their pompous weighty arguments. And what did he care for the British class system, for the marquises and the misters, the honourables and the cloth caps and mufflers?

Archie was American. True, few from across the Atlantic would have recognised his classless drawl as the end result of a boy born on a wintry day in a brownstone apartment in the Bronx thirty-six years before. Maybe it was because Archie had been born American, been brought up within the English class system, and seen at first hand the result of class and political intolerance that made him enjoy so much the debunking work he did.

Archie's father had been a gag-writer, sometime commercial writer and continuity-scriptwriter with a small Manhattan radio station. In 1947 David Taylor, a second generation immigrant of English extraction – the original Taylors hailed from Staffordshire – lost his job for a gag on a radio show which offended the local Tammany Hall politicos. He packed his wife and child and all their possessions into a 1938 Buick and drove to California in six weeks, camping on the way.

Archie remembered the green valleys, the great plains and big skies, the endless waving corn and camping in the open, smelling the fresh, clean air. California was warm and full of oranges, just as the songs had said, but life was still hard. More and more were flocking there in search of the golden dream and Archie's father had to take a job scripting commercials on a Pasadena radio station. They lived cheaply but comfortably in a rented two-bedroomed apartment. From his bedroom window Archie could reach out and touch the leaves of a palm tree. He thought it was paradise after the cold winters and tough Italian kids of the Bronx.

David Taylor got up at 5 a.m. and took his portable Remington into the un-air-conditioned kitchen to sweat over his film-script before leaving for the radio station at 9 a.m. Script after script came back, but for David Taylor the Hollywood dream came true one August morning. A film company not only wanted to buy an option on his script, but hired him to the payroll of the company as one of the permanent scriptwriting team. They left the apartment and Pasadena and headed for Bel Air. It was swimming pools and convertibles now. Archie remembered looking out of his bedroom window late one night and seeing girls in bathing costumes, shrieking with laughter as they were hurled into the pool. There were giggles and the chinking of glasses, but somehow his father didn't seem to be around as much, and his mother never seemed to smile.

One spring afternoon in 1953 his father came home unexpectedly from the studio and shut himself in the television room with the curtains drawn. Archie heard the noise blurting through the locked door. A raucous voice was ranting, accusing. He heard the words . . . 'Communist' . . . 'fellow traveller'. His father didn't go to the studio after that. The rantings of Senator Joseph McCarthy and the infamous Army-McCarthy hearings had seen to that. An indiscretion of fifteen years before had reached out and shattered David Taylor's career. For a brief heady moment in 1936 at the outbreak of the Spanish Civil War, David Taylor, with two workmates, had joined the Communist Party in a drunken, optimistic afternoon they soon regretted. He had torn up his party card and posted his resignation four short weeks later, but the sin had been committed. No one would touch him after the hearings when he answered that infamous question: 'Are you or have you ever been a member of the Communist Party?' David Taylor had believed in truth, justice and the American way and had answered, honestly: 'Yes, for four weeks in 1936.'

He would have been as well to admit to having leprosy.

The convertible was the first to go, then the horses, and soon they moved to another rented apartment without air-conditioning in the San Fernando valley.

One day, Archie's father sat down and told the boy he was being sent to England to school. It was a public school – but what the English meant was that it was private, a private school. They both laughed. There was an aunt, a family relative, who'd see him from time to time. His mother and father were going to New York to try and get work and theyd come and visit him as soon as they could. It was for the best. He'd get a good education in a country where it didn't matter that his father had once, briefly, belonged to the wrong party. They put him on an aeroplane. It was the first time any of them had flown and he, the youngest, felt proud to be the first. It was an adventure. He'd see his mom and dad soon. He watched them, tiny figures, as they stood in the dust at the edge of the runway, the whine of the propellers blocking out their shouted goodbyes. At La Guardia an uncle met him and took him to the docks. The boat was the biggest he had ever seen. It was raining and he stood on the deck with his little suitcase and cried, the tears rolling down the small, sun-tanned face.

They'd said England would be green, but it wasn't; it was grey and damp. He longed for the sunshine of California, the freedom to run and ride, swim and fish. He was taunted about his accent. The boys called him Yank and cowboy and Roy Rogers. He learned to defend himself with his fists and soon gained their respect. He learned to play rugby – it was a bit like American football, although many was the time he was admonished for tackling an opposing player who didn't have the ball.

Then came the day when he was called to the head's study. There had been an accident and his father was dead. His mother was fine and sent all her love. She would write soon. There were no more details.

Archie was sixteen years old when he walked into a bookshop in Worcester, determined to read about the horrors of the Army-McCarthy hearings, and learned on page 357 how his father had really died.

David Taylor, penniless, heavily in debt, and blackballed by every studio in Hollywood, had gone back to New York and failed to get a job. His health failing, he had gone to a small gun shop in the Bronx and bought a snub-nosed .38 revolver and a packet of shells. He only needed one. He locked himself in the bathroom while his wife was visiting relatives, and with his trusty Remington wrote a passionate and moving denunciation of discrimination and intolerance. He then put the pistol in his mouth and blew the top off his spinal cord. Archie's mother lasted two years before her mind went and she was sent to a State institution in Rochester, upstate New York. She died three days after Archie's twenty-first birthday.

At school he gained many friends, some the sons of titled men, others the offspring of wealthy businessmen, and was accepted as one of them. Despite it, he hated the English class system, and saw in it the seeds of the intolerance that had killed his father. He hated the subtleties of rank where wealth counted less than descent. He vowed that when he finished school he would return to California, taking his mother with him. But soon he was taking 'O' and 'A' levels, and it was his aunt's dearest wish that he try for Oxford. He tried – and failed – settling instead for London University. It was the swinging 'sixties and a great time for a young man to be alive and in London. He had an allowance, a small second-hand MG sports car, and a girlfriend called Penelope who made his nights interesting.

So he started selling bits of gossip to the daily papers. Thirty bob here, two quid there, but it all helped. And sometimes they took you out to lunch, always paid, and pocketed the bill.

With some frantic last-minute swotting, helped by a minor bust-up with Penelope, he managed to get a second. But Bachelor of Arts degrees were thick on the trees. Thank God for those lunches. The London *Evening Express* were looking for a man to join their diary pages. Thirty quid a week and an average six quid on expenses. Archie jumped at it. Before inflation became a household word, a single man could have a high old time on money like that. The man who despised the British class system and its old school tie manifestation didn't realise it, but he was wearing one. He got invited to parties, hunt balls, point to points, and all the social occasions of the London and country calendar.

He met Sir Peregrine Hamilton and they shared a taste for fine wine and not-so-fine women.

He'd gone over to the *Courier*. They were expanding, revamping the paper, and they'd paid to get him. The number one on the diary knew why they'd hired the young American, but was polite about it. Six months after the vulture had flown in to settle on his shoulder, the number one took his pay-off and left Fleet Street to open a bistro in Cirencester. As all his erstwhile colleagues cheerfully and maliciously pointed out when they'd drunk his farewell champagne at El Vino's – though not of course in his earshot – if he was as good at running a bistro as he was at running a diary, then remind them not to eat in Circencester.

And they'd all laughed and patted Archie on the back and said how they were all looking forward to working with him.

And Archie laughed too and bought more champagne and mentally worked out which faces he didn't want. And they went too, at intervals in the months following, and on those occasions there was no champagne.

Archie was on five figures now, and virtually wrote his own expenses. 'Talk about People' was *the* gossip column. They'd been sued a few times, paid out a few thousand here and there, but it was all worth it, the proprietors knew that. He'd even coined a new term, 'to Archie' meaning to rat on someone. He liked that. Some idiot had once taken a riding crop to him because he suggested the man's daughter was shacked up in a commune. Archie was riding high and it looked like going on for a long time. As long as there were people like Mike Daniels to help with Archie's revenge on McCarthy and the stultifying years in an English public school.

Archie knew it wouldn't last for ever, though. One day

he'd lose his touch or the informants would dry up, or they'd hit that too-big-to-ignore libel action, or maybe gossip columns would simply go out of fashion. But he'd be okay. There'd be a pay-off, a big one. He'd probably go to France or somewhere. Archie had a novel inside him, he felt that, and he'd write it. He'd write about Fleet Street and its inside secrets. He sipped at the champagne and looked at Daniels, deep in thought. And what would he be? Villain or hero?

'Mike?'

Daniels looked up, startled.

'Tell me something. Nothing personal and I'm grateful you did, but what made you rat on the old man? Aren't you a bit worried he might pin it on you?'

Daniels shook his head. 'Not really. If he's poured it out to me he must have done it to someone else. Besides, too many people are privy to it, I'm surprised it hasn't come out before. And why did I do it? Well I've flogged stuff to you before so I've no qualms in that direction, but I probably wouldn't have done it to Grenfell. But do you know what the old bastard did? After he'd sobbed on my shoulder and drunk my tea he calmed himself down and coolly tried to get me to knock £50 off the price of the escritoire. Friend of your mum's, old chap, all that nonsense. So I made a decision. I gave him the discount and decided to recoup it some other way.' He winked at Archie. 'Bit of a bastard, aren't I?'

'No,' said Archie, 'you're just surviving. Besides Mike, if you'd only admit it, you hate them as much as I do.' Archie finished his glass. Daniels picked up the empty bottle and looked at the clock. ''S only five to, Archie, fancy a third?'

Archie put his hand over his glass: 'Sorry Mike, got to stay sober and upright. Tonight, so my debauched friend Sir Peregrine Hamilton tells me, I am going to witness the birth of a great fighter. One Tommy Booth, with whom I am not acquainted. But I would like to see the fight without closing one eye.'

They parted and Archie went quickly back to his office,

made some notes, and started to make phone calls. He set in motion events that would result in a late-night knock on a Bridgetown apartment by a man flown in specially from New York to investigate Archie's tip.

Archie opened his bottom drawer, took out a half bottle of brandy and a small glass. He poured himself a shot. 'God bless all rats,' he said aloud.

Margot, swathed in white mink, rushed down the stairs of San Lorenzo, a pretty Italian restaurant hidden amongst the old traditional antique shops of Beauchamp Place. She was breathless and late as usual. Vivien Trowbridge rose from the table to meet her friend and kissed her on each cheek.

'A bottle of champagne love?'

'Oh why not, it's not that often we see each other.'

Vivien beckoned to an attractive Italian woman who was talking to a group of celebrities at the next door table. 'A bottle of Perrier Jouet and a carafe of fresh orange juice, please Mara.'

Mara moodily disappeared to return a few minutes later with their order.

Margot sipped her drink. 'Mara darling, why are you in such a bad mood today? Has that naughty Lorenzo been giving you a bad time again?'

'Ha, men,' said Mara, her broken English heavily accented, 'you can't trust any of them, they're all lazy good for nothings, including Lorenzo.' She sulkily sauntered off to talk to another table of famous faces, leaving the two friends to catch up on the gossip.

Margot nursed her drink. 'So there it is, Vivien, the whole exciting panorama of the eight months since we last met.'

'You sound bored.'

'I'm not. I can honestly say I'm not bored, it's just, well . . .'

The blonde woman looked shrewdly into Margot's dark eyes. 'No problems with that wonderful thing called sex, by any chance?'

'Vivien!' Margot affected shocked surprise.

'Don't pull that little girl shocked face with me, darling, we shared a dorm, remember? Oh, Vivien from whom no secrets are hid. Blasphemy. If the adultery hasn't done it already, that should bar me forever from the Kingdom of Heaven. Come on old love, Dudley not quite Clark Gable?'

Margot took a long drink before answering. 'Vivien you are absolutely impossible. You take me out to lunch on the pretext of catching up on all the latest gossip and the next thing I know you're probing me about my sex life. This is absolutely the last lunch I shall ever have with you.'

'Until the next one, I know, love.'

A waiter brought a large plate of home-made pasta.

Margot toyed with her fork. 'No, Dudley's fine, he hardly ever has headaches,' she laughed. 'I wonder why it's always supposed to be women who have headaches? No, he does his duty. Trouble is, Viv, I think that's just how he sees it. A real duty.'

'Wham, bam, thank you mam?'

Margot spluttered through a mouthful of food. 'Vivien you're impossible! Look at that old dear – I'm sure she thinks we are a couple of good time girls.'

'Wouldn't mind, could be fun. But seriously, is everything all right in the longevity stakes?'

Margot clutched her Buck's Fizz. 'Oh yes, he plugs away, waits for me then off he goes, all very satisfactory, but mechanical. No, it's fine, really it is, it's just that, well, sometimes – oh, I don't know! Get on with your lunch.'

Vivien shovelled in a forkful of spaghetti and said through the mouthful of food: 'What you need, my love, is an affair.'

'Oh Vivien, belt up, there's a dear.'

'No I mean it. Bit of spice in your life, excitement, passion, intrigue, secret meetings. As a matter of fact, I'm having one myself.'

'Vivien, you're *not*!'

'Cross my heart. It's been going three months, it's reached the curve and I estimate it's the downward path from now on; I'll give it about another seven weeks. Doing me the world of good. Lost pounds, I really have.'

'Andrew?'

'Doesn't suspect a thing, but he *has* noticed a change in me, and in turn he's responding. Between you and me I think he's been doing a bit of reading up on the subject. I'll get him to lend Dudley the handbooks.'

They giggled like naughty schoolgirls, attracting stares from the surrounding tables.

'But haven't you, Margot?'

'Haven't I what?'

'Don't be coy, sweety. Had an affair?'

'No. As a matter of fact I haven't.'

'Ever considered one?'

'Vivien my love you can't just go down to Harrods and order one. "I'm thinking of having an affair. What have you got in stock? Yes that's fine, deliver him will you?" ' They giggled again.

'No, I somehow thought the whole idea was total fidelity, one partner through life and all that.'

'You sound less than convincing.'

'Perhaps. But anyway there's my photography. I'm damn well determined not to be just a decorative addition to Dudley, a politician's wife, shaking hands, kissing babies, applauding politely at the right moments. I've never been as involved in anything, Viv, which is probably all that *is* saving me from boredom. I'm determined to be the best photographer around, bar none.'

The waiter took their empty plates.

'So you see Vivien, my friend and confidante, I *am* having an affair – with a Nikon and a Leica.'

'I am a camera,' said Vivien, on cue.

'Me no Leica,' said Margot in perfectly rehearsed reply, and they convulsed with laughter.

'You remembered?'

'How could I forget?'

They parted on the corner of Curzon Street. Vivien kissed Margot's cheek.

'Take care darling and let's not leave it eight months this time.'

''Course, love to Andrew. And . . . let me know how the other thing works out.'

Vivien winked lasciviously: 'Full report darling.' She swirled in the road. 'And don't rule it out for yourself, look what it's done for me. Adds a bit of spice.'

'I shall proposition the next Harrods deliveryman who is lucky enough to come to our door, and that is a solemn promise.' The commanding arm of the blonde woman waved down a passing cab.

'No, Vivien, laughed Margot. The only body I'm about to get involved with is a new Nikon – I've got the lenses already!'

# *Chapter Two*

Smoke from the countless cigarettes hung like an autumn mist, caught in its swirling layers under the harsh, cutting lights. The crowd was bored; and bored crowds are restless. In a massive, unknowing unity they swirled like a sea, moving, fidgeting, shifting in their seats. Their murmured conversations rose and fell like the kiss of night-time waves on a shingle beach.

The two boxers seemed not to notice. They fought their own private duel bathed in the unforgiving light. The whoosh of expelled air as each landed a punch, and the whiplash of leather on flesh punctuated their ritual dance. There was a flutter like so many disturbed pigeons as hundreds of programmes were simultaneously lifted and leafed through. And still the two men fought on before their bored patrons, two modern gladiators satiating the blood lust of any 'seventies Caesar with enough readies to get himself a seat at the ringside. The boxers were young men, slim and muscled, but their faces had a dulled look, the finer features blunted, like the faces of statues weathered by wind and age.

They were standing now, toe to toe, the dancing energy gone, power left only in the last, strongest bastion of their arsenal – the arms. Like two armies wasted by attrition, equally matched, equally powerful, equally weary they stood, toe to toe, and slugged it out. They punched and hit, got punched and were hit. Each blow came over like a shell, seemingly slow, but just as unavoidable.

Each hoped he could strike the one. The one blow, the blow that would be enough to crumple the enemy opposite.

It came at last, and, as though they sensed the kill, there was an almost inaudible sigh from the crowd as the first took off on its arc. It carried with it all the strength the fighter could muster and exploded on the other's chin. He seemed to shake like a tree that has taken the final axe blow and refuses to topple. For an age he seemed to hang there, his opponent too weary to raise anything more than a feeble cluster of punches to the man's arms as a follow-up. Then he toppled. The legs went first, their strength gone. He was on his knees, the referee holding back the other boxer, protecting the stag at bay. The stricken boxer looked up, but there was no pleading in the look, only resignation, defeat. Then he slid sideways, an arm flailing to protect himself, and lay like a drunken man, at angles to himself on the canvas. The count was unnecessary and the other man threw two tired arms aloft, a hideous look of happiness and pain on the bruised face.

The bored crowd applauded politely.

Klein leaned across to Margot and Dudley in a wreath of cigar smoke. 'What do you think Margot? Like the fight game?'

Margot arched an eyebrow and leaned forward confidentially. 'A trifle rougher than I'm used to, Lewis, but I could get to like it.'

Klein laughed. 'Bit like life really Margot – or politics, hey Dudley?'

Dudley laughed. 'Some of these lads wouldn't last five minutes at Question Time.'

'When you're Prime Minister, Dudley, I think you'll see them off at Question Time like our Tommy is going to see off this lad tonight.'

'I sincerely hope there won't be any blood, it would look awful on the front bench,' and Dudley laughed his short politician's laugh again.

Margot looked without fear into Klein's eyes and held them. 'And when he is our gallant P.M., Lewis, you wouldn't just be hoping for a little old knighthood would you?' She waved a hand down the row to her left, where Sir Peregrine was fondling the ample bust of an unknown blonde who'd turned up with him that evening.

'What with Perry *and* my husband rooting for you I would have thought there'd hardly be a problem?'

Klein shook his head in mock sorrow. 'You're a sweet girl Magot, but much too Machiavellian for me. I'm just a simple lad from the East End made good. You aristocrats are always under the impression everyone is after something.'

Klein slid back in his seat and Margot whispered in her husband's ear. 'Watch him Dudley, he's using you, you know that. You and Perry. As soon as you turn the key in Number Ten he'll be knocking on the door begging for a trip to the Palace.'

Dudley spoke out of the side of his mouth, but neither need have worried, for Klein was already half out of his seat talking to a knot of boxing promoters. 'For God's sake darling, don't talk about it now. The man is a friend. You know how much he donates to the party – outside the big boys he's probably the single biggest contributor, and he has been a significant help to us in the East End. You know what happened at that by-election; do you think for a minute we'd have stood a chance without his help? We gave them a bloody shock, I can tell you. Their majority down from 13,000 to 617. At the General Election they'll have to devote time and money to what used to be a safe seat. Every bit helps, and in that arena it is all down to Klein's personal pull. So don't knock the man to me. And afterwards, if he wants a trip to the Palace, well, maybe it can be arranged.'

'God, you really want that job, don't you?'

Dudley unconsciously clenched both fists, and Margot saw the knuckles whitening. 'Of course I want it. I deserve it. This bunch of incompetents and the clown who's sitting there at the moment aren't fit to run a chicken farm. I could be a great P.M.,' he turned to Margot, 'you know I could.'

She took his hand and gently unclenched the fist. 'And you wouldn't let anything prejudice that ambition? Would you sweety?'

Dudley thought guiltily of Emily. 'Nothing.'

But Emily was more than just a lover – if the word love could ever be applied to The Honourable Dudley Creighton. No, he thought, she is my power. Inspiration. I am the articulation of her thoughts. The political *nous* of the woman was amazing. She could spot trends, discover what people were thinking, the way politics was going. Without her, without her hidden force, deep down, he knew he'd never make it to Downing Street. Just another back bench MP wasting away with useless questions in an empty, uncaring chamber. Her savvy had got him to be Leader of the party when the old man had stepped down through ill-health.

'Be the elder statesman,' she'd told him. 'Don't throw your hat in the ring straight away, but don't look as though you're frightened. "If my party needs me, reluctantly I'll serve", that must be your stance.'

So he'd waited and let the two main contenders wear each other to a standstill in three ballots Then he stepped in. With dignity but with energy. And the party had fallen for it, and now Sir Dudley Creighton was an election away from Number Ten Downing Street. In his terrifying, inward-looking moments, he knew that Emily was his power, his dynamo, his political brain. All he had to offer was looks, wealth, the ability to speak – and a Presidential wife. Nothing would prejudice his ambition. But Emily wasn't a risk; she was a necessity. It was a political relationship. That's what everyone thought, even the bitchy cynical Westminster crew with eyes ever alert for a lingering touch, a stolen glance that would indicate an affair.

Not Emily, they all thought, bloody frosty virgin. The papers had done their bit on Emily leaping out from the Cessna. Little mousy Emily, dwarfed by the helmet and parachute pack, the tiny features peering out from behind the visor. Who'd want to go to bed with that! Not Dudley, with a wife like he'd got tucked up in bed waiting for him.

No, he was safe from any hint of gossip on that score.

Klein turned to Archie: '. . . if he wins this fight – pardon my lack of faith, *when* he wins this fight – he is going to get the best offer an amateur boxer ever had, and, as they say in the Mafia, it will be an offer he can't refuse.'

Archie looked alarmed. 'Christ, Lew, you're not going to threaten him?'

Klein managed to look perplexed and disgusted at the same time: 'What do you think I am Archie, a criminal? No, it was a figure of speech. A joke. Oh, forget it. What I mean is the offer will be so good he'd have to have half a brain to refuse it. And this boy, I assure you, has one hell of a brain in good working order. No, he'll agree tonight, and then we'll have a big press conference, with champagne – thanks for that little piece of advice, Archie, I always thought pressmen preferred halves of bitter – and we'll announce it then. Lunchtime tomorrow. Your paper'll look good and we'll have a nice spread in the London evenings and the national dailies the day after.'

'If he signs.'

"He'll sign. Because, you know what we're offering him? I'll tell you. We're offering him something money can't buy. We're offering to help him realise his ambition. To be world champion . . . heavyweight champion of the world.'

Archie said, 'I don't know that much about boxing, Lew, but isn't that a bit ambitious? He's still an amateur.'

'And I'm sure Columbus used to play in rowing boats but he still managed to discover Australia.'

Archie let the remark go. 'You must be sinking a lot of cash into him; you sure he can make it?'

'Absolutely. It'll take a couple of years, perhaps more, but he'll do it. And there's not only me with faith in him. Perry's in it too – off the record at this moment Archie. He's going to invest heavily in this boy. He'll have his own training H.Q. on Perry's estates, he'll have skilled dietary advice, doctors, the best machines to train on, everything a boxer could wish for. He'll be the best prepared boxer in the world when we're finished with him. And – our secret weapon, this – he'll have old Maxie Wellington, who knows more about the fight game, from the inside, than any man around today.'

'Isn't he the guy you pulled out of the gutter? I thought he was a bit punchy! What do you want with an old bum like that? I thought,' there was a trace of sarcasm in Archie's voice, 'this was a scientific operation.'

Anger glinted in Klein's eyes. Shitty little muck-raking pencil pusher, he wouldn't be able to take a fiftieth of the pain Maxie had taken. He put a firm hand on Archie's shoulder, and the gossip columnist felt an uncontrollable surge of fear rush through him like a mild electric shock.

'Maxie was a good fighter. I remember him. One of the best, he was. Game, a good puncher. But in those days nobody cared too much for fighters. They were working class, you see. Stout fellow, salt of the earth, but when they got mismatched and punched out, they were thrown back on the scrap-heap where they'd come from, and then some other young hopeful was conned into believing he was going to make it to Madison Square Garden. But don't run Maxie down to me, Archie, never. If it was now and I was his manager, he'd have a bloody big house at Chigwell, I'd see to that. As it is he's going to get it anyway, when he helps Tommy to bring home the bacon.' His hand left Archie's shoulder, and the gossip columnist shivered.

'Yeh, sorry about that Lew, he sounds a nice chap.'

'Nice is a good word for Maxie.'

The man in the monkey suit was speaking into the microphone. 'Ladeez angennelmen . . .'

Lewis pointed to the corner on their left. 'That's Tommy, isn't he magnificent?'

Archie nodded. Tommy was, even to an untutored eye, a magnificent figure of a man. But so, he observed ruefully, was his opponent. A West Indian, skull closely cropped, body sheening black in the lights, tight and muscled, the legs sinewy, the hanging arms speaking of hidden danger.

Perry ignored the introductions. He had his hand in the blonde girl's blouse, stroking the nipple of her left breast. For modesty, her fur stole hung over her left shoulder, but it was little more than camouflage. Sir Peregrine wasn't interested in the ritual. He had come for the action – and the results. At the sound of the bell his hand left the American girl's blouse like a fighter darting from his corner. His eyes blazed excitement. With searchlight intensity they focused on the young white man sparring cautiously with his opponent. Tommy and the West Indian knew each other. They'd sparred at the same club. The West Indian knew how good Tommy was. Very good. The West Indian knew he had only one chance. Catch him cold. He'd seen Tommy hit in the first twenty seconds of a fight, almost as though he took time to concentrate. The West Indian moved in and the two men traded cautious punches. Then the West Indian hooked with his left. The punch got through like a pistol shot to Tommy's nose. Blood sprayed in an arc onto Tommy's white vest. The crowd bayed like hounds sensing a wounded fox. The fight was just forty-seven seconds old. Tommy danced back, ignoring the blood. But this was an amateur fight, albcit a championship one.

The white-shirted referee stepped in and separated the two boxers. He pulled Tommy aside and as the crowd gave a collective groan, fearful it might be robbed of its sport, he peered at Tommy's nose. Klein gave an audible sigh of relief as the referee waved them on.

Tommy seemed unconcerned. The blood had stopped flowing now, but a red smear down the white vest showed that first blood – literally – had gone to the Jamaican. They were still fighting cautiously, and the crowd was getting restless. At this level – even from amateurs – they expected action. It was to come.

At the end of thc first round, Maxic took a long, hard look at Tommy's nose. 'Nothing serious Tommy, just a bleed. Just like when you was a kid.'

'I know,' said Tommy calmly, 'lucky strike. I've got the measure of him, don't worry about it.' He took a pull from the water bottle and spat it in a long waterfall into the waiting bucket.

Yes, thought Tommy, I've got your measure my son. I remember you from way back and you haven't improved much. You're unwieldy. You lack balance. Something about you West Indians that makes you different from the black Yankee fighters. You think it's a bloody limbo dance; they know how to fight. All the same, his nose stung, and bizarrely Tommy didn't try mentally to mask the pain. There'll be more like this. Get used to it, this is nothing compared to what's got to be taken in the future. The pain roused him, set his senses alight.

Maxie was speaking into his ear. 'Watch those hooks Tommy. The bastard's got long arms. Get in close and work him over.'

Tommy nodded and was on his feet as the bell went.

The two men closed and Tommy saw with a glint of triumph the hardly masked look of fear in the other man's eyes. You've blown it, my son. You were going for the quick one weren't you? Well you haven't got it, have you, so now let's see how you shape up.

The West Indian danced back, left and right arms going in a poor imitation of Mohammed Ali. Not enough my son, you haven't got the speed. Tommy closed quickly, sending jarring punches to the arms before he got inside the guard.

The West Indian was trying to protect his body and his head. But he didn't have the sense of timing to do both. Tommy would feint a left to his head and the two long, black arms would go up like a fortress gate. Then Tommy's Trojan right would strike like a piledriver under the guard and into the ribs. The other fighter winced. They were hurting. Right, let's do some damage. Tommy was getting through with punch after punch, but the West Indian was still alert, putting up some sturdy reply punches and still making an attempt at evasive footwork.

The referee was watching him closely though. These lads weren't in it for the money. They wanted no A.B.A. contestant in a coma. The black man was breathing heavily but stormed out of his corner with a flurry of punches that hit Tommy like a snowstorm.

Life in the old dog yet, okay, try this for size. The West Indian was having trouble defining the range of his punches. Some he was flinging over Tommy's shoulders. Others were battering air inches from the fighter. Tommy stepped back onto the ropes and the West Indian came on lured like a rookie cavalry patrol into the ambush. Tommy gave him a straight right. Some instinct told the West Indian it was coming and he jerked up his chin. But the punch took him full on the throat. He staggered back. Tommy stepped in, brushing aside the arms waving like jungle vines. He hit the Jamaican with a salvo of punches to the body. He felt the black man wince in pain and drop his arms. Then he saw the chin, jutting towards him like a black rock of Gibraltar. It isn't often in a fighter's life he gets such an opportunity. The right started at Tommy's waist and came upwards at an angle with all the power of a steam shovel.

A split second after the punch connected something happened to the Jamaican. One sports writer was reminded of a decapitated chicken who keeps running, headless, on surviving nerves. The man's legs buckled, then they seemed to right themselves. Then a quiver ran down the length of his body as though he had been given an electric shock, and the legs took off in a two-second obscene, jerky two-step: back, forward, back again. Then he toppled sideways and hit the middle rope. The weight of his torso began to take his body through in a sliding arc, out of the ring and onto the press benches. The quick-thinking referee grabbed his leg, and a couple of pressmen – knowing the fight was over – pushed him bodily back into the ring and onto the canvas.

A doctor was called.

Tommy stepped, dripping and stark naked, from the shower and into a mini-arena of noise, smoke and champagne.

Maxie thrust a glass into his hand and hugged the boxer affectionately, spilling half the champagne. 'Drink it you little bastard, you've earned it. Just the one, mind.'

Tommy sipped the champagne and felt the stinging of the bubbles in his injured nose, a sweet reminder of his triumph. The circle of faces around him were grinning, smiling at him. People were speaking to him, but the words seemed jumbled together, he couldn't seem to make out any individual sentences. So this was what it was going to be like from now on. He took another sip from the champagne glass. He decided he didn't like the taste but, like the pain in the ring, it was a symbol of the way ahead. He drank again.

A figure detached itself from the mêlée. Lewis Klein. 'Tommy, congratulations my boy. An excellent performance. You saw him off in style.'

'Thank you Mr Klein. Maxie told me this morning you might want a word with me.'

'I do Tommy, I do. I have a little business proposition to put to you.' He put his arm around the naked fighter and steered him to a quieter corner of the dressing room. The men spoke for several minutes.

Behind the champagne bottles, the cigar smoke and the noise, Lady Margot Creighton stood with her husband, Archie Taylor and Sir Peregrine. With a look of healthy curiosity, but somehow detached, she watched the naked boxer. She took in the powerful shoulders, trim, muscled waist and sturdy legs. The limp penis, brown against the mound of blonde pubic hair caught her eye and a thought within made her smile and look away.

Archie nudged her. 'Good looking little bastard, isn't he?'

Margot nodded. 'Quite the Greek God. I wouldn't mind going fifteen rounds with him myself.'

Archie swigged his champagne. He was feeling drunk now. He'd called the office: Grenfell's kid had coughed all, they'd got pix, and it would be a damn good show for the day after tomorrow, so he'd decided to relax a little.

'Speaking of normal human beings, Margot, there's always me. Bachelor gay, or rather, in this day and age, delete the gay. Pity about that. It was a good word, gay.'

Margot kissed him softly on the cheek. 'You're adorable, Archie, you know that, and if ever Dudley divorces me I'll come running round to your flat before you can say Jack Robinson. Deal?'

Archie took another swig. 'Deal, Margot.'

Tommy was still sitting in the corner, naked, talking to Klein. She wondered what he was like as a lover. Just a boy really. Clumsy, rough perhaps, and yet she almost sensed a quality of gentleness in that rippling body. For a moment she daydreamed. Imagining the young boxer thrusting into her, burying the blonde curly head in her breasts. Her teaching him, guiding, helping, bringing him to new heights of pleasure. She was jerked out of her fantasy by the words: 'Ladeez an gennelmen.' There was a ripple of applause for Klein's mock introduction . . . 'I give you Tommy Booth. Amateur Boxing Association heavyweight champion.' More applause.

Klein hushed it with an outstretched hand. 'And may I say that Tommy has, in a way, achieved two landmarks tonight . . . he's just agreed to turn professional under my management.' Burst of applause and a sporadic rendering of 'For he's a jolly good fellow'.

'Who?' wondered Archie, with drunken moroseness, 'Tommy or Klein?'

'This information,' said Klein, 'may I add, is not for the benefit of the press until noon tomorrow, so I would urge everybody in this room to regard it as our little secret.'

Everyone who knew Klein – and everyone in the room knew him – was so urged. The words were wafting over Tommy's head now. He was high on a mixture of pain, champagne and exhaustion after combat. Her heard words . . . 'future world champ' . . . He would be that. HE WOULD BE THAT. And then . . . 'my good friend Sir Peregrine . . . substantial investment . . . training centre . . .' They connected with words Lewis Klein had spoken to him just minutes earlier. He would be the best prepared fighter ever. Yes. And the best trained and best advised.

Then through the heads he saw the face of a woman. His first reaction was annoyance and embarrassment. Who'd let a bloody bird in here? He'd banned his own girl from the fight, let alone the dressing room. But someone just had to let their bit of crumpet in. He was no bloody peep show, and roughly he pulled on his dressing gown. She was watching Klein and Tommy watched her. She was good looking. But more. Her face had . . . Tommy searched for the word . . . class? He hated that word. No, style. Style.

There was a round of applause and someone held Tommy's hand high. He smiled into the sea of faces. Then Klein took him by the arm and steered him towards the woman.

Klein made the introductions. 'Tommy, I want you to meet Lady Margot Creighton and Dudley Creighton.'

Tommy stuck out a hand and Dudley took it. 'Pleased to meet you, young man, congratulations on tonight.'

Margot's hand was soft and warm, but she took the boxer's hand firmly. 'Tommy, it's a pleasure.'

The boxer stammered for words under the confident gaze of those large, brown eyes. 'Hope you enjoyed the fight?'

'A novel experience, neither my husband nor I had seen a live boxing match before.'

'No,' said Dudley, 'didn't realise there was so much noise. Anyway, young man, we must be leaving soon,' he laid his patronising politician's hand on the boy's arm. 'It's been a pleasure meeting you; if you're ever near the house, don't hesitate to call in.'

Tommy hesitated. He could feel the blood rushing to his cheeks. 'Your house? But . . . but I'm afraid I don't know where you live.'

Dudley smiled reassuringly: 'Definite article Tommy, THE House, House of Commons, Mother of Parliaments, all that.'

'Yes, yes, of course. Thank you.'

Margot looked at Tommy. To think this powerful man, this fighter who did so much damage in the ring less than an hour before, could be put out by Dudley. The vulnerability of the giant. She could visualise those arms, those legs, that body crushing her down, defenceless, beaten, subjugated.

She turned to her husband. 'I'd like a few more words with Tommy before we leave, dear. Business, remember?'

Dudley nodded: 'I'll wait in the car. Don't be too long. I want to be there by midnight. Bye Tommy.'

'Bye Dudley.'

Margot took the boxer's arm, feeling the power as it gave against her touch, and guided him to a corner of the dressing room.

'That was quite a fight tonight Tommy. You're the best boxer I've ever seen.'

Tommy laughed, but his eyes held hers. She's from another world, he thought. She makes my girl seem, what? Drab, dull. Just ordinary. Her skin was alive, it glowed. He'd never liked make-up, hating the dull plaster of paris face powder, the thick black mascara of the girls down in the East End. But she was made-up, soft oil on her face, gentle marking round the eyes, soft moist lipstick. Instead of blotting out her beauty it seemed to enhance it. Tommy could feel his hand shaking. She still had her hand on his arm.

Bravely he said: 'How many boxers have you seen Mrs ... I'm sorry, Lady Creighton?'

'Margot. Call me Margot. And to tell the truth, just the ones on the bill before you.'

'Not really a fair comparison. I'm just an amateur.'

'Correction Tommy. As from tonight, if I hear aright, you're a professional.'

'Yes, I mean that I haven't actually fought any professional ...'

'I know what you mean Tommy.'

Tommy moved his arm. He could feel the passion rising in him and he remembered he was only wearing a dressing gown. He'd never wanted a woman so much in his life. And another man's wife. It was always the bloody same. You could never have what you wanted, it always belonged to someone else. Then he remembered the World Championship. An East End boxer couldn't take away the wife of a Tory politician, that wasn't on. But he could, *would* take away the title.

Now that *was* on.

'Tommy, you're miles away.'

Tommy shook his head to calm his passion and clear his head of dreams. 'I'm sorry. Can I get you some more champagne?'

Margot looked at her empty glass. 'Some other time, Tommy. We'll be seeing a lot more of each other from now on.'

Tommy thought of her watching him naked and failed to suppress a smirk. 'Well you've seen all there is to see of me. Will I get as good a view of you?'

Margot tried to look stern. 'That's cheeky!'

'I'm sorry. Why . . . why will we be seeing more of each other?'

'No doubt Perry – Sir Peregrine – hasn't got round to telling you yet. My sideline is photography. I'm being modest, I do it rather well, actually. The only thing that stops me doing it full-time is those bastards in the N.U.J. They don't think a woman whose husband earns a small fortune – that's how they see it – should get a union card.'

Tommy stared at Lady Margot in surprise. Never before had he heard such a woman swear openly in front of a man. In the East End it was only slags on a Saturday night out at the local who swore, and yet here, standing in front of him, was this elegant beauty coolly calling people bastards. And yet in some inexplicable way he found it exciting.

'Have you had any pictures published?'

'Lots. Magazines here and there – West Germany, France, the States, some advertising work – that I *am* allowed to do. But anyway, Perry and Klein want a comprehensive photo-record of their budding champ.' She poked a finger at Tommy, 'That's you, chum, and they decided to use me. They know I'm okay, but frankly they know that no other photographer can spare the two years odd it's going to take, off and on, hanging around you. So I'm stuck with it.'

Tommy looked hurt. 'Don't you want to do it?'

'Of course I do, it was only a turn of phrase. Tommy, if you're going to be the next Mohammed Ali you'll have to learn to spot sarcasm, wit, irony, *double-entendre* and all the other shit our gallant media friends will throw at you once you're in the running. Don't worry, I'll give you a hand. I've mixed with the best – bitches that is, and contrary to James Herriott they come in all sexes.'

Tommy took her arm, emboldened by he wasn't sure what: 'So if you're going to be my official photographer you'll be seeing more of me. But only if I can see some more of you.'

Margot raised her eyes in mock surprise. 'What do you expect? I'm a respectable married woman!'

Tommy took his hand away. 'I'm sorry, I didn't mean anything rude. Please don't get the wrong idea.'

Margot took his arm. 'I didn't. See you very soon. I must dash or Dudley will divorce me.' She leaned across and her lips brushed Tommy's cheek in a strictly acceptable 'hello darling', 'goodbye sweetheart' kiss. Then she was gone.

Tommy felt the mark of her lips on his cheek and inhaled the scent of her perfume. Expensive. No girl he'd been near had ever smelled like that. He sat down heavily on the bench. I've never been k.o.'d by a bird before: that's for sure.

'Everything all right, Tommy, my son?' It was Maxie.

'Yes fine, fine.'

What chance have I got? Bloody East End boxer, I can't string two words together. She must be ten years older than me. She's mature, she's travelled, husband a bloody politician. I wish he would divorce her. Christ I couldn't go out with a married lady even if I wanted to. My mum and dad'd kill me. It'd be the talk of the street. And anyway, no chance son, no bloody chance. Blot it out of your mind. He screwed his eyes tightly closed. He wanted her. *He wanted her*. And I've got the time. The time to wait. Wait to win the championship and I can have anything I want. I've seen the gorgeous birds who hang around the big-time boys. Glamorous groupies, they are.

And Tommy Booth, East End boxer, realised, almost with irony, that he stood a good chance of getting Lady Margot Creighton.

The chauffeur-driven Daimler purred through Knightsbridge, round Hyde Park Corner and down Constitution Hill past Buckingham Palace. The Royal Standard was hanging limply from the flagpole, showing the Queen was in residence.

'Must you go to the House darling?'

'Important division, dear. I have to be there, you know that.'

They sat apart in the cavernous waste of the limousine, like strangers on an empty bus, putting the maximum of space between them. Not crossing the critical distance.

Flushed and excited from her encounter with the boxer, yet hardly recognising her own motives, Margot said evenly, 'It has been three weeks since we made love. Is something wrong?'

Dudley coughed into his hand and addressed the glass panel dividing him from the driver. 'You know what a session this has been. Have you any idea of what these late night sittings do to you?'

She put a hand out to stroke his, but stopped it halfway on its journey. 'Of course. You need a holiday. I'll fix something for the recess if I'm not involved on the Tommy Booth thing.'

Dudley spoke the words in front of him. 'Smashing. Somewhere warm.'

At the House of Commons he stepped from the limousine without a word, a wave or a goodbye glance. As the car pulled away from the kerb Margot shut her eyes and leaned back in her seat. Waves of images of the boxer swept over her and she felt powerless to resist them. She shifted uncomfortably, the feeling surging through her. Oh God, I need the real thing. She slipped her hand under the fur coat, inside her blouse and stroked her nipple, firm and erect. God Almighty, I can't bear it. Her other hand had wandered unconsciously to her thigh, feeling her own soft flesh above the stocking top.

She didn't want this. She clenched her eyes firmly shut. She wanted . . . she couldn't bring herself to mouth his name. It was absurd. But she wanted him. The car was going past thc Tatc Gallery, the moon shining into a full and heavy Thames. Her painted nails slipped under the silk panties and touched a mound of tightly curled hair.

The two men stood on the deserted pavement, the white of dinner shirts peeping from overcoats. Their bow ties hung loose like party streamers. They were both a little drunk.

'So, what do you think of your investment Perry?'

'It's a long trail, Lewis, a very long trail. But it's a good start. He certainly dealt with our dark friend.'

'In style, Perry, and that's the way he's going to continue.' Klein put out a hand. 'When he becomes the heavyweight champ I'll buy you the best, oldest, finest bottle of claret at your club. Deal?'

'Could set you back the cost of a new mini, what I hear.'

Klein swept his arm to the skies. 'If you prefer a new mini, Perry, I'll buy you that. The choice is yours.'

'I'll settle for the claret. How about a 1945 Chateau Lafite?' Sir Peregrine took his hand. 'To our success Lewis.'

'To our success.'

'I'll call you,' Lewis shouted, disturbing several sleeping pigeons who cooed uneasily.

'Do that.'

Lewis climbed into the Jaguar, rubbing his hands. 'Turned into a bit of a bastard out there, get the heater going for Christ's sake.'

Graham coughed the engine into life, set his steely blue eyes on the road, turned the heater to 'Hot' and cruised through Knightsbridge, heading for the East End.

'Monique's?'

Klein nodded. 'I'm stopping in town. Your flat. Remember I told you and remember the night.'

Graham tapped his leather-gloved fingers on the steering wheel, 'Can't think why you bother with the pretence, Mr Klein. She'd never find out. Don't think she really knows what day it is.'

The Jaguar lurched across the white line, sending a Cortina scuttling onto the pavement as Klein's fist slammed into Graham's head. The car screeched to a stop.

'Jesus! You could have killed us.' Graham was holding his head. Klein grabbed him by the hair, dragging his face an inch from his own.

'You get this straight, sonny Jim. You may have worked for me for the last hundred and fifty years, but you don't talk about my wife like that. Savvy?'

Graham nodded as much as he was able. 'Sorry Mr Klein.'

'And so you should be. My wife suffers ill health and isn't robust enough to carry out certain marital obligations. Because of that I regard it as my duty not to bother her. Monique and I have an understanding. But that does not mean . . .' he tugged at Graham's hair to emphasise the point . . .' that I do not take marriage seriously or treat my obligations lightly.'

'Sorry Mr Klein.' Klein released his hold.

'Now bloody drive before some filth takes it upon himsel to relieve his boredom by talking to us.'

Graham drove down Constitution Hill, down the Mall, round Trafalgar Square and down the Strand towards Fleet Street. At a news stand opposite Bouverie Street, halfway down Fleet Street, Graham stopped the car as he was instructed. Klein bought some first editions with story and pictures of Tommy's triumph. He read them in silence until the car stopped outside a flat above a bookmaker's shop – his own – in a side road off Poplar High Street. He took out an envelope and handed it to Graham.

'Birthday present.'

Graham opened it and spread the £200 in twenties like a fan.

'There's no need boss, you know that.'

'Bonus, Graham. Do a good job on him. I want that cunt to shit himself when he hears my name.'

Graham nodded. 'I could blow him away Mr Klein, easy as cracking an egg.'

'Who do you think I am – Al bleeding Capone? No, this is better. Kill the bastard and everyone will forget in a month the way things are going in this town. This way is much better. And don't forget to tell him, if he so much as breathes a word to the filth – not that he will have one iota of proof, Graham my son – but that if he does we'll not only waste him but his wife, his kids and his fucking mother-in-law. Don't forget to tell him.'

'I won't Mr Klein.'

'Who you using, Andy and Dave?'

Graham nodded.

'Yeh, they're reliable. Don't piss it up, Graham.'

'No danger.'

Klein shut the car door, took a key from his pocket and slipped into a door at the side of the betting shop. He took the stairs, two at a time. You're still in shape Lewis, old lad.

She was waiting at the top of the stairs wearing just bra and panties. He hugged her neck and she kissed him on the lips.

'Hello love. Hungry?'

'Hungry for love.'

She laughed. 'Life in the old dog yet, eh?'

'Bet your bottom dollar. Good night at the club?'

She swivelled her hips in time to imaginary music, pouted and thrust out her pelvis. 'I wasn't exactly Margot Fonteyn, but then the Starlight isn't exactly Sadlers Wells.'

He hugged her close. 'Not to worry love, wait till this Tommy thing gets off the ground, then we'll get you into proper cabaret. We'll have you at Las Vegas yet.'

Monique clenched her fist. 'Positive thinking. Las Vegas here we come.'

Klein slipped off his coat and began to unlace his shoes. 'How's your mum?'

'Much the same. I got a letter day before yesterday. I think she misses me, and pines for me dad. That's the main story.'

Klein delved into his inside pocket and tossed a white plastic wallet into her lap as she sat opposite him.

'What's that?'

'Open it.'

She did and held out two blue and red tickets with the words 'British Airways' on each.

'What's this?'

'You sound like a bloody parrot.' Klein leaned across and flicked open a ticket, he closed it and opened the other. 'Can you read?'

'Lewis, I'm not a savage.' She mouthed the words, 'Miss

Monique Derand . . . London – Mauritius. Lewis, you sweet thing!' She flung herself round Klein. 'I can see my mum, oh Lewis, thank you, thank you!' She looked at the ticket. 'Twenty-eight . . . god, that's, that's Friday. Lewis the club . . .'

'It's been arranged. Now don't you want to see who's going with you?'

She snatched at the other ticket, then flung herself back in his arms. 'Our first holiday. I can't believe it. My mum's gonna love you . . . not that she approves of white men, mind you, but I think she'll make an exception in your case. Oh Lewis, you darling.'

She pulled away, momentarily sombre. 'What will you tell . . . ?'

'It's business. She's going to Frinton to her sister's. She likes Frinton.'

Monique crouched down and rested her chin on Klein's knees. 'How anyone can ever say a bad word about you I will never know.' She stood up, took him by the hand and led him to the bedroom door. 'Oh boy, have I got something special in store for you.'

As a Mr Lewis Klein, businessman, and a Miss Monique Derand, entertainer, sipped champagne in the First Class compartment of a British Airways 747 jumbo jet as it cruised south through the darkness, Graham was piloting a stolen Mercedes through the heavy Friday night West End traffic.

Dodd didn't look like a criminal, still less a psychopath. His well-tailored clothes, expensively cut hair, hand-made shoes, shirts from Turnbull and Asser combined with his height and undoubted good looks to give him the style of a newspaper ad clipped from a glossy Sunday magazine. The vicious four-inch scar on his right cheek would, of course, have denied him that, but still it failed to hint at any trace of criminal activity. Casual observers thought of stirring sabre duels at Prussian universities rather than nasty bar-room brawls.

But Graham was a criminal, poured into the mould from

the East End streets before he was old enough to sit his 11-plus. Sweets from the corner shop, fruit off the cart. Then lead, then a bit of pickpocketing down at West Hampstead Football Club and a trip to the juvenile court and two years of boring, well-meaning, totally ineffectual probation officers.

Then at fifteen, the fights. Dance halls, pubs, gang brawls.

He was just fifteen when the Hell's Angels pushed into him outside the Dog and Sparrow. It would have been like a scene from *The Wild Ones* except that this was for real and the biker got a broken nose and a fractured skull. The first, Graham was ready to admit, was from his knuckle-duster, but the second he continuously maintained was a blow from the kerbstone. The court didn't agree and Graham found himself with short back and sides, in short trousers and boots – this time without steel toe-caps – in one of Her Majesty's Borstals.

On the seventh night he was awoken by a face near his, and a hand groping at the bedclothes. He struck out and was rewarded by a splash of blood on his hands.

'Dirty bastard!'

A week later they came for him. Seven of them. He fought but he couldn't stop them. Five held him down while two of them – his visitor from before and another – sated their repressed, perverted lust on his imprisoned body.

The dark horrendous secret never left him. Those who had violated him were released. But Graham never forgot or understood. And one terrible night he crept from his own bed to that of the blonde boy who had joined the dormitory two nights before.

Self-loathing seeping through every pore, Graham slipped beneath the blanket, a hand over the blonde boy's mouth. 'Make a noise and I'll kill you.'

'I won't make a noise, I promise.' The blonde boy didn't need to be held down. He even put an arm round Graham's neck and stroked his hair.

Later Graham went back to his own bed and sobbed silently, praying for the dawn.

He had exactly 3s 4d and owed two weeks' rent at his digs when Klein hired him at his betting shop.

'You been inside?' Klein asked him roughly.

'Yes,' said Graham, without shame.

'What can you do?'

'Anything,' said Graham, defiantly. 'I'll do anything.'

'Yes,' said Klein, 'I do believe you would. You're hired.' He gave him £50 there and then to pay his digs, have a proper meal and buy a suit. That sealed Graham's affection for Klein. Now – although his criminal career hadn't up to now included the ultimate act – he would kill for the man.

Graham touched the scar on his face as he eased the Mercedes through the dawdling commuters. Got that for Klein, he thought proudly. They'd been coming out of a restaurant in the King's Road. It was a surprise. They might have expected it in Poplar, but they'd been lulled into a false sense of security among the boutiques, the tourists and the bistros. It was some old quarrel but whoever it was had sent one of his lads with a razor – thank Christ it wasn't a shotgun, thought Graham later.

Graham had just seen the glint of the blade in its downward curve and threw himself in front of Klein. He took the blow on the cheek, feeling it open up to the bone. He felt no pain, kicked the assailant in the groin, and as the man lay groaning on the pavement, kicked him twice in the ribs, and stamped harshly and expertly on the outstretched fingers that had wielded the razor. It was some minutes later, as Klein and his friends drove him to hospital, that Graham realised why his shirt was soaking wet. Everyone knew, including Graham, that there would be a scar. He seemed the least concerned, and wore it now like a badge of courage, a symbol of his loyalty to Klein.

He remembered the cutting from the *Daily Express*. The man had three broken ribs and four crushed fingers on his right hand. The index finger, Graham recalled with relish, had to be amputated. He wouldn't be using razors any more.

Graham threaded the car through the City traffic, watching the lemming-like hordes streaming out of the offices, banks and city institutions for the railway stations at London Bridge, Fenchurch Street, Cannon Street and Liverpool Street. And then the packed cattle-ride home to semis in Romford, Croydon, Brentwood, Southend, Bromley, and an evening, tired and lethargic, slumped in front of the television. He shuddered in disgust.

In the secret corner of his mind that he kept locked like a forbidden cupboard he remembered Danny. They had nothing in common. Graham had made himself an expert on art. He'd devoured every book on the subject he could find. Anything to separate himself from what he regarded as the ignorant scum he'd been brought up with. Graham was determined to have class. He now boasted of the fact that he'd visited every major art gallery in Europe. He was privately building himself a collection of fine watercolours. If ever Klein teased him about it, Graham referred to it as 'just my little hedge against inflation, Mr Klein'.

A complete contrast to the world where he'd met Danny. The forty-year-old ex-boxer ran a small gymnasium off the Mile End Road where young hopefuls could get a work-out and some advice. Graham hadn't realised about Danny. And he thought, too, that his homosexuality was dead, finished, left behind at the Borstal.

But Danny had been having dinner at Graham's flat in Whitechapel opposite the Blind Beggars. They were both drunk. Graham felt the blackness loom again and was powerless to stop it. He soon knew why Danny spent the long hours watching the young muscled boxers working out in the gym; towelling their perspiring bodies.

Once a month, sometimes more, when desire became too strong, instead of suppressing the urge he would visit the gym and watch the fighters, sparring with them in an attempt to assert his masculinity. But instead he found himself sexually aroused. Then Danny would drive with him to his flat.

They never spoke of their relationship, even as they sipped wine from Graham's cellar or ate the food Graham prepared in his well-equipped kitchen. And tonight, after this is done, I'll call Danny. Graham shuddered. We'll just talk. This time we'll just talk. And he knew, deep inside, he was lying.

Andy and Dave were waiting in the car park behind the cinema. They got out of the brown Cortina estate and approached the Mercedes.

'Got the plates?'

'Yeh.'

'Well put 'em on, quick.'

In the dark of the car park the two men expertly screwed the false registration plates onto the Mercedes.

'Okay. Let's go.'

The car, with Graham and Dave in the front and Andy in the back, headed towards a north-east London suburb.

After a long period of silence Andy said, 'What's he done Graham?'

'Not the faintest,' said Graham. 'Well that's not true, I do. He's been pissing round Monique again at the club. Man's a fucking lunatic, he knows what happened last time.' Graham tossed the words to the back seat. 'Got the gear?'

Andy held up a joiner's bag and jangled it: 'All here Pontius.'

'Shut your fucking mouth Andy, I want comedians I'll watch the Marx Brothers. You're not carrying, either of you?'

Andy said: 'For Jock? You must be joking. What would I need, fucking water pistol?'

Dave leaned across. 'Not just Monique, is it Graham? Come on, give it. I heard Jock put in a bid for old Manny's shops over Romford.'

Graham didn't speak.

'And I heard further, my son, that when Klein told him to desist he told Uncle Lewis to go stuff himself. Do I get first prize?'

Graham laughed quickly: 'I heard it was domestic, just shows how much Mr Klein trusts me.'

'Leave it out,' said Andy, 'he tells you everything. You're a close bastard Graham.'

Graham took a left down a dual carriageway. 'We know what we've got to do, it doesn't matter a tuppeny toss why, okay?'

'As you like my son,' said Andy, and winked at Dave in the front seat. Graham saw it in the rear view mirror. It didn't matter. They'd do the job.

The little Scotsman upended his Scotch and waved to the barman. 'Till tomorrow Eddie, take care.'

'Cheers Jock. All the best.'

The cold night air hit him like a slap in the face and he turned his coat collar up. He felt for his car keys and jangled them reassuringly in his pocket. Hope the little boys in blue with the plastic bags aren't too thick on the ground tonight.

He was a car length from his Jaguar when the man stepped from the shadows.

'Mr McCulloch?'

'Yes.'

'Detective Constable Munroe. Few questions I'd like to ask you, sir, just routine, shouldn't take a minute. Car's right over here, sir.'

The Scotsman looked at the man in the half light. 'I don't know you. You're not local. Which station are you?'

The man's coat pocket sprouted a gun shape pointed directly at the Scotsman. 'Get in the car or I'll shoot you where you stand.'

He pushed the Scotsman to the Mercedes, opened the door, bustled him in and the car moved silently away. The man who had stepped from the shadows pulled out his hand from his coat pocket, the two fingers extended.

'Bang, bang, Jock, you're dead.'

'You bastards! What's the bloody game? Where are you taking me?'

'For a ride,' said Dave in the front. 'Yes,' said Graham, 'and you make one fucking sound to try and draw attention and we'll fucking shoot you, I promise you that.'

The Scotsman went white. 'Christ you're going to kill me! It's a bag job!' He slumped back in the seat.

'Don't worry,' said Graham reassuringly. 'We ain't going

to kill you. We'd've done it by now. So just sit there and keep quiet.'

They turned onto an industrial estate and into a burned-out warehouse. Graham stopped the car. He turned to face the Scotsman.

'Know why you're here Jock?' He didn't wait for a reply. 'I'll tell you. You know that bit of business with Manny?' Andy and Dave smiled. So that *was* it. 'Well do Mr Klein a favour and call it off.' He put up a hand to silence the Scotsman. 'I'm not interested in your reply, just call the business off. Oh, and Jock, if you so much as set foot near the filth even to ask the time of day we'll cut you and Maureen off at the knees and your little kiddiwinks had better watch out taking sweets from strange men.'

'You're a cunt Graham,' said the Scotsman sullenly.

'The finest,' said Graham, 'and when this night is over you'll need a new dictionary to describe me.'

At precisely 4.51 a.m. – the constable, seven months on the beat, logged it exactly – P.C. Dennis Westerman heard a noise from an alley containing garages behind a row of terraced houses in Chingford.

On proceeding into the alleyway, and shining his torch to ascertain the source of the noise, he saw a middle-aged man sprawled against a garage door, covered in blood, his arms splayed upwards and outwards. The man had been severely beaten and was barely conscious. On checking the odd position of the man's arms, which appeared to be self-supporting, the constable discovered they were held in place by two six-inch nails which had been driven through the palms of both his hands.

What the constable did not put in his report was that when he saw Jock McCulloch, the officer said: 'Jesus. They've crucified him.'

And was promptly sick down his almost new uniform tunic.

# *Chapter Three*

'. . . are all aware that the government has sadly mishandled the grave economic crisis in a manner that brings discredit on this country and upon its people . . .'

The right arm of Dudley Creighton thrust accusingly across the Commons at the Prime Minister, the finger like a dagger point. The Premier's normally bland, grey face flushed as the attack stung home. '. . . and it was a far greater Englishman than I who used the words on another occasion when our nation was in peril. But I make no excuse for repeating them this night. In the name of God, sir, go!'

'Resign! Resign!' The shouts echoed through the chamber, and bounced into the microphones, making the Commons reporters wince and clutch their ears. The seething ranks of Tory M.P.s, waving their order papers, bellowed at the boiling mass of Labour members on the other side of the political divide, like Greeks and Persians they stood, waiting to plunge into the Macedonian river and do battle.

Sir Dudley sat down, face suitably sombre, and the Prime Minister, looking bent and old, rose wearily to his feet and leaned on the Mace for support. The Speaker was calling for order as the thin, reedy voice of the Prime Minister started its reply: 'I am sure the Right Honourable Gentleman will forgive me if I remind him and his party . . .'

Dudley closed his eyes. There would be no battle, just blunted words, empty phrases. The swords had been sheathed in this chamber long ago. He could hear in the background two M.P.s from the opposing parties hurling abuse at each other, oblivious of the Prime Minister. Like belligerent school children, safe within the packed ranks of their own gang, they postured.

And afterwards? Well, Dudley thought, a drink together in the Members' bar, a pat on the back, 'Gave you a hard time tonight eh Reg?' Then dinner in the Members' dining room – subsidised of course. A choice of *canard à l'orange* or veal *cordon bleu* tonight. And the rabid political opponents would probably split a bottle of the house claret. Not at all bad.

Dudley permitted himself a small smile. I'll probably have a drink with the P.M. if he's not rushing off. He doesn't look at all well. Can't think why he doesn't pack it in and go back to Cambridge. His wife hates politics, always did. Poor girl, thought she was marrying a don and looking forward to dreaming spires, college teas and nothing more vitriolic than a bit of college politics. And now you can't pick up a newspaper that hasn't some cartoonist vilifying the poor old devil. Must really get to Marjorie, poor girl. Go back to Cambridge, Bill, or you'll be dead in eighteen months. Whatever way, thought Dudley, in less than two years I intend to be sitting across there, and then we'll start to have a little sanity back in the nation.

The thin voice droned on. '. . . and it ill becomes the Right Honourable Gentleman, a landed aristocrat, to lecture a government of the people on the way it should perform its duties.'

Dudley winked across at the Chancellor, who twitched an eyebrow in reply. Now come off it, Bill. I thought that approach had gone out with Harold Wilson and his 'sixties white heat technology. No my dear, aging Socialist friend. Landed I may be, and my forefathers, and aristocrat of sorts I suppose. But we were no robber barons or crusaders thrown a few million acres for making the trek to the Crusades, and well you know it.

Earned it, Bill, every penny, every square foot, every blade of grass. Through industry, enterprise and risk-taking out in the colonies. While your great-grandfather was cobbling shoes in Newcastle, mine was catching malaria and sweating out his dream-laden fever in Lucknow. Buying, selling, trading, travelling, risking, Bill, risking. Nineteenth-century capitalism. And uncles, risking all on a small factory, and then working ten years with never a day's break and then risking the whole pile on another factory. And the voters know it, Bill. Now I'm leader they're going to realise just what it was that made Britain great.

He watched the old man's feeble attempt to pound the despatch box. We gave our blood Bill, our blood for this nation. Crimea, Spion Kop, two elder brothers dead within six weeks of each other on the Somme. And my bit too. An M.C. with the Gloucesters on the Imjin. What did you do in the war, daddy?

Back-room boy, secret operations, beat the Jerries with clever words and a trick or two. Dudley shook his head, eyes still closed. He was growing drowsy. The vote was a foregone conclusion but it wouldn't do to fall asleep. Nation's future leader. Alert. Vigilant. He permitted himself the luxury of thinking about Emily. With Margot at Sir Peregrine's taking pictures of the young boxer, – what was his name? Booth? Tommy Booth – maybe I could risk that weekend I've been promising Emily.

She had a place down on the coast, near Brighton. No pressure and hardly anyone for miles. It was a risk. But why not? It had been a risk, hadn't it, on the Imjin. Bren white-hot jarring into the hip as he fired it into the yelling masses of Chinese P.L.A. troops, whistles, shrieking, bugles blowing. As risk when he stabbed at that yellow mongolian face and felt the bayonet sink into the man's throat and then the Chinese soldier's own bayonet piercing his calf. And a risk to lie as though dead, in the stifling, suffocating heat with the stench of his dead comrades putrefying around him. You didn't get a Military Cross by not taking a risk.

He looked across at the Mace and the grey face of the P.M. And Emily is my trump card, Bill. For your job. She's the one who gives me the ammunition I fire. So I have to take a small risk, don't I?

But Dudley Creighton, with the caution that had enabled him to rise through the minefields of promotion in the Conservative Party, reminded himself to think up a very, very good cover story.

*

Tommy Booth pushed the cup of cold coffee moodily across the plastic-topped table. Back and forth it went, the dirty brown liquid with its hint of froth like a dirty lace petticoat, slopping dangerously towards the rim. The harsh neon cast a pallor over his face and that of the girl opposite, washing out the colour, deadening the features. The acrid tang of hot fat and frying onions hung in the stale air.

Sylvia picked up her own cup and pretended to sip the cold coffee. She put the cup down and left a smear of pink lipstick like a calling card on the rim.

'Will I be able to come and see you Tommy? We've never really been separated before.'

There was something in her tone of voice, the hint of a whine, that irritated Tommy, plucked at something deep down within him, jangling his nerves.

'Look Syl, we've been over this a thousand times. Mr Klein says I can't have visitors, not even me mum and dad or even you. I'm a professional now, it's not a game any more, it's how I earn my living. Can't you understand that?'

She put a hand on his, arresting the monotonous, pointless back and forth journey of the coffee cup. He felt the touch, warm, moist, yet somehow lifeless. He remembered the vibrance of the hand Lady Margot Creighton had placed on his arm, and wondered what he had ever found exciting in Sylvia.

'Couldn't you train down the gym, love? You know, like you used to. Then we could go on like before.'

Tommy moved his hand away, and the girl's fell like a dead weight onto the surface of the table.

'Syl, listen to me, love. Things have changed. I'm going to be fighting real boxers now, not kids, amateurs. If I'm going to be a success I need the proper training, the proper equipment and advice, and I can't get any of that down the gym four nights a week and then on to the Palais with you, can I?' Tommy went on: 'Every minute of every day is going to be planned out for me; what I eat, when I go to bed, what time I get up. Mr Klein and Maxie, they've got it all worked out for me.'

A small man in a red nylon jacket and with dark Mediterranean features appeared at the table and pushed two plates in front of them: 'Two cheeseburgers and chips.' Tommy murmured a thank you.

'Don't you understand Syl? Don't you want me to make something of my life, be somebody?'

The girl tossed her head coquettishly and the tall, lacquered hairstyle teetered dangerously. 'You know what they say, don't you? All work and no play makes Tommy a dull boy. It doesn't sound all that much fun to me, the life you're going to be leading. Sounds more like you're training to be a monk than a boxer.'

Fun, thought Tommy. And is it fun with you Sylvia? The back row of the Odeon on Saturdays, heavy snogging, perhaps a hand up your blouse, and then the shoulder of my jacket plastered with face powder and mascara and knowing looks from my mud and dad. Or back at your sister's, baby-sitting so help me, and you with your bra round your neck and me getting all worked up like hell and then 'Tommy, no, please, not here, we mustn't', and you wedging my fingers in the top elastic of your tights to stop me going any further. And then when we did get round to it, lying there like a bloody corpse in the dark, and then afterwards not speaking, like we'd committed a crime. And then tears and nail-biting if your period hasn't arrived by the end of the month.

And then the knowing looks as we walk past H. Samuels, and how you pretend to want to look at the digital watches, when all the time it's the engagement rings you've got your eyes on.

Is that your idea of fun Sylvia?

'Syl, if I become world champion, you know, like Mohammed Ali, will that be fun? Won't it be worth it then? I'm prepared to invest time in it, won't you?'

Sylvia picked up a chip from her plate and nibbled at it like a cocktail straw. 'My, we have got big ideas now, haven't we? World champion. Well I never. Aren't you getting just a little bit big for your boots love? Shouldn't run before you can walk.'

Tommy felt the blood rush to his cheeks. He took her free hand and gripped it hard in his mighty fist.

'And why not? Why not me? Do you think Ali was born a champion? He was a little black kid in Louisville when it wasn't a good idea to be black in that part of the world. But he was good and so am I. And if he can make it, so can I. What makes us any different, eh? I'll tell you. We just don't *think* we can do it. We've always been told we can't. Ever since we were kids there's been somebody telling us we're nothing. Just dirt. Rubbish. You remember at school, Syl? Nobody talked to us about being doctors or lawyers, going to university, did they? No; bloody labourers and factory workers for us and sewing machinists in somebody's sweat shop or working behind the counter at Woolies for you.' He tightened his grip: 'Look at the bloody houses we live in, the shops we shop in. We get the worst of everything, no wonder we don't think anything of ourselves.'

'Tommy you're hurting me!'

The boxer released his grip and Sylvia rubbed her hand, a hurt, peeved look on her face. 'Well, I'm not ashamed of what I am, even if you are. I like working at Woolworths. And there's nothing wrong with our home, mum and dad have kept it very nice and dad's never had a day out of work all his life and mum works part time. And I'd . . .' she faltered, '. . . I'd always keep a good home for you, you know that.'

Tommy put his head in both his hands, his inability to explain eating at his heart. He looked up, leaned across and took both the girl's hands in his, gently this time. 'Sylvia. There's more to life than this.' He nodded at the cooling, congealing cheeseburgers. 'There are all kinds of good things that we only see on the telly or at the pictures. Cars, holidays, houses, restaurants, thousands of things. Well I want some of those things. I'm not going to spend the rest of my life in the East End. And if I have to give up things to make it, then I'll give them up.'

He looked intently at her, struggling for the right words.

'And Sylvia, if you're not prepared to make some sacrifices as well, then I'll give you up too. Do you understand?'

She nodded dumbly, biting at her upper lip. Then the tears came. Silently they spashed down from the dark, painted eyes, running long, mascara-stained rivulets through the face powder. They caught on the lips, diverted and dripped down from her dimpled chin onto the plate below.

Tommy realised for the first time, just how ugly she looked.

And wondered in amazement how he had ever loved her.

Klein's dark red Jaguar XJ12 saloon swept between the brick-built pillars. The tall, wrought-iron gates had been opened and held back by the elderly gate-keeper who had come from his small cottage just inside the entrance at the sound of the car's horn.

The car crunched up the drive, a screen of rhododendron bushes on either side. On the right, between the trees, the car's occupants could glimpse the flat expanse of water with its two small islands where the wild ducks nested. Sir Peregrine was fond of referring to it as 'my little duckpond'. Behind and beyond it, out of their vision, were the acres of woodlands, then the farm house and its outbuildings, and the rich meadows rolling down through the Wiltshire countryside. That was 'my little tax loss' to Sir Peregrine. The car rounded a bend in the drive after half a mile, and in front of them was Whyman Hall. Sixteenth century and handsomely restored and maintained, it was built like a letter H with the cross-bar nearer to one end.

Tommy had seen only one house like it. As a schoolboy on a day's outing by motor-coach he had travelled from the East End of London to the Bedfordshire countryside. That day he'd handed over his silver coin and, clutching his bag of sandwiches and bottle of lemonade, had traipsed through wood-panelled halls, while his schoolmistress recited the names of the severe-looking men in grey-curled wigs who glared down from the massive oil paintings. And now he was to live in such a house. Graham slid the Jaguar smoothly to rest in front of the large, double door, set mathematically in the centre of the cross-bar portion of the hall. Klein leaned across from the front passenger seat and tapped Tommy jovially on the knee. 'Got to put your name down early on the council housing list for one of these, eh my old son?'

Tommy laughed and slid the catch on the door and stretched his big frame out of the car. He felt a little cramped after the 120-mile journey from London and consciously flexed his muscles, then relaxed them.

Klein spread his arms in mock puzzlement. 'No Perry, no champagne, no red carpet, well I never. Graham, this young man is going to welch on his contract if we don't do better than this.'

Graham smiled nervously, stepped forward and hammered three times on the brass knocker set into the head of a tiger.

Thirty seconds later two bolts slid back behind the closed door, there was the click of a well-oiled lock, and a man dressed in black jacket, grey and black striped trousers, white shirt, black tie and immaculately polished black shoes with toecaps stood before them.

Before they could speak he said: 'Mr Klein and Mr Booth. Sir Peregrine asked me to apologise for not meeting you personally. He is on his way back from the farm at this moment. Come this way please.' Recognising a fellow servant in a way that only one who has spent his life waiting on the English upper classes can, he ignored Graham.

The three men followed him through the panelled halls, along the squeaky, waxed floors to a room at the end of a small corridor. The room was furnished simply but expensively with a writing desk, small coffee table and a leather sofa and two chairs. Hunting prints adorned the walls.

'Please make yourselves comfortable, Sir Peregrine will be with you shortly.' There was no hint of emotion or even humanity on the man's beaky, polished face. He put out a hand to no one in particular, palm upwards. For a moment Tommy thought he was expecting a tip.

'If you will let me have the car keys, I'll bring in your luggage and put it in your rooms.'

Graham looked coldly across at him, contempt in his eyes. He tugged the keys free from his pocket where they had become entangled with his handkerchief and tossed them, the aim deliberately bad, at the outstretched hand.

'Catch!'

The keys fell into the undergrowth of the carpet and the butler bent down to retrieve them, then left the room, closing the door behind him, without saying a word.

Graham spoke deliberately while the man was still in earshot. 'Bloody stuffshirt! Yes-man! Sodding contry's full of 'em, no wonder we lost the bloody Empire!'

Klein fixed Graham with an arctic smile. 'Mind your manners, Graham. We're only here a few days but this is going to be Tommy's home for a long time. Doesn't do, upsetting the hired help. Savvy?'

Graham nodded. 'Sorry Mr Klein, just got under my skin a bit that's all.'

Klein blinked quickly as though bringing a blind down on Graham's action. 'Sit down lad.' The three of them eased themselves into seats, Klein and Tommy on the sofa, Graham in one of the easy chairs. Klein scratched his head as though something had just occurred to him.

'That's a point to remember Tommy. Lesson one if you like. Treat Perry's people right, okay? Be firm. If they're here to bring you stuff, and that's their job, then they do it. But no rudeness, and no pushing them about. It's a known fact that the staff in these sort of places are the worst kind of tell-tales and if you do anything out of line, they'll all be rushing off to the papers with it. So we want you to be Mr Nice Guy. That's your image from now on. You're white, you're British, you're the people's hero. Tough but fair, you know the kind of thing. Every mother's son, everyone's kid brother, the one the kids can look up to and the one the dads all wish they'd had as their son instead of the layabout they've got.'

Graham interjected hesitantly, afraid of upsetting his boss: 'We don't want to make him too nice, do we boss? I mean, they'll all think he's a pushover.'

Klein did him the honour of answering his point. 'But that is just it, isn't it my son? All right, he knocks over some European, British if you like, first off. But in the States they'll think he's just another Limey pushover, a nice guy who's going to finish last. But we know different. The first Yank he gets he's going to get a good purse and a decent venue. Then he's going to knock shit out of the guy in such a way that'll wipe the smile off their smug Yankee faces and make him a name overnight. Okay, some of the promoters won't want to know, might win a few, get the picture. But he'll be a serious contender, and they'll know he can perform. Mr Nice Guy outside the ring – Mr Savage in. Remember Graziano? Forget it. Well he was a tough little bastard, vicious in the ring, Yanks loved him. Tommy's going to be twice as vicious only scientific with it. Graziano didn't know boxing from chess, he was all guts and no style. Our Tommy is going to beat the shit out of every Yank they put in front of him, do it in style, and leave him wishing he'd never set foot in the ring.'

He turned to Tommy: 'You follow my pattern son?'

Tommy followed all right. They'll think they're putting an English gentleman complete with rolled umbrella in the ring and then I'm going to knock seven kinds of shit out of the poor bastard. And I can do it.

'Yes, I understand you Mr Klein. I'm polite, I don't swear, I'm soft-spoken, nice to the reporters, sign autographs. Then the first American I get you want me to work him over, cut him, not just finish it. Make it go a few rounds. Right?'

Klein spoke softly, awe in his voice. 'I picked right when I picked you. And these pictures Margot is doing. I've told her, gentle stuff to start with. You with a horse, you with a dog, you holding a flower. The gentle giant. And no bird. You're Mr Clean. By the time you get to Madison Square Garden the Yanks will think you're a poof.' He laughed throatily and Graham coughed into his hand. Seconds later the door swung open and a medium-sized man, running to fat, hair thinning, entered the room.

He could easily have been mistaken for the gardener in his green woolly sweater, hole in one elbow where the shirt poked through, blue cord trousers tucked into knee-high Wellington boots caked with wet mud. It was probably the fact that he was oblivious to the mud which smeared the rich carpet that indicated he ran the place, not worked for it. Sir Peregrine Hamilton, 17th baronet, thirty-two years old, city financier, property tycoon, part-time farmer, sports lover and sexual adventurer wiped the back of a mudstained hand across his perspiring forehead. If a combination of breeding and money is a powerful aphrodisiac then this man was extremely sexually attractive, despite the early paunch, incipient double chin and rising forehead. He scorned many of the old traditions for, unlike most of his aristocratic friends, he had enough money to make his own rules. He knew real power lay in a nation's banks, in its city institutions, in its vast fortunes multiplying themselves and looking for avenues along which to flow.

The Hamilton fortune had been made first in the nineteenth century on the respective backs of wiry, underfed men who hewed the black gold from the seams of coal that criss-crossed the subterranean map of northern England, and the women who toiled in the tea plantations of Ceylon halfway across the globe to supply the drink that was fast becoming a national addiction. True, they had been aristocrats since the days of King Richard the Lionheart, but the Hamiltons were not too noble or haughty to sully their hands with business. They saw the writing on the historical wall a hundred years before their contemporaries, who thought servants would always cost £15 a year and take one day a month off.

They sold two-thirds of their valuable agricultural land and bought a coal mine in Derbyshire. Then another, and another. A member of the Hamilton family visited Ceylon and promptly sunk a fortune into tea plantations. And the money rolled in. They proved adept businessmen over the years. They had that quality of vision, the ability to spot a change in the wind that makes for success. Twenty years before the mines were nationalised by a Labour government, the Hamiltons sold to willing buyers and plunged their money into shipping. They sniffed the growing scent of Asian nationalism while their contemporaries were telling them over the after-dinner port that the British Empire would last for a thousand years. They sold their plantations to a huge tea conglomerate for a massive profit and the money went into steel in time for the rush rearmament programme forced by Hitler's adventures in Czechoslovakia. The Second World War, which visited death, ruin and destruction on so many millions, simply set the seal on the Hamilton family fortune.

With steel nationalisation the family went into property and made millions on speculation in the late 'sixties and early 'seventies as property values in London soared. And then got out before the bubble burst. So too with shipping. Five supertankers bought with a massive risk-all loan paid for themselves in two years after the Six Day War closed the Suez Canal; and were shrewdly re-sold before the oil recession that left hundreds of the giants in mothballs at ports all over the world. Sir Peregrine had become 17th Baronet at twenty-five, when a big, grey hunting horse called Gulliver put his feet in a rabbit hole and catapulted the 16th Baronet to an instant death from a broken neck. Sir Peregrine, with the *sang-froid* for which the British aristocrat is renowned, remarked at the funeral, to anyone who would listen, that his father's biggest regret would have been that the fox got away.

A millionaire many times over now, if one cared to count – and no one did. One of the few British aristocrats to have kept his ancestral home without having to offer sightseeing tours and cream teas at £1 a head to be able to afford it.

And Sir Peregrine – Perry to his ubiquitous, fun-loving friends – had also inherited the bawdy streak from his ancestors that had kept a steady stream of bastard Hamiltons sired through the centuries. There were no chambermaids to bed now, or serving wenches to tumble in the hay in this modern welfare-state Britain. And if there had been they would have promptly run off to a Sunday paper and sold their story for a tidy sum.

But in the London clubs – not the kind where you paid a couple of pounds for instant membership either – there were girls a-plenty. Girls only too anxious to jump into bed and cater for any predilection their wealthy friend might have. And, unusually for a man who could get more or less anything he wished, it was a fact that at least two call girls in Mayfair – had they declared their incomes to the tax authorities, which was doubtful – had reason to thank the generous wallet of Sir Peregrine for a large proportion of it.

He made no secret of his liking for prostitutes. With amazing candour he would tell all who wished to know: 'Tarts? I love 'em. Makes it more fun somehow, paying for it. Gives it a bit of edge. And it means I don't have to be polite about it.' And he would laugh heartily and pour out more champagne and fondle the breasts of his latest companion in full view of any who cared to look, daring the girl to complain.

If the man who stood before them could be said to have hobbies, then sex and boxing were those hobbies.

On trips to title fights in the United States he would combine the two, hiring the most expensive hooker in town to be his companion until he jetted out. Perry could afford it.

He put out a hand to the young boxer.

'Welcome, Tommy. I'll show you the kind of training facilities we've got for you, then you can have a look at your quarters. I think you'll like what you see.' He kept Tommy's hand in his and cocked his head at Klein. 'Well Lewis, they say the Hamiltons haven't made a bad investment yet. World champion is he?'

Klein held Perry's gaze: 'Sure thing. Why not ask the boy, though?'

Sir Peregrine looked back at Tommy, feeling the boxer's firm grip: 'Well?'

'Yes, Sir Peregrine. I'm going to be world champion. You can bet on it.' Sir Peregrine squeezed the boy's hand warmly but there was a hint of warning in the eyes. 'I already have son, and my stake will be about a hundred and fifty thousand by the time it's finished. So don't,' he paused for effect, 'don't let me down.'

Tommy lay on his bed, eyes closed, breathing slowly. He felt a deep sense of physical and mental satisfaction. In the four weeks he had been at Whyman Hall, he had realised the difference in fitness between a good amateur – as he had been – and a professional – as he was now.

Now his muscles vibrated with tone, his reflexes were sharper than they had ever been, and he could feel the new strength in his legs.

No boxer could have wished for better facilities. A vast gymnasium had been created in a wing of the hall, with every item of exercise equipment, a boxing ring and luxury showers, jacuzzi massage bath and changing facilities attached. A walk away from the gym was an Olympic-sized swimming pool with glass roof that slid back to take the sun. Tommy's mind reeled with the details. A dietician flown from California to plan Tommy's eating habits and due to return a month before each fight to supervise personally every meal eaten, every vitamin swallowed. A rigorous medical that confirmed Tommy was as fit as a horse and a check-up planned for each month to ensure he stayed that way. Two sparring partners, one a tough Texan, expert in close-in work; the other a wiry Puerto Rican to make Tommy dance, run and weave.

The training had been gradual, breaking him in gently to the rigours of 5 a.m. road work, followed by a mind-jarring plunge into Perry's 'duck pond'. A sparring session with the Texan, filmed by Margot with a specially-hired video and then played back in Perry's private movie theatre and analysed by Maxie and Klein on his weekly visit. And then long talks with Maxie and the Texan. What to watch for. The thumb in the eye, the stamp on the foot, the close-up butt with the referee unsighted.

Maxie, who had tasted that particular Yankee fight game

dirty trick, literally winced when the Texan recalled it. The arm round the neck, the Texan told him, designed to wear you down, tire you, annoy you. You lose concentration, next thing he's pulling your head onto his left. Turn away, go sideways so the arm slips – and rap him a couple to warn him not to do it again.

Psyching Mohammed Ali style. The big stare when the ref introduced you, then the talking in the clinches. Bullshit. It worked for Ali 'cause Ali was the best and they knew it. The other guys trying that stuff are chickenshit. They don't think they've got what it counts and they're trying short cuts. Let 'em talk. Keep *your* mouth shut. The more they talk, the less breath they have to run.

When a man's cut over the eye, every chance you get, clinch. Then rub heads, grind the forehead into the cut, make the motherfucker hurt, close the eye. Make the bastard work and sweat so the perspiration goes in the eye, stinging, blinding. Then work from his blind side so he's always pivoting to try and find you. Bait him like a wounded bear. But don't get cocky – wounded bears can be dangerous. And when you hit him good, look at the eyes. If they go glazed you've got the sonofabitch. Then destroy him. Don't let up, nineteen, twenty, however many punches it takes. But aim them, cut down on the number if you like, but make every one count. Watch for the counter-punch, don't leave yourself open. Just in case the bum's doing a Brando on you. Acting, Tommy, acting, and the Texan laughed.

The first fight is lined-up, Tommy thought. The German, Goettman, at the Albert Hall. He was ranked number one in his own country and ranked twelfth in the world stakes. Done fifteen rounds with Ali in his youth. Tommy knew the rumours, read them in the sporting press. Everyone thought Klein was off his rocker lining up the German for Tommy's first fight. Klein knew that Tommy had heard the rumours and had spoken to him quietly after a sparring session, as Maxie towelled the boxer down.

'He's a good fighter, Tommy, make no mistake about that. But he's slowing, just a fraction, but it's there. It'll give you the edge you need to get used to the pace, seeing as how it's your first pro fight.'

Tommy listened patiently as Klein outlined the German's history while Maxie started to knead the muscle-knotted shoulders.

'They like him in the States too. The Panzer, they call him, fights like a bloody tank, too. You'd heard that, I suppose?'

Tommy nodded.

'When you've beaten him, we'll try for a date with Carson. He had a stab at the new champ six months back and got stopped in the eleventh, but he's rated and the fans love him, another gutsy lad. Game, good punch, but you'll deal with him.'

Tommy wiped sweat out of his eyes: 'Yeh, I saw him on the box. Fast. I liked his style, but I reckon I can cope.'

Klein said, 'You'll manage. But the first job is Goettman, fucking Kraut, give him one from me. Never could stand Germans. We've got as many of his fights as we can on either film or video, so we'll really take a good look at him.' He patted Tommy on the shoulder. 'Your party tomorrow – and then down to the real thing. But enjoy yourself tomorrow. Couple of drinks, that's all, but let your hair down, have a bit of a dance. Pull a bird if you want. All work and no play, eh son?'

Tommy remembered the last time he'd heard that phrase.

He lay on the bed remembering the conversation. The party was tonight. He knew why they were holding it. To introduce Tommy Booth, professional boxer, to the right people. He'd seen the guest list. Boxing writers, TV pundits, columnists from the back pages of the heavy Sunday papers, gossip columnists – Archie Taylor, the man he'd met briefly after his A.B.A. championship win, he was on the list. And society editors from the glossy magazines, and a sprinkling of film and TV actors and actresses and a handful of models for glamour.

Tommy grinned to himself. And all to celebrate me. But he also remembered the wise words of his host.

'We want to get you known,' Perry had told him – it was Perry now, not Sir Peregrine. 'Launch you into society as it were. Makes you sound like a fucking deb I know, but there you are. We'll fill these greedy bastards full of champagne, caviare, lobster and all the rest, and we'll get a publicity start-out we couldn't buy for a hundred thousand pounds. And it'll sell tickets to your fight. Remember, like Lewis told you, polite, friendly, and don't stay too long in any one place. Don't talk too much and if you get in deep water or you think someone's trying to put words in your mouth, make an excuse and leave, as they say in the Sunday papers. They'll be a snide lot of bastards on the quiet, the media always are, so don't give them any more opportunity than they'll already have by simply being there.'

Tommy opened his eyes and looked at the ceiling.

Lady Margot was going to be there. She'd been working with him on and off this last month. Cool, professional, almost sombre. It only made Tommy think of her more. He tried to remember every line of her face. The smell of her body; her touch. She was everything a man could want in a woman, he thought, picturing the way her long black hair would cascade down her naked body. He only wished he knew what to make of her. Over these past months she'd been cool, detached – almost deliberately hiding her personal feelings behind her camera. But from time to time he'd caught those deep brown eyes fixed speculatively on his body, and when he'd attempted to hold her gaze she'd looked away, embarrassed, and briskly taken up her professional stance again. But he was sure she fancied him; he just didn't have the courage to make the first move. His mind wandered to Goettmann.

You'll see, Herr Goettmann, you'll be the first. You'll see how much of a nice guy I am. You're the first obstacle standing in my way to that crown and I'm going to smash you out of my path.

It was an hour before the first guests were to arrive. Tommy wandered into his private bathroom and turned on the hot and cold taps to run himself a bath. He peeled off the clean, fresh blue tracksuit and pulled off the jockey shorts. He stood naked in front of the full-length mirror on the bathroom wall. Looking at his body gave him pleasure only in that he knew of its potential. But he looked with satisfaction at what professional training had done for him. The extra-trim stomach with its hard-ridged bed of muscle, the shoulders and biceps visibly stronger from the hours of weight training. He wandered back into his bedroom while the bath filled and caught sight of the letter on his dressing table. He must reply to Sylvia, it was only decent. But he could think of no words with which to reply to the sugar-sweet, hackneyed, Valentine-card phrases of love she'd poured into her letter.

He walked back into the bathroom and slid luxuriously into the warm water and lay almost immersed, only his face above water.

In a couple of hours I'll see Margot again. He felt his heartbeat increase. Christ, it's like a first date.

He closed his eyes and conjured up a picture of her. What would it be like to walk with such a woman, hand in hand. Yours, loving only you. The pride, the feeling of happiness. To sit with her in a darkened cinema, her head on your shoulder, safe in your arms.

He shook his head silently. Imagine walking into a pub or restaurant and all the heads turning. My woman. Mine. To feel her soft sensual body when you woke in the morning.

And to walk into a room and say, 'I'd like you to meet my wife.' Wife. The picture was perfectly formed and focussed as any photograph and even though he knew it was pure fantasy, he carried it with him as he bathed and dressed. It was ridiculous that he felt so committed to her. Would she, he wondered, ever feel the same?

There must have been five hundred people in the dining room, but there was no crush or jostling as the guests ambled back and forth to the long linen-covered tables to replenish their glasses with punch and champagne or fill their china plates with a selection from the vast array of food. Girls, some carrying trays with fresh glasses of champagne, others with trays loaded with canapes, circulated among the guests. From a room which led off the immense dining area with its tall, crystal chandeliers, Tommy could hear the sound of beat music coming from a mobile discotheque hired for the evening.

The night was warm and sultry and the French windows were open wide. Some guests stood on the terrace, or sat, glasses in hand, on the steps leading down to the neat lawns, flower beds, fountains and ornamental ponds.

The dinner suit fitted perfectly. Tommy had never felt so smart. The tailor had been back for three fittings. The crisp, light blue dinner shirt felt smooth and cool on his skin – Perry himself had tied the velvet bow tie for Tommy. That was one thing, the boxer reflected, he didn't think he'd ever get used to.

A figure detached itself from the edge of the guests, took a fresh glass of champagne from a passing waitress, and Perry took Tommy's arm. 'Tommy you look super. Got some people just dying to meet you.' He gave the boxer a warning look: 'Remember what I said.'

'Sure.'

'Tommy, meet Martha Quick, the love of my life. If only you would let me make you a Lady, Martha.'

'Perry, you flatterer! You know nothing could make me a lady!' She turned to Tommy. 'Hello.'

The small dark woman with the ample bust took his hand limply. Crikey, she was off the telly; what was it called, that spy thing, Sunday nights? She was always giving crooks karate chops, and then throwing them over her shoulder. Forever leaping out of helicopters, parachuting into East European castles or swimming harbours with a knife strapped to her leg. She looks smaller in real life. But wait till I tell my mum and dad I've met Martha Quick.

'Pleased to meet you, Miss Quick. I really enjoy your TV programme.'

'Thank you, kind sir.'

A suntanned man in a cream suit and with a pronounced northern accent said, ''Ow are yer Tommy?'

Tommy stuck out a hand: 'Dave Garrity, isn't it?'

The comedian looked around in mock amazement: 'And they say boxers have no brains.'

Perry pushed a small man with wisps of white hair and a shifty look on his face towards Tommy.

'And if,' said Perry, 'or rather, should I say *when* you become *really* famous, Gerald here might just have you on his chat show. Mightn't you Gerald?'

The small man took in the boxer's physique with a none too surreptitious glance. He put out a hand, warm and dry and without strength, which Tommy took. 'Be delighted Tommy.'

Heard all about you, mate. One of the limp-wrist mob by all accounts. Make my flesh creep. Still, they say they're all like that in show business. Takes all kinds to make a world.

Perry backed away into the crowd. 'Must circulate, loves. Back in five. Don't dominate him Martha, I know what you're like.'

The chat show host pouted at Tommy as the boxer took the first sip of his champagne. 'Drinking? I thought you were in training.'

'One night off. And only a couple of drinks, then it's back to the grindstone starting tomorrow.'

Martha Quick spoke in that husky whisper Tommy remembered from the television series. 'I really don't know how you do it Tommy. All that punching and violence, and all the training and running about you must have to do to keep fit for it. Quite beyond me. Must wear you out.'

Tommy grinned. 'Yes, but you get used to it. Still, I mean, you're being a bit modest. You do karate and judo, and all that swimming and parachuting and stuff. You must be pretty fit yourself.'

The actress laughed her throaty, famous laugh and Dave Garrity guffawed loudly. The chat show host simply raised his eyes to heaven. Tommy felt the blood rushing to his cheeks. What had he said that was funny?

'Tommy, darling, you shouldn't believe everything you see on television. Good God, you don't really think I do all that rough stuff do you?'

Tommy stammered out, 'Well, I thought . . . I didn't see why . . .'

'Oh no love, I have a dear, sweet girl, ex-commando or something, who does all that for me. I couldn't karate chop a kitten, my dear.'

Garrity spluttered through his champagne. 'Now what was I saying about boxers?'

Tommy was getting redder and he felt the sweat break out on his forehead. His collar felt hot and tight. 'But I've *seen* you throw someone over your shoulder.'

Martha patted him on the shoulders, reaching on tiptoes to do it. 'Camerawork sweety, and my ex-commando friend, who from the back looks remarkably like your little Martha.'

'I never realised.'

'That's me. Not quite the Randy Brown Secret Agent you know and obviously love.'

Tommy forced a smile. 'You live and learn.'

'Yes,' said the chat show host, with an air of resignation, 'that you do. But tell us Tommy, we're all absolutely dying to know, what on earth makes anyone become a *boxer*?' He stressed the last word as though it was 'whore' or 'hangman'. Tommy's eyes grew cold and every muscle in his body tightened, he felt like hitting this schmuck.

Then Tommy spotted through a jumble of faces several yards away the figure of Margot. She was wearing a pale purple beaded evening dress. She was looking straight at him. Help me. Please help me. They say like minds can pick up telepathic vibrations, and as though he had actually shouted the words, Margot detached herself from a knot of drinkers and came towards him. As she walked, the light caught the beads and, turning them into a thousand and one stars, enhanced her dark beauty.

'Tommy, how wonderful to see you again.' She kissed him softly on the cheek, and the fragrance and the memories of that goodbye kiss at the Albert Hall came flooding back to him. She nodded, a shade curtly, at the three inquisitors. 'Martha, Gerald.' She turned to the comedian. 'I don't believe we've met.'

'Dave Garrity.'

'The comedian. Of course.' The speed with which she launched into her next words was comment enough on the status of the comedian. 'Tommy darling. I've got someone absolutely longing to meet you. Martha, Gerald, Mr Garrity. You will excuse us, won't you.' Tommy wished he had the knack of putting people down with a few well-chosen words like Margot was able to do. With a hand on his elbow, she steered Tommy from the quicksand into which he'd so quickly plunged, and out onto the terrace. She took a glass of champagne from a passing waitress and gave it to Tommy. The boxer thankfully drained his first glass and put it on the tray. 'Thanks, I needed it.'

'You look hot. You can sip that one.'

'Who do you want me to meet?'

Margot paused and smiled before speaking. 'Will I do?'

Tommy realised her subterfuge with gratitude. 'Thank you,' he said, 'I was getting in a bit of deep water there. It's crazy, I'm frightened of no one in the ring, but that lot put the fear of God in me.'

'Yes,' said Margot gently, 'you looked like a frightened rabbit. I've never seen you like that before. Why?'

Tommy sipped the champagne, feeling the effervescence and remembering again that night at the Albert Hall. 'I don't know. I'm just not a very good conversationalist. It must be obvious I didn't have much of an education. And they are famous, aren't they?'

'Well known is what they are Tommy. She is well known for jumping into bed with any casting director in town and for being a very poor actress. The second no doubt accounts for the first. She's pushing forty-five and rumour has it she won't be Randy Brown Secret Agent for much longer. And Gerald? Well, a poor little homosexual who fears falling ratings and death in that order. Garrity? He's just nothing. He's well known for what he does best, being vulgar and crass. In short, for being himself. Collectively they shouldn't frighten a moth. The difference between them and you is that they know the rules of this silly game that passes for social chit-chat. Don't take it too seriously and watch your back. To make matters worse, you're on your way up and they're on their way down. They know it. Ergo, they try and humiliate you.'

She laid a hand on Tommy's arm. 'Lovely, there isn't one person in that room you need to be frightened of. A lot of them are self-made men and that is what you are. Just because you have left school doesn't mean you have to stop learning. In fact most of us learned all we know *after* we left school, and we keep learning every day. You can read and hear, so you can learn. Sorry about the speech, but I'll tell you something else as well, because I think you should know. You are frightened, in part, because you think that lot,' Margot pointed over her shoulder towards the milling guests, 'are all one mass and that you are an individual. Well, that's not the case. They're all individuals, cruel, lonely, happy, unhappy, brave, cowardly. And in all honesty – and if this hurts your ego I'm sorry – they don't give a damn about you either way. If you're successful you'll be one of them, if you're not, then they couldn't care less. It's like a nettle Tommy, remember? Brush it, be frightened of it, and it stings. Grip it without fear, and you'll be okay.'

Tommy smiled at her. And thought how much he would like to have her style. 'Thanks for your advice. I'll think about it. You know, I wasn't only being polite. I really did think she did all those stunts herself, Martha Quick I mean. Made a bit of a fool of myself, I suppose.'

Margot looked at him in the summer moonlight, and felt a strange, almost foreign feeling, as though something way back in her childhood had reached out and touched her. He *is* a gentle giant. He saves his viciousness for the ring, not like that pack of sharks in there.

'Come on Tommy Booth, take me for a walk in the gardens and tell me your life story. I've been so wrapped up in those bloody photographs that I've hardly given you a thought.'

They linked arms and walked round the fountains and through the moonlit gardens. He talked as he had never talked before to anyone – his mother and father, Lewis, Maxie, Sylvia – of his hopes and dreams.

She listened, speaking only infrequently, to comment or enquire. Margot was aware of her desires. True to herself she tried neither to forget they existed nor to suppress them. But for the moment, she realised, they must wait. He was, she concluded almost with disbelief, a strong, decent man. He would be a strong lover, considerate, inexpert perhaps at first, but a good strong lover, giving as well as receiving. They sat down on a rustic seat beneath an ivy-covered stone wall that shielded a section of the gardens from the house. The air was heavily scented with jasmine. Neither spoke, but Tommy watched Margot's face, half in shadow, half in moonlight, the silver sheen on her hair.

A strong, terrible feeling he had never experienced before took hold of him. A feeling not of sex but of tenderness.

'Margot.'

She turned and her face came fully into the moonlight.

'Margot, I –' Quickly but with dignity she put a finger on his lips.

'Not now Tommy. There'll be time enough. I'm not going anywhere.'

Tommy trapped the words, unsaid, in his heart. Slowly he brought his face close to hers and kissed her on the lips. For an eternal second he held his lips to hers, feeling the moisture and the softness, then pulled away and took her head in his massive hands, his heart beating as it never had before. He put her face to his chest. Her hair cascaded over his wrists. I love you Margot.

Reluctantly Margot pulled away from Tommy's grasp. She looked into the boyish face so full of expectation.

'I think, Tommy darling, that you'd better go to bed before you say something we might both regret.'

Margot fought hard to regain her composure. She felt a great surge of love well up inside her. This was a feeling she'd never experienced before. Not with her husband, not with anybody. She tried to suppress it with all the effort her will could muster. She felt out of control and frightened. It was like some tidal wave that had overtaken her. God, this is ridiculous, I'm so attracted to him. But she knew it wasn't just attraction, it was deeper than that. She tried to banish the thought from her mind.

She saw disappointment cloud his face. She took his hands, closed them together and patted them. 'After all, it's an early start for both of us.'

Tommy felt he was being patronised. It was the same tone of voice the local vicar's wife used when she came collecting, stepping almost gingerly into the two-up, two-down terraced house that had been home until the council got their bulldozers to work and consigned the tenants to concrete birds' nests in the sky. The voice of the woman in the department store in Knightsbridge when he'd made a trip up West to get Sylvia her first Christmas present. It said, 'You're sweet, you're cute, but don't try and be like us. Go back to where you belong.' And now he was getting it from Margot. The last person, the very last person, he expected it from. She stood up. 'I'll see you in the morning. Six sharp. Go and get your beauty sleep. It's nearly ten.' She smiled at him and was gone.

His stomach churned with confusion. He flushed with rage. What kind of person was she? What did she want? He determined that from now on what she'd get was a big helping of nothing. He'd never been treated like this by anyone before. He felt lost and alone, and longed to put out a hand and touch a familiar object or look up and see Maxie or Klein, or even – even Sylvia. He choked down the thought, his longing for the things he knew. It was a new life; he had to adjust. Perhaps I should behave differently towards her. I'm treating her too bloody well and I've done that with a bird before. Don't let them see you're interested, son. That was how it had been when he'd knocked around with the rest of the lads. And now? Christ, I mustn't show I care, particularly to her kind. If they see just one chink in my armour I'll be a loser even before I've got a swipe at my next opponent. They're all waiting for it. One slip Tommy boy and all your grand aspirations will be over. No champagne and smart cars for you then fella. Just a short swift drive back to that dump called home. It might be all right for Sylvia, but I always knew there was a better way of life and now I've seen some of it, I want it. I'll buy mum a lovely house in Chigwell. There'll be a Rolls parked in the drive for dad. Mum will be covered in diamonds – no more selling fruit and veg in markets for her. No, it will be a long time before I show my emotions to the likes of them in there again. Tommy looked towards the terrace where Margot had just disappeared – and especially to that stuck-up bitch.

She won't get it even if she begs me. She bloody fancies me, too. I'm sure of it. I know she wants me; why doesn't she react like any normal woman? It's been months now with us working together. I can feel her eyes on me. I can feel her react when I kiss her. I love her, but I don't understand her. She'll destroy me if I don't pull myself together.

Tommy swore savagely under his breath. 'Well sod her.' From now on I'm playing no more games with Lady Margot. The fighting is all that matters. The goal. And no bird is going to screw it up for me, not Sylvia, not Lady Bloody Margot. This bunch of people, I just don't understand them. They don't seem to have any real feelings, not like back home. There's no . . . he struggled in his mind for the right word . . . no warmth, that was it, no real warmth.

Like Perry. Right away, it's call me Perry, and I get the run of the house. But he never seems to get *really* friendly, like he's talking like this all the time to people, maybe 'cause it's convenient for him, or something. Just like some of the teachers at school. Most were right bastards and you knew where you were with them. It was the others, the friendly ones who'd help you out a bit, or take you all on trips outside school hours. They seemed to care but they never got really close, even if you really rated them. Like as though they didn't mind being a bit friendly, but didn't want to get close in case some of what you were rubbed off on them.

He's got that look with me, like I'm a car he's bought, or a racehorse. How good is it? Will it go all right? Will it break down? I'm just an investment to him. How can you be like that with people? Now Mr Klein, they all say he's a hard man, a villain, he's had blokes buried in concrete, all that nonsense. They all spin a yarn down the East End. Bloke once told me he reckoned as how Klein was really Jack the Ripper who'd taken a youth drug; and then fell about laughing into his beer. He was a hard man was Mr Klein, but he was okay. A good friend. He'd give you a boost, tell you you were working well, put his arm round you, crack a few jokes, put you at ease. And Maxie too, good old Maxie, no bloody edge there. Margot, Perry – even Archie and he was a Yank, they could be so cool, so detached.

What was it Mr Klein had said? 'Upper classes? Load of wankers, my son. Treat 'em like shit and they love it, eat out of your bloody hand. Show 'em any respect, kindness and they'll walk all over you.'

He'd only been young then, Tommy, fifteen or sixteen, and was listening respectfully down at the gym as Mr Klein held court for a dozen or more youngsters on the thoughts of Chairman Klein. But Tommy had remembered that.

'No respect, treat 'em like shit ' He said the words aloud to the empty moon and got up from the rustic seat where just minutes earlier he had felt so warm and loving towards Margot. His face was set in a determined expression, a mask of coldness, not unlike the one that settled over his features when he set foot in the ring. He went back into the house, pushed firmly through the crowded celebrities, ignoring the arms that clutched at him like clinging vines And went to his bedroom alone.

Margot crossed through the crowded room and took a glass of champagne. He'll hate me now. He doesn't understand. Dammit he doesn't understand. An affair, yes It would be the first time, but yes, why the hell not? But love? It was too much, too soon. Impossible. But if only she could have explained. He wouldn't understand, he wouldn't. She could tell by his face she had wounded him. Hit at some vulnerable spot deep within him. She downed the champagne, in a reckless determination to forget the hurt look in his eyes.

*

The maid padded across the darkened room and swished back the curtains with one hand. The other held a tray set with cup and saucer, milk jug and teapot As the grey, misty light seeped into the bedroom, she laid the tray on the bedside table and whispered, 'Madam'.

Margot opened her eyes, instantly awake, unease flickering on her face It was too light.

'What time is it?'

'It's eight o'clock madam,' the maid replied, without looking at her watch. 'I've brought your tea.'

Margot sat bolt upright in the bed, oblivious of her naked breasts. She said, 'Never mind the damn tea, why in hell's name didn't you wake me earlier?' Her face was ablaze with anger at her abrupt and tardy awakening.

The maid took a step backwards, disconcerted at the tone of the question and at the woman who did not even have the decency to cover her breasts in front of a stranger. 'Because madam,' the maid tried to keep the anger out of her voice, 'I was given no instructions to do otherwise. I thought after the party last night . . . and on Tuesday, if you remember, I was reprimanded for waking you too early.'

Margot stepped naked from the bed, took a pair of panties from a drawer, slipped into them and began tugging on a pair of jodhpurs. She rounded on the maid. 'For God's sake don't answer me back. Just go down to the stables and get the boy to saddle me a horse – the chestnut mare.'

'Yes madam.'

Margot dressed hurriedly and angrily, not bothering even to do her face. Shit! I should have been at the meadow by six, to do pictures of Tommy starting his training run. It had to be right, just right. The dawn breaking, the early morning light, the right feel about it. These pictures are going to be right if I have to sleep in that damn meadow to be there on time. In the meantime the best I can salvage from this bloody débâcle is some general shots when the run is over, to prove – she tugged with exasperation at the leather riding boot – to prove I'm as damn professional as they are. She screwed up her face in annoyance. I should have been there at six, damn that butler. I gave him strict instructions I was to be woken at 5.30 a.m. Damn servants!

She slung two black-bodied Nikons, one with telephoto lens, round her neck. The horse was waiting, held by the stable boy, and stamping impatiently on the cobbles, its breath wraith-like in the cold morning air. The boy legged her onto the horse, she took the reins and galloped with a clatter out of the courtyard. A thin mist hung like floating grey cotton at waist height over the meadows. The horse stepped cautiously into the shallow rolling grey sea, then, spurred on, it went into a canter, breath billowing in steamy spurts from the flared nostrils. In the distance she saw the disembodied figure of Tommy emerge from the woods, the top of his body in the bright-red tracksuit the only splash of colour on this battleship-grey morning. Seconds later a horse gingerly picked its way out of the wood and into the meadow, the figure on its back poised awkwardly with all the lack of grace of someone who has learned to ride late in life, and reluctantly. Maxie. She reined in her horse within a few yards of Tommy. His head was dropped as he stood there, hands hanging loosely, sucking air into his tortured lungs. Maxie dismounted clumsily and held the reins of his horse tightly as though afraid the animal might bite him.

They remained unspeaking for a full minute while Tommy regained his breath. Three figures, two horses, in an ethereal ghostly tableau, the only sound the regular breathing of Tommy, the snorting of the horses and the occasional call of the woodpigeons.

Tommy looked up and there was something written on his face that Margot didn't recognise. 'Nice lie-in?' There was all the cockiness of the school smart alec in his voice.

She ground her teeth in frustration. 'Perry's domestic help arrangements leave a lot to be desired.'

Tommy wagged a finger. 'Ever heard of alarm clocks?'

'Oh piss off. It wasn't my fault. Anyway, I'm here now.'

He wouldn't let it drop. 'If you didn't go to parties and stay out late, you might be able to get up in the morning. I went to bed like I was told, and look at me. Fresh as a daisy.'

Maxie was taking a great interest in the condition of his horse's head. He wanted no part of this.

'Now maybe that's why the N.U.J. don't want you. Not because of Dudley's money, but because you're not quite up to it. Not professional enough.'

She dismounted without speaking, unslung a Nikon with the 35 mm lens and wordlessly shot ten frames of Tommy as he stood, hands on hips, cocky look on his face, up to his waist in swirling mist. She remounted the hourse without assistance. And none had been offered. Maxie was still learning about horses from close range.

'You, my young friend, have yet to prove how professional you are. So it ill becomes you to criticise anyone else.'

Doggedly, unsubtly, like a bulldog he pursued her: 'Then how come, as I was saying, they won't let you in the National Union of Journalists? I would have thought with a friend like Archie you could have swung it if you'd been any good.'

How dare he? Working-class little upstart! She brought the riding crop down with all the strength she could muster. Tommy dodged with ring sharpness, and the crop plucked at the tracksuit cloth on his right arm. His hand shot out and grabbed the crop. He tugged, and for a moment it looked as though she would fall from the horse.

But she released her grip in time and grabbed at the reins. She was too good a rider to fall for that trick. She turned the horse and dug her heels in savagely. As she cantered off across the meadow, the horse still treading warily into the mist and resisting efforts to make her go faster, she was aware that Tommy was behind her, running, almost catching the horse. She turned and looked. There was a sardonic grin on his face. Treat 'em like shit, Klein had said.

'Race you back.'

She threw the words over her shoulder. 'You're on. At least you can show me you're good at something.'

She could feel the tension and irritation mounting in her but slowed the horse until Tommy was alongside, resting his hand on the pommel of the saddle as he jogged.

'We have a nice old saying in the East End – "If you don't

like the sentence, don't rob the bank" – You sure you can take the pace Margot?'

'I can take it, Booth.'

'Booth?'

'Mister Booth, then.'

'Right, *Lady* Margot.'

Her face broke into a devious smile. 'Take care you always address me that way or next time I'll really horsewhip you.'

Tommy held up the crop that was in his left hand. 'What with?'

'I'll buy another.'

'You can't afford it, I heard as how your old man was bankrupt.' He laughed and broke into a sprint as the stables came into view. She spurred the horse and cantered easily round him to clatter into the courtyard first. As he loped in she dismounted and the stable boy took away the horse, again without a word being spoken. Tommy noticed the natural assurance that there would always be someone there to take the coat, take the horse, open the door. Invisible, not really human. There was no expression on the stable boy's face but he looked once, quickly, at Tommy.

'Bit slow aren't you?' Margot teased.

Tommy nodded.

She looked deeply into his eyes. They no longer seemed to be making love to her, as they had done only twelve hours before, when they were in the garden. Yes, that mood was gone from him now. She wondered if she'd ever be able to rekindle it. She knew she'd gone too far. He is a man and I treated him like a boy. He wants love and all I did was verbally to slap his face. I should have taken more account of his feelings. Had she turned off that depth of feeling in him forever? If she had, Margot didn't know if she could cope. Things had suddenly got far too serious for just a casual affair. If only he realised the tangle her emotions were in.

'Tommy darling let's take a stroll down to the lake. When the sun breaks through it'll be absolutely gorgeous. I can shoot some super stuff of you swimming.'

He tossed the words offhandedly: 'I'm excused my plunge this morning. I've got to spar at ten so I'm taking a nap.' And then he was gone, loping out of the courtyard in the direction of his own quarters.

Well, he knew he'd won that round but it was somehow worse than being in the ring. He always knew he'd come out from those ropes a winner but with Margot he wasn't quite so sure. All he did know was that the only way to win with Margot and her friends was to fall back on that East End gut toughness that Sir Perry and his like called chippiness. But, my God, without it Tommy knew any working-class person mixing in this group was a goner. He remembered Bert, a friend much older than himself, who was involved in the protection business. Tommy had met him through Mr Klein. Well, he got mixed up with one of these toffs – a right little beauty she was too. Next thing you know he'd topped himself in a club by cutting his wrists in front of her, just to shock. And you know what, nobody moved a muscle to help him. He died later – of septicaemia in a National Health hospital bed.

Cold, hot, hot, cold then bloody hot again. He felt a deep well of frustrated passion boil inside him. I just don't understand her. He felt violence swelling inside him for the first time in his life outside a boxing ring.

# *Chapter Four*

The Albert Hall was packed. Not bad, as the boxing writers would later say, for a boxer's first professional contest. But Goettmann was a good crowd puller. A German who looked every inch the jingoist's dream of the archetypal Hun. Square-jawed, close-cropped hair, dull grey eyes and a physique like a storm-trooper. He'd never been beaten on British soil – or by a Briton for that matter – and he was a headline writer's dream. 'Davidson Blitzed' and 'Fritz the Panzer crushes the Welsh Fusilier' were just two of the headlines after he'd put two British fighters on the canvas on his last trips from Munich.

Add the fact that Goettmann's father had been in the Waffen SS during World War Two and that the boxer himself was known for expounding his right-wing views in Munich beer cellars and it was easy to see why all but Goettmann and his seconds had come to see the German get his come-uppance.

If the press were looking for a hero to turn this contest into a struggle between Good and Evil, then blonde and handsome Tommy Booth was their man. A carefully orchestrated campaign, backed by Perry's money, Klein's brain and Margot's photographs had made him a national favourite before he even stepped into the ring.

Tommy loved animals. Tommy loved his mum and dad. Tommy was everyone's friend. The newspapers loved it, even if their seasoned boxing writers were a trifle sceptical. But they saw him sparring and realised there was steel behind the soft build-up. At a no-holds-barred session with the Puerto Rican, Tommy put the battle-hardened ex-pro on the canvas with savage onslaughts even though his opponent was protected by pain-absorbing headgear.

Unknown to everyone, even Tommy, Klein had paid the Puerto Rican a bonus to insult Tommy before the sparring session to be watched by the press. In heavily accented English the copper-coloured boxer goaded Tommy about his inability in two areas – boxing and lovemaking. The lovemaking angle Tommy dismissed with contempt, but he decided to point out with his fists to the Puerto Rican that his second comments were unjustified. Quickly, scientifically but with a savagery that shocked even veteran boxing writers, Tommy dropped his man three times onto the canvas, making the hapless Puerto Rican wish he'd turned down the extra padding to his wallet. So the writers went away and pounded out the message on their typewriters. That this was no powder-puff boxer, all image and no punch. He could fight on the face of it, had a thirst for victory. Could take a punch and mix it. They knew better than anyone that sparring partners in the later years of their fistic careers were one thing and Goettmann was another. Yet, they'd been around the fight game long enough to spot a good boxer. And their noses fair twitched at the sight of Tommy.

So the scene was set. Goettmann the dragon came to breathe fire on the fair St George. Other knights had failed to slay him. Did Tommy have the sword and the courage to do it? The cameras were there to put the fight on record for the next night's television, so they could hail a new boxer or bemoan, with the benefit of hindsight, another failure as they played back the action replays for the critics to analyse and dissect.

Margot sat at the ringside with Klein. She hoped with all her heart Tommy would not get hurt. She had tried to hide, quite successfully up until now, the truth of her feelings for Tommy. But it was no longer possible. She smiled to herself and thought, I might have won a few battles but I've certainly lost this war. Since the night of the party she'd known she could no longer pretend her involvement with him was just professional. They weren't even simply sexual longings, which could be rationally dealt with, and hidden behind a Nikon camera, any longer.

She felt a shudder go through her when she thought of him being bruised and torn, clubbed and whipped by unforgiving fists. She knew what damage a pair of gloved fists, wielded by an expert, could do to another human body. Since taking on this assignment she'd devoured every book she could lay her hands on on the subject of professional boxing. She knew how the brain was jolted back and forth in its protective case by the power of punches. She knew how this vital internal organ of the body reeled under constant pounding. She'd read of what happened to some fighters. Going punchy, brain damage, vision impaired, their speech slurred and slow. She'd read of Goettmann and what he'd done to others who were, on the face of it, every bit as good as, if not better than, Tommy, and with more ring experience to boot. What would happen to her Tommy, Tommy who had kissed her as clumsily as a schoolboy only the other night? What, she thought with an icy feeling in the pit of her stomach, if the German just walks out of his corner, brushes aside anything Tommy can offer, and rockets him into oblivion? Tommy's career would be over. Who could Tommy look in the face after such a demise of his career?

She turned to Klein. 'Any time now?'

Klein nodded. 'Shouldn't be too long.'

Seconds later there was a deafening roar as Tommy jogged into the arena, Maxie behind him, and climbed through the ropes into the ring, wearing a blue silk dressing gown with his name embroidered in white letters on the back. He looked staggeringly handsome. Margot's heart leapt into her mouth. He bowed politely to all four sections of the crowd and, seeing Margot in the front row, waved a gloved hand in greeting. She felt his blue eyes piercing into her very soul.

The German climbed into the ring with the crowd virtually silent. Fight crowds do not boo a visitor, as football crowds will. The boos might come later, if the German got up to any of his dirty tricks or sneaked a dubious points verdict. But in their silence the crowd said more than they could have with a crescendo of jeers.

Margot watched Tommy intently as the referee spoke to both fighters following the M.C.'s introduction. There seemed to be something different about him. Something she couldn't pinpoint, a look on his face, or lack of it. Lack of it. That was it. It was as though the boxer was Tommy's twin, but lacked that hint of kindness, compassion, tenderness in the line of his face. This face was the same one she'd seen as Tommy had dealt savagely with the Puerto Rican. With an intensity that thrilled her with an almost orgasmic force, she saw the naked aggression in his eyes. The human, redeeming qualities had been put aside as redundant, irrelevant, almost harmful in that small cockpit of pain bounded by the nylon ropes and the waiting fans. She felt a deep sexual urge for the man standing in the ring, and realised she could not put off much longer the moment when she would, must, have him.

Maxie was whispering urgently into Tommy's ears as they waited for the bell. Tommy, passive, immobile, filing away in his mind the last-minute instructions. Margot could sense Klein fidgeting next to her, his nervousness communicating itself like an earth tremor.

Yes, Lewis, if Tommy lets you down tonight, you lose too. It's goodbye friend Perry, maybe even goodbye Dudley. An end to your dreams of real fame and that trip to the Palace, back to your sordid little world of crooks, casual violence and betting shops.

And maybe I lose too. If he is beaten out there tonight it will change him so drastically, rob him of his self-belief, and leave what? The husk of the man I want.

The bell cut through her thoughts as Tommy and the German came into the centre of the ring and touched gloves. Margot could feel her heart start to pound. She could not remember anything affecting her in this way before. The ring had become a harsh square of light and colour in a sea of velvet darkness broken only by the tiny red dots of lighted cigarettes like fireflies on a warm Asian night. The two men circled cautiously. Then the German came forward quickly and unleashed a salvo of punches. Tommy took them on his arms and gloves and dodged quickly to his right. The German followed, but a shade slowly, like a tank turret traversing to find its target. Tommy threw a straight right which clipped Goettmann's head. The crowd, anxious for some evidence to believe in their man, roared lustily.

A chant went up from the back of the hall: 'To-mm-y To-mm-y'.

Tommy moved forward as both men sent out exploratory feeler punches. Then the young Englishman gave a right, left, right combination of astonishing speed, which broke the German's guard and sent him reeling against the ropes. Goettmann put up the shutters again and Tommy retaliated with a volley of punches like piston-strokes to the unprotected stomach, but the steel-hard muscles took them with ease. The German clinched, pulling Tommy into his sweaty embrace, tucking his head into the side of the Englishman's and attempting to pin Tommy's arms to his side. The referee shouted 'Break!' but the German held on. The referee leapt in and parted the two men, wagging an admonishing finger at Goettmann.

'When I say break, break. Now box on.'

The German barnstormed forward, crowding Tommy, looking for an opening. A punch got through, catching Tommy on the right cheekbone. For two minutes they punched and mauled, Goettmann continuously holding Tommy and trying to push him onto the ropes. The crowd were booing heartily at every attempt. This was what they loved to hate about Goettmann. In Zagreb he'd needed a police escort out of the ring after he'd pushed Miljanic through the ropes, helping the hapless Yugoslav on his way with a rabbit punch to the back of his neck.

But Tommy was too strong. Every time Goettmann pinioned his arms Tommy would extract one arm with all the ease that goes with super strength and rap a right to the German's head in retaliation, then pull himself free.

There were twelve seconds to the bell when Tommy saw

his chance. The German unleashed a right, a wide, swinging punch full of power. But Klein had been right, Goettmann was just that shade too slow. Tommy lifted his left arm to block the jarring punch. At the same time he shot out a straight right. The German had dropped his left a fraction to balance himself and the punch went straight through the gap like a crossbow bolt. The punch jerked Goettmann's head back like a marionette and he fell unceremoniously onto the seat of his pants. The crowd was in ecstasy. Klein was on his feet, shouting words drowned in the sea of noise. Tommy stepped back, the only calm man in the Albert Hall. The German got onto one knee, breathing heavily. The referee was over him counting, 'One, two, three, four, five, six...'

The bell cut through the count and the revelry like a knife. Goettmann's seconds rushed out and helped their man back to his stool for some instant repair.

Tommy casually sat on his stool and took the plastic water bottle. He spat a fountain of water into the plastic bucket and let Maxie wipe the sweat from his head and chest. As Maxie worked he took a quick look at Tommy's cheek. Discoloration, slight bruising, nothing to worry about. He spoke quickly to Tommy as he worked.

'Not bad, not bad at all. Think you've got him. Don't get cocky. Stand off and punch him. Watch the clinches. No need to mix it. Watch the clinches. He'll have lost confidence and he'll want to come back. You're working well, keep it up.'

At the bell the German came out at a rush, dignity hurt but everything else seemingly intact. Tommy stood off and jabbed, keeping the German at bay. There was a collective moan of disappointment from the crowd. They thought the German was dead and now their man was jabbing him like an exhibition bout. They screamed for action. Goettmann tried a few long range shots, but was content to stand off as well, gaining strength, hiding the hurt.

Tommy could sense the crowd's unease and decided to take the matter into his own hands. He had the strength, he had the power. He eyed the big German, looking for the weaknesses. Then Tommy went into Goettmann like a fair-ground fighter. The crowd bayed. Tommy and the German traded punches toe to toe for a full sixty seconds. They stood like two giant battleships sending over shell after shell to burst on the ironclad enemy. The crowd was on its feet now, yelling, screaming. This was the fight game. This was why they came. Klein was shouting himself hoarse: 'That's it Tommy, kill the bastard.'

A spurt of blood came from the German's mouth, spattering Tommy's chest and then Goettmann's gumshield went, a white blur flying into the line of reporters shouting into the telephones at the ringside. Goettmann's punches seemed to have no effect on Tommy, but the German was slowing, Tommy's punches hurting, sapping energy. And each punch he threw drained further that great reservoir of energy in his shoulders. He tried to clinch Tommy and the crowd booed, but Tommy ducked contemptuously out of his clutches and rained more blows on him. He caught Goettmann with a mighty punch that threatened to take the man's head from his shoulders. And Tommy saw the eyes and remembered the words of the Texan. The grey eyes of the German had gone glazed, unable to focus. He was there for the finishing. In for the kill now and watch for any Brando caper.

Tommy unleased one, two, three, four, five punches with alternate hands. Three caught the German in the face, sending him reeling backwards. Two exploded harmlessly in mid-air as Goettmann ducked and weaved, using all his professional know-how to try and escape the punches which came at him like guided missiles. Don't let up, nineteen, twenty, however many it takes, the Texan had told him. But aim them, cut down the number if you have to, but make every one count.

Tommy hit a straight left to Goettmann's ribs and saw the German wince. The man was back-peddling now, searching for a refuge. They can run, as one famous boxer once said, but they can't hide. There was no hiding place for Goettman. Nowhere to go to escape the lashing, stinging, punishing fists. Only the canvas below him, and the German was standing up now almost by pride alone as Tommy's ruthless fists hunted him out. One, two, three, four, five, the punches rammed home. The Kraut had guts, the crowd knew that, but go down you bastard. The German teetered and Tommy hit him flush in the face. More blood and soon the face was a grotesque mask of red pain. The crowd could see the blood, almost smell it. They remembered what Goettman had done to Davidson from Stepney, and Williams the sandy-haired Welshman from Pontypool. Now taste your own blood. Like Romans at a savage gladiatorial contest they screamed, blood-lust high in their throats.

The referee was watching Goettmann carefully. Much more and the fight was going to be stopped. Tommy settled the matter before that necessity arose. A right hook, one in a long series he had been hurling at the German, ended it. Goettmann's eyes were closing before he started his long sideways fall to the canvas. Ruthlessly, efficiently, Tommy hit him again with a vicious left hook as he was halfway down. You're not getting up from this, Goettmann.

The referee pushed Tommy aside and raised his hand. A count was irrelevant. The Albert Hall was a cauldron of seething, bubbling humanity as Tommy's arm went skywards.

Goettmann was stretched out like a corpse on a slab, a bevy of seconds, officials and a doctor crowded anxiously around him. Maxie was kissing Tommy on both cheeks to the delight of the cameraman who had clambered into the ring. Then Klein was in the ring too, his arm round his protégé.

Over Klein's shoulder, Tommy caught Margot's eye. He shot her a look of pure triumph, registering her sparkling eyes, her parted lips, the almost sexual excitement on her face. His victorious smile was unmistakable. 'He did it for me,' Margot thought, wonderingly. 'He won that fight for me.'

'Just one more Tommy.' 'Let's have another Tommy.' 'Arms round him again Mr Klein.' 'Big smile Tommy.'

Tommy broke away to bow politely to the applauding

delirious crowd and wave to them with the same gloved hand with which he had greeted them on his arrival in the ring, those short minutes ago.

Margot sat limp and exhausted, drained of emotion, stunned at the impact the fight had had on her. Tommy came to the edge of the ropes, smiled and waved a hand, free now of the gloves, at the crowd.

His face had changed. The warmth was back. The tenderness back in the young face, despite the ugly bruise on his cheek.

The newspapers were to have a field day. 'British Tommy stops the Panzer in his Tracks.' 'Boxing Booth does it for Britain.'

But Margot's thoughts as she looked at the boxer were far from his chosen profession or the stunning victory he had just achieved. There was a warm liquid feeling deep within her. She ached to hold him in her arms. She wanted to surrender herself, the due spoils of war, to him. I want you Tommy, she thought. But how? Why? The arguments raged back and forth in Margot's head. Logic battled emotion, reason tussled with passion. He was good looking, strong, young, a magnificent man. He may be a slow, inexperienced lover, but she could guide him, teach him, lead him. And God it wasn't as if she was getting sexual satisfaction from her marriage. Dudley's thrice weekly sex-by-numbers. Was that to be her life in the bedroom for the next twenty years? Maybe Vivien had been right that lunchtime, maybe an affair was what she needed. But an affair with an East End boxer barely out of his teens? And what of the risk? Of someone discovering and using it to ruin Dudley's career.

God, if her husband had just been something in the City it wouldn't matter. But the Leader of the Opposition! The Tory party didn't take kindly to adultery, they'd seen it hit at their electoral chances too often.

And with Tommy, she knew deep down it wouldn't be just an affair, couldn't be. Something strange, illogical warned her.

She thought wildly of making a balance sheet, this column

all the reasons for, that column all the reasons against. Tot up the pros and cons and go with the winner.

She smiled to herself for she knew, unerringly, that if the result went against her, she would cheat.

It was one of those hot, cloudless summer days that made it a joy to be alive and living in the English countryside. Birds sang, the grass and trees were a luscious green and the scent of honeysuckle hung in the air like rich perfume. Klein leaned out of the window of his Jaguar, Maxie next to him in the passenger seat.

'Sure you won't come Tommy? It'll only take a couple of hours and then you can see your mum. Perhaps have a bit of a kiss and cuddle with Sylvia,' Klein winked lasciviously, 'and you'll be back here tomorrow night. You said you'd come, they'll be expecting you.'

Tommy shook his head. 'No, it's okay Mr Klein. I gave me mum a ring this morning, told her I'd changed my mind. I'll do a bit of sunbathing instead.'

'Up to you lad,' Klein coughed the powerful car into life. 'There's only Winfield on duty, and he's over in the east wing. You know the drill. If you want anything, buzz him on the intercom from your room.' He wagged a finger admonishingly at Tommy. 'Don't miss a meal. Winfield knows what you should have and he'll serve it up prompt. And bed sharp at ten.' Klein jerked a thumb towards Maxie. 'Just 'cause your chaperone's away doesn't mean you take liberties. Savvy?'

'Okay Mr Klein.'

The car powered down the drive, sending spurts of gravel in the air as the wheels bit home.

Tommy breathed a sigh of relief. Alone for the first time in months. He felt a glorious sense of freedom. No one telling me to run, punch, skip, lift, swim. No one telling me what time to go to bed – well not in person anyway – what time to get up. No one pumping information into my brain as we watch yet another video of the next fighter I meet. Twenty-four hours of relaxation, to lie in the sun and do nothing, think about nothing. Perry was in Switzerland, Margot in London, back tomorrow; half the staff were away, just the lonely figure of Winfield with the polished billiard ball head to cook the steaks and chill the orange juice.

Tommy walked towards the pool. The water shimmered green in the sparkling sunlight. He pressed a red button on the wall and there was the hum of an electric motor and the pool roof began to roll back to reveal a ceiling of blue, dotted with small cotton-wool clouds.

Tommy peeled off his shirt, pulled off the training shoes, stepped out of his trousers and jockey shorts and dived naked into the cool water. Its freshness brought him alive and he surfaced, snorting with well-being. He moved into a powerful crawl, cutting through the water with long strokes. He did ten lengths and hauled himself out of the water and onto a sun-lounger. He could feel the sun's rays on his wet skin.

His mind wandered to the thought of Margot. If only she were here now. His mind dwelled on the image of her body, emerging from the pool. The full breasts he had only seen beneath blouses or dresses. He moved restlessly, feeling the arousal in him as he imagined her glistening with water from the pool, there before him, inviting his caress.

He closed his eyes and pictured her naked, the sun warming her brown body. Kissing her softly, then passionately, his hands touching, exploring her. Swimming together naked in the pool, the cool kiss of the water on their skin, burying his head between her breasts, or watching the blurred outline of her body through the water.

He shook his head to clear himself of the image and plunged back into the water to cool his ardour. He did two more lengths and climbed out, Margot banished from his mind.

Was it betrayal not to want to go home? Not to want to sit in that cramped flat, high in the empty sky and listen to the gossip; of neighbours, new babies, marriage break-ups and the cost of food. Not to want to be alone with Sylvia to listen to her entreaties of love and receive the clammy kisses and fumbles and acceptance that encompassed her knowledge of the art of love. A guilty thought stabbed at him. Had it been to see Margot, would you have gone? 'Come and see Margot in London', would that have made it different? He knew the answer and strangely it didn't make him feel too guilty. I'm changing, he thought, I'm changing.

Within minutes he fell asleep in the sun and dreamed of Goettman. The German was in uniform and carrying a gun, but Tommy still hit him and remembered the look in those eyes after the killer blow. He awoke with a start, the dream cheers of the Albert Hall crowd still ringing in his ears. His mouth tasted bad, his head felt muzzy and his naked body tingled from its exposure to the sun. He climbed off the lounger and padded through the sliding door to the shower room, in an adjacent outbuilding. He turned the jet to 'Cold' and let the icy needles wash away the sourness of sleep. A minute later he let the water go warm and began to soap his body and hair luxuriously.

And so he failed to hear the black Porsche Targa, with Margot at the wheel, come to a halt outside Whyman Hall. Margot slid out of the car. She was hot from the drive, despite the well-chosen cool white linen suit. She wore no bra or stockings, and her full breasts swung tantalisingly as she walked towards the pool. A swim had been her first priority ever since the first traffic jam on the Chiswick flyover, barely out of London. She thirsted for the water's cool kiss on her body.

They were all away: Perry in Switzerland, Klein, Maxie and Tommy back in town. She'd just had to get away, Dudley was at some seminar on the south coast. London was hot, humid and crowded with tourists. So she'd started out a day early. She would swim naked. The pool was once again flat, calm and green, the tremors of the last swimmer settled. She slid out of her suit and left it where it fell, first kicking off her white leather strappy high heels. She put her Cartier watch and gold bracelet on the floor next to the lounger and quickly slipped off the brief silk pants. She stood naked and poised at the edge of the pool. Frequent long holidays in the sun had burned her skin a deep russet colour. Only the edges of her breasts were milky-white, pinpointed by the rich pink nipples.

She cut the water cleanly and swam under the surface for the length of the pool, her hair streaming out behind her. She surfaced, turned and swam a leisurely crawl back down the pool. The water felt like champagne on her skin, refreshing and invigorating. She rolled over onto her back and felt the sound of the water lapping round her ears as she gazed at the blue sky. She closed her eyes and lay in the water's cool embrace.

Tommy let the hot jets stream the soap from his face and hair. He turned the water slowly to 'Cold' again and felt his body tingle with the change in temperature.

Margot climbed out of the pool and walked towards the shower room. She was five paces from the open door when she saw the pile of clothes at the poolside and heard the sound of running water at one and the same time.

It could only be Tommy.

A tremor ran through her and she shuddered as though hit by a cold wind. She could feel the blood begin to pound in her temples. She smoothed back the thick hair, raven black from the water.

Tommy turned off the shower, and glowing with well-being stepped into the small room to pick up the large bath towel hanging on a heated rail.

Margot crossed the threshold. Her mind was now clear; certain as to its purpose.

The boxer turned, and for a fraction of a second the instincts of a lifetime nearly triumphed as his hand reached automatically for the bath towel with which to cover himself. But, unblinking, Tommy drew back his hand. Unashamedly he stood as the desire rose visibly in him. Margot stood transfixed, animal longing burning within her, fuelled by the display of nature she was witnessing.

The boxer walked slowly towards her like some magnificent animal; without a word or a gesture he took Margot's head in his hands and kissed her softly on the lips. Then his tongue was probing, searching. His hands hunted urgently, stroking the firm breasts, then pressing, crushing, squeezing. Gripping the small firm cheeks of her buttocks, crushing them to her. Now his fingers, touching, probing her. She was so wet. And then they were inside her, moving, working. His mouth was on her neck. Now her leg was raised to his thigh as his fingers probed deep inside her. She could feel him, ramrod stiff, and hot against her thigh. Her hand found his prick, gripped it and stroked its length. She heard a sigh from deep within him.

Suddenly – so suddenly she was terrified something was wrong – he pulled away. He smiled in reassurance, though his face was flushed with excitement. He took a long gymnasium mattress from its place on a ledge and unrolled it on the floor. He picked Margot up with contemptuous ease and laid her gently on the mattress. He lay down beside her and kissed her hungrily, his hand on her right breast, the second finger gently stroking the nipple. The warm, molten feeling grew like lava inside her.

'Tommy, I want you inside me.'

He rolled over and she could feel his chest crushing her breasts before he took his massive weight on one arm. His breath was on her face, and rivulets of water from his hair tumbled down to mingle with the tiny globules of moisture on her face. She felt him shift position slightly. She must not help. Then he was inside her. She gasped. He began to drive into her, rhythmically, methodically, terrifyingly. She felt she was being fulfilled for the first time in so long; her body was not her own. Her whole being had been occupied by this magnificent invader, this frightening, beautiful thing that tore into her. He could not go deeper, there was nowhere left in her soul to go.

Her legs gripped him round the waist. Her eyes were closed, arms alternately clutching his shoulders and splaying out in helpless ecstasy. It was building like a dangerous volcano far within her. She felt the terrible power start its slow surge from her loins through her whole body. It exploded with cataclysmic force, the shock waves rolling through her; wave after wave of indescribable pleasure, surging into every corner of her body. She felt suspended in a void of warm blackness, floating on a sea of pleasure. Every cell of her body was pervaded by this beautiful sensation. And still it went on like a series of tidal waves. And still the man above thrust into her helpless prone body. She was screaming, everything within her liberated, fulfilled, revealed – but no sound came, just the crescendo of her own pleasure deep in her consciousness.

Then she felt a tremor run through Tommy. He gave a low moan and there was a strange choking noise in his throat. She clutched his face to hers and held him tight, her legs a vice round his thighs. The tremor became a shock wave and suddenly his whole body stiffened, he let out a long 'aaaaaagh . . .' and she felt him explode within her. His body jerked spasmodically, then he lay still, his face buried in her wet hair.

Like exhausted swimmers cast on the shore of a desert island, they lay there for what seemed an eternity, lost in the exhaustion and bliss of lovemaking.

Eventually Tommy leaned up on one elbow and gazed in disbelief at Margot. 'I didn't think you were coming till tomorrow.'

She looked into the blue eyes, at the face with the age-old look of the satisfied male written upon it. She said, 'As a romantic quote, Tommy, that gets a big zero.'

He leaned over and kissed her on both eyelids. 'But I'm glad you did. In both senses of the word.'

Her face went serious. 'I didn't plan this. I didn't know you would be here. But I wanted you, you know that. It was just a matter of time – for both of us.'

'I hoped.'

'You're a wonderful lover, Tommy – and not a bad boxer, I'm told.' She laughed.

There was little boy pleasure on his face. 'Am I? Am I really?'

She kissed him sensuously, running her tongue over his teeth. 'You betcha.'

'I think I love you Margot.'

Margot sighed deeply, she was confused but oh, so happy! She climbed to her feet and put a hand out for Tommy. 'Let's shower.'

'I just have.'

Margot laughed deliciously. 'Not like we're going to shower, you haven't.'

The warm water cascaded down them as they stood, mouths locked, bodies entwined like some erotic Greek statue. Margot quickly disproved Tommy's belief that it was over for a while and soon his body was aroused and stiff. She soaped him, running her hands over the firm muscles, then gently caressing his penis, wondering at its power. Through the falling curtain of water she reached up and whispered to him, 'Your turn for a little pleasure.'

He watched as she slid down to his waist. He'd never done that. Sylvia wouldn't. He'd wondered. Now. He couldn't believe...

His back arched and his face broke in a rictus of pleasure as she took him. His hands reached down and plunged into her hair.

It was better, better than he could ever have imagined.

As the surge of pleasure convulsed him he realised almost with disbelief that the woman kneeling before him giving him unashamed pleasure was someone else's wife. The wife of the man who must shortly become the Prime Minister of England.

They could hear the sound of the sea as it sucked and hissed at the pebbles on the beach. The wind moaned in the trees like a giant whisper. Emily was propped up in bed on one elbow. Dudley was sitting up with the pillows bunched behind him. Their lovemaking had followed its usual pattern. First they had eaten, mouthfuls between the constant talk of politics. Sips of wine sandwiched between exchanges on the mood of British politics, apathy among the voters, Tory attitudes to the trade unions, the potential Liberal vote. Their hands had never touched during dinner, only their minds met and caressed like friends and lovers. Quiet, momentarily, as they sat in front of the blazing log fire sipping the Remy Martin, Emily had said finally:

'Are you sure you hadn't better get back? It's a risk. You're going to be P.M. Nothing must spoil that.'

Dudley swirled the cognac round in his glass. 'It's all right, I'm certain. The seminar finished at 9 p.m. and they all headed off to the bar to get drunk. By the way, remind me to speak to Smithson, he's been hitting it a bit heavily lately. We don't want any slip-ups during the campaign. Press'd love a drunken shadow Defence Minister. Anyway, I told them I was visiting an aunt who lives in Newhaven. It so happens that I do have an aunt in Newhaven. If I leave here at five, I'll be back in the Metropole before I'm missed.'

'What about your room key?'

He patted his jacket pocket.

'And if anyone sees you going in?'

'Simple. Couldn't sleep. Drove to Peacehaven for a walk on the cliffs. Thank God you don't have neighbours.'

She laughed and kissed him. He took her roughly, there on the rug in front of the crackling, spitting fire. There were no words as they quickly took off their clothes, piling them in neat bundles. As he squeezed her breasts she closed her eyes and sat astride him. She did not open them until the quick orgasm had ripped at her and she felt his body convulse and then become still. They'd gone to bed straight afterwards, their minds sharp and rekindled, nothing now to mar their conversation, the exchange of their knowledge.

He knew she was nowhere near as beautiful as Margot. She was, one could almost say, mousy. The short brown hair cut in pageboy style. Freckles, small nose, dumpy schoolgirl figure with the two pert mounds held high and straight by the strict bra. But she had power, dynamism, an animal strength which flowed out of her when she spoke to criticise, evaluate and analyse. She had produced for him a devastating report on his Shadow Cabinet. Analysing in detail their strengths and weaknesses. Who should go and why? Who should be brought in and why? He has a poor brain but the public love him. Keep him until after the election and then send him to the Lords. He's ambitious, sees himself taking the Premiership off you in two or three years. Promote him beyond his capabilities, he's not as good as he thinks he is. Give him a Ministry, Environment perhaps, then make sure he blunders. Not something big enough to harm the government seriously, but enough to chop him. An election in eighteen months, probably sooner.

Emily briefed him on the latest Labour strategy, how she thought they would try and woo the voters and how to counter that strategy with a vote-getting campaign of their own.

'Darling you really should have been born in the United States. You'd have been the first woman President.'

She laughed heartily like a high school prefect who had been told a clean joke: 'Never could stand Washington.'

He stroked her hair tenderly. 'When are you playing Superman again?'

'Superwoman you mean.'

'I thought that was a book by Shirley Conran.'

'All right, Superman then. Saturday. You really should try it, it's very liberating. Britain's only parachuting prime minister. You could drop in on your constituency.'

He laughed. 'My supporters would love that, but I wouldn't. Far too dangerous.'

'Nonsense, Dudley! I'd hate to quote you statistics but it's much more dangerous to cross the street than to make a parachute jump.'

'Says who?'

'Me, and to prove it I've been crossing streets and jumping out of planes for years and I've never been run over yet doing either.'

'You're impossible. But doesn't it scare you?'

'A little. I suppose that's part of the thrill really. But secretly it's all Freudian I'm sure. I must be sublimating something.' She laughed. 'Besides, as you know, I'm a great believer in law and order. So just once in a while it's nice to break the law – even if it's only the law of gravity.'

They talked until the early hours, the only sound to disturb the tranquil murmurs of the night a car crunching down the narrow track, its headlights arcing across the ceiling of the small low-beamed bedroom. Once, the sudden urge to take her high in him. he put his hand on her breast as she spoke. She was talking of the present Prime Minister, his strengths and weaknesses and her instinct that the Labour Party might try to ditch him in favour of a new young face to put on the posters and woo the young mums. Leadbetter, perhaps, or even Tyson. Incredibly she seemed not to notice his arousal, though his sex was thrust against her. But by some thought process she quickly ended her analysis and said, 'You don't think your wife suspects? Suppose she calls the hotel?'

Dudley flopped wearily back on the pillows. It was 4 a.m. He'd have to leave soon. He was going to be damned tired but it had been worth it.

'I doubt it. She's down at Perry's place in Wiltshire. She seems to spend half her life there now. I sometimes think she fancies that little punk, Booth. It would just about fit in with her tastes.'

She kissed him gently. 'That's not important. But getting you to Number Ten is. You're going to be a great P.M., Dudley, a great one. This country's been going downhill for too long. You can stop the rot, Dudley, you really can.'

Her brow was furrowed with determination as Dudley slapped a fist into his palm. 'I know I can do it. I know. You believe I can, you believe in me?'

She looked at him long and hard. 'I wouldn't be here if I didn't.'

He tried to inject a note of flippancy into his voice: 'I had thought you just may have been a teeny-weeny bit in love with me.'

She snorted in disgust. 'Love? Love is an illusion. I had love at Oxford. It was straight out of the poetry books. Long dreamy afternoon being punted along green rivers, trailing my hand in the water. Then nights of passion with my young lover. Then suddenly I'm pregnant and the love is gone and so is the lover. Just me left, and this thing implanted in me.

The day I walked out of that nursing home in St John's Wood, I vowed never to believe in love again.'

Dudley took her hand: 'I never knew.'

She closed her hand over his and said wearily. 'Something went wrong. Now I can't have children, and children are the only thing that gives love meaning. The rest of love, the hearts, the flowers, the vows – like I said, they are an illusion. The only real things are power, responsibility and respect. I find that in you.' She squeezed his hand. 'You don't want love from me, I know that Dudley. Sex, yes, and I'm happy to give it, for you don't believe it means more than the act. You and I are alike. We're mature enough to go on without love. We're a team and by God between us we're going to change the destiny of this country.' She bent down and kissed him. 'Am I right?'

'You always are.'

The phone rang on Archie Taylor's desk.

'Diary.'

'Archie? Tony Duggan, *Brighton Argus*.'

'Hello Tony, how you keeping?'

'Mustn't grumble.'

'Wife and kids?'

'In the pink.'

'Got a good one for me Tony?'

'Not sure really, but I thought I'd give you a tinkle. Might be something, might not. You know the Leader of the Opposition's secretary, Emily something-or-other?'

'Carstairs.'

'Emily Carstairs. Well she bought a little place down here not so long back. Little cottage, off the beaten track, near the beach. Well, I was down there the other night 'bout midnight I suppose. To be honest, it was a bit of naughty. I adore Cath and all that but a man's got to have a bit of variety, right?'

'Too right.'

'Still, long story short, when we drove past there was a car parked in the trees next to the cottage. Almost looked as though someone was trying to hide it. On the way back, it was still there. Daimler Sovereign it was, dark. Maybe nothing in it, but if one of our local worthies is knocking off Emily I thought you'd like to know. I gather she's a bit of a power up at Westminster these days, shades of Marcia and all that.'

'Wait till Dudley gets to Number Ten, she'll make Marcia look like an amateur. Did you get the number?'

'Just because I retired to a quiet life by the seaside doesn't mean I've lost my touch. Got a pen? It's KMB 736T.'

Archie suppressed a little whistle of surprise. 'Thanks Tony I'll check it out.'

'Do me a favour Archie, if you ever bump into me when I'm with Cath, not a word, there's a mate. She thinks I was on an all-night mission with the Territorials when in fact I was on a low-level bombing run over this bird who's just started on the local radio station. Tits like melons she's got.'

'You're a dirty sod Tony. Not a word, don't fret.'

'See you soon Archie.'

'Take care.'

Archie put the phone down. Well, well, well. Who would have thought it. I've seen that car a dozen times with Dudley at the wheel. So Margot isn't enough for him. And I always thought he preferred politics to sex. But Emily when you've got a wife like Margot? He must be bloody insatiable.

I'll have to let Tony in on it. He'll keep his mouth shut for two hundred. Ex-Fleet Street man: he'll not blab if he's paid. Archie tucked the jewel of information safely in the strongbox of his mind and leaned back in his revolving chair. And allowed himself the luxury of thought. Now just how best can I use this information?

Margot sipped her white wine. The dinner had not been a success. It was two weeks since they'd been together and now they sat like strangers forced to share a restaurant table, avoiding each other's eyes, smiling nervously when their glances did meet. And yet Margot was not nervous. She felt no guilt about what she had done. Tommy had appeared on her horizon. She knew she loved him. She knew herself. Conscience, the guilty sort, was for when you did something that was wrong and hurt someone. She did not feel she had hurt anyone or done any wrong. After all, she concluded, what could penetrate that cocoon of ambition and lust for power that her husband had spun around himself over these years? Each mental thread building into a cage that it seemed no love or fear or longing could penetrate. Yet her smile had a nervous feel about it, like a fault in the hem of a dress, which tugged, pulling the garment out of shape. It was something of Dudley's nervousness, she decided, which sprayed at her like shrapnel, peppering the surface of her calm. His knife and fork rested neatly, pointing towards her like daggers across the plate.

'Delicious darling, how nice to taste your cooking again. Mrs Melling is an angel but she's hardly *cordon bleu.*'

He put his arm across the table and the slim, elegantly manicured fingers touched hers as they curled around the stem of the tall, cut-crystal wine glass. But there was something in the gesture, something awkward, like that of a bad actor cramped with stage fright.

She smiled at him and felt again the tug at her facial muscles.

He said, 'How are the pictures coming along my dear? I thought you would have had an album full by now. Couldn't you spend a little less time down in Wiltshire? The house doesn't seem the same without you.'

'Well, darling, it seems Tommy Booth is going to go a long way, and that means I follow in the footsteps, dutifully clicking away. Perry and Klein – and how I hate that little gangster – are convinced Tommy is a really hot property. A book of exclusive and different pictures of him could be a very good publishing proposition if he does make it to world champion.'

Dudley poured them more wine.

'You hardly need the money darling.'

'It's not the money, it's a chance of recognition for my work. You know what absolute bastards the National Union of Journalists have been because I don't earn x per cent of my money from full-time journalism, or some such nonsense. This work could establish me as a recognised photographer.'

Dudley repeated the words, his eyes narrowing into sarcasm: 'Recognised photographer?' He looked across the polished table, measuring his words like arrows for range and force. 'It is just possible this country's voters would prefer the wife of their potential Prime Minister to spend just a little bit more time with the husband she loves and wants to help into Downing Street.'

A burst of fire like that from a blast furnace gushed in Margot's brain. 'And perhaps, just perhaps, your loving voters would all like to go out and fuck themselves.'

Dudley pulled a face. 'My, we must be rattled. You don't normally have to fall back on Anglo-Saxon to make your point.'

Margot closed the furnace door on the tongue of flame. The words came over, measured and calm. 'And you Dudley, are not addressing a party conference at Brighton or making the Party Political Broadcast on behalf of the Conservative and Unionist Party, as I believe the caption reads.'

'*Touché.*'

'Besides,' she added, 'you never struck me as someone who needed the proverbial little woman at the kitchen sink. You knew the way I was when you married me.'

They lapsed into silence while Margot served coffee from the silver jug into the tiny, patterned china cups. Unwittingly she broke their uneasy truce, accidentally firing a shot which struck home.

'Speaking of Brighton, party conferences and all, did you have a good time at the seminar?'

'Sorry?' Dudley could feel the red begin to creep from below his ears.

There was a crisp ting of china meeting china as Margot replaced her cup. 'I said, did-you-have-a-good-time-in-Brighton?'

Dudley wondered for a millisecond how a professional

politician like himself who regularly lied with a straight face, as professional politicians did and must, could be disconcerted quite so easily.

'Not bad, quite productive.'

'Drink a lot?'

Dudley's face furrowed. 'Not really.' What was going on?

'Just thought you might have gone on a bit of a bender. Your insomnia.'

Dudley reeled mentally. He was like a boxer being hit and not only being unable to fight back but not even knowing from where the punches were being launched. There had to be a step forward, if only to restore confidence.

'Darling, you're talking in riddles.'

'Freddie Clare, darling. I saw him in Harrods today. Said he thought your insomnia might be back. You know how bad he is. Don't look so mystified dear, he saw you popping into the Metropole close on six one morning, and presumed you couldn't sleep. Only *I* know what causes your insomnia and he doesn't.'

She spread her hands in a gesture of genuine innocence. 'That's all. I just presumed you'd hit the brandy bottle. I wasn't checking up on you or suggesting you were screwing the chambermaid or something. You weren't were you?'

Dudley's head had cleared. 'Oh, of course, I make a habit of it, it's the pinafores.' How much does she know? Damn that man Clare. How could you trust a man with a sensitive job like the Home Office – which is what he was in line for – when you can't trust him not to blab to your wife. And presumably told her about Aunt Phoebe in Newhaven. A card to sacrifice before it's seized. 'If you must know I did have a few that night. I couldn't face boozing with that mob after three days cooped up with them at the Metropole, so I told them I was going to Phoebe's at Newhaven. In fact I went over to see Teddy Alexander – Korea, remember? – his wife was in Antibes so we had a sort of bachelor supper. I'd been working hard and he's under the most awful pressure at Tomlinsons, so we rather let our hair down. I got back at three, couldn't sleep, walked along the beach to clear my head, then got a couple of hours.' He grimaced. 'After which, of course, I made love to the chambermaid. I expect the *News of the World* will be knocking at the door any moment. Does the District Attorney have any more questions? And by the way you *can* check with Teddy.'

Thank God for caution. Emily had been right. A fall-back cover story. Teddy was watertight, he had indiscretions he didn't wish revealed. So it worked out. Men lie to their colleagues every day. And to their wives. But rarely at the same time and about the same incident.

Margot was genuinely puzzled. An offhand query and Dudley reacted as though he'd been stung by a wasp. Slowly she said, 'I'm sorry. I was just curious.'

'Forget it, I'm worn out. I over-reacted. It's these late night sittings.'

She thought of Tommy. Of lying exhausted in his arms. And although there was still no guilt, she recognised the justice in not being suspicious of Dudley. After dinner they listened to music, and once, just once, Dudley's hand went round her shoulders and traced a line in the soft hair at the base of her neck. But like a nervous, unsure visitor it departed, and they sat, untouching, bathed separately in twin pools of music.

She put on her prettiest nightgown of pale-blue satin, her breasts showing soft and round through the plunging divide. She lay in the crook of his arm, her left hand tracing the contours of his body like the fingers of a blind man might. How different he was from Tommy. There was power, but it came from the soul, the heartland, its only symbol the messages of nerve which warned the toucher not to be deceived by the outer ramparts. Power, said the nerves, lies at the centre of the fortress. The proportions were different; no hard-ridged muscle or firm hillocks of bicep. Rather, slim and white – she could feel the colour as though her fingertips had eyes. The body of a city man – fine and in shape but with the tell-tale soft ripples of fat collecting at the base of the ribs like sand from a crumbling dune.

He kissed her in silence, and his kiss spoke of guilt. It had too much passion. It said, 'How good to be home – how different – to be back from that other mouth . . . for a while.' It was a guilty visitor, happy at the reunion, but knowing it would soon depart for other doors.

As he entered her Margot shivered. It was one thing she had never considered of Dudley. Infidelity seemed no part of his make-up, any more than he would sneak off to drive stock cars or get his fingers and clothes dirty tinkering with the engines. But Margot could feel the effect of her own infidelity. It tightened her, gripped at her feelings, making it difficult, almost impossible, to act naturally, or react instinctively instead of with calculation. She had used to feel that Dudley was mechanical, sex-by-numbers. But wasn't she guilty of the same offence?

It was like a profit-and-loss account. For every moment of abandon and spontaneity with Tommy, something was lost with Dudley. Had he guessed and decided to hit back with an infidelity of his own? In the past she felt she honestly would not have cared. And yet now? The thought didn't shock her, stun her or send her cold with fury as it might some women. But she felt a cold touch of unease, a restlessness that had never affected her before. Then it sprung from hiding like an evil imp and jumped into her mind. She hated it, tried to chase it from her head. It had no place in her powerful, organised, sure, sure mind. But the thought stayed, and nagged at the corners of her brain, waiting to be acknowledged.

Her poor, dear, passionless, ambitious Dudley might – just might – be making love to another woman. And enjoying it more than he did with her.

# *Chapter Five*

Klein cupped Monique's right breast in his hand and stroked his thumb backwards and forwards across the brown nipple, firm and erect. She knelt on the bed, eyes closed like a contented cat, almost purring with pleasure.

'Nice?'

She nodded, eyes still closed. Then she opened one eye mischievously and leaped like a surprised tiger, pinning Klein back against the pillow, her tongue searching for his ear, flickering round the lobe, then nibbling and sucking at the hanging flesh. He turned her over roughly and kissed her wetly and fiercely.

She said, 'You randy old devil, haven't you had enough? I'm worn out.'

Klein laid his head on the pillow next to her and tickled her chin with his right hand. 'You must be joking. I've only just started.'

Her eyes widened in mock surprise. 'We've been at it for hours. There's a limit to everything Lewis,' then she giggled luxuriously and rolled swiftly and agilely out of the bed, evading his clutching hands. She stood there, hands on hips, naked and beautiful in the soft light of the bedside lamp. 'If I don't get changed and out of here in thirty minutes the Starlight Club is going to be short of its star attraction.'

He was silent looking at her. She was one of the few things – few people – Klein felt any real affection for. His wife and son, certainly, but in a distant way. They were a responsibility, a burden he gladly shouldered, but they were kept in the business corner of his mind. Birthday presents, a new home, holidays for them, schooling for the boy, pounds and pence to be dealt with like an accountant. I look after them, profit, I fail to look after them, loss. Klein liked profit. But Monique. Monique was different.

He'd met her in the Manhattan Club at Upminster. He'd been with Jock McCulloch. They'd been uneasy friends then, linked by numerous shady deals but no love lost. Jock had very little muscle, Klein knew that, but he was ambitious and could be dangerous. Jock brought her to the table where they'd been drinking.

'Lewis I'd like you to meet my favourite wog.' Klein saw her eyes tighten behind the smile.

He took her hand. 'Lewis Klein, it's a pleasure.'

'Monique.' She joined them at the table and held Klein's eyes firmly.

In halting English she told him briefly and without embellishment, of how she came to be at the Manhattan. She was twenty-two years old from Port Louis in Mauritius. French father, native mother, the last two years of her life spent singing in a club in the Vieux Port district of Marseilles. A visiting club owner had offered her a cabaret spot at his West End nightspot and she agreed to come to London. She had wanted to leave anyway, she told Klein, and he saw her tense as she spoke the words.

The club owner had told her to tell immigration if they asked – which they did – she was here for a three-week holiday. The work permit was a formality, he explained. But neither her English nor her singing, it seemed, was up to Flamingo, Bond Street, standards – and the work permit failed to materialise and she ended up singing at the Manhattan, courtesy of Jock McCulloch.

Klein could read people, see the vibrations fly off them and he could tell one thing: she hated the Scotsman. Stick a knife in him as soon as look.

She excused herself and headed for the powder room. McCulloch leaned across and Klein smelled the Scotch and halitosis on his breath: 'Not a bad bit of the old tarbrush, eh, Lewis?'

Klein looked at him with a mixture of pity and contempt.

Repressed little Scots berk. Soon as his fat wife's back is turned he's out screwing everything in sight. He'll get nowhere there.

His elbow nudged Klein's. 'I'm on there, Lewis, sure as eggs are eggs.'

'She wouldn't touch you with a bargepole Jock, and you know it.'

The Scotsman smiled a smug smile.

'Unless you've got something on her.'

McCulloch picked up his Scotch, took a sip, then picked up his champagne glass and drained it. Enjoying the silence. 'Well Lewis, it's like this. Without a work permit she can't get work and she gets deported. If little Jock gets her the permit she's got to be grateful.'

'One snag, Jock. You haven't a hope in hell of getting her a work permit. The only connections you've got in government is that bent surveyor down the town hall.'

McCulloch pulled down the skin below his left eye. 'You know that Lewis, and I know that, but our little bit of black ass, she doesn't know that. And the message she gets is that if she doesn't drop her knickers by next week she's on the way out.'

'Why don't you go up to Shepherd's Market, Jock, or down to Brixton? You can get all the black chicks you want. You can afford it. Why pick on her?'

''Cause I fancy her and it'll be a bloody sight cheaper. So don't come that holier than thou stuff with me Lewis, you've pulled dirtier stunts than that in your time.'

'Not with women.'

'She's only black trash, Lewis, and half French black trash at that. The two things I can't stand are niggers and Frogs. But I reckon she'll screw like a rattlesnake so I'll make an exception in her case.'

The champagne bottle would probably have fractured the Scotsman's skull had it connected, but with an agility astonishing for a man of his age he dodged sideways as he spotted the green blur out of the corner of one eye. Instead the bottle shattered harmlessly on the edge of the chair.

McCulloch was spattered with champagne and fragments of green glass. Monique stood before him, her voice quivering with rage. 'You ever speak of me like this and I kill you.'

The Scotsman's face was white with shock. 'I should watch yourself, darling, or you'll get hurt.' A man in a dinner jacket hovered uneasily at the Scotsman's elbow. 'And I think you can consider yourself fired, eh Jimmy?' The manager nodded nervously.

Klein watched in silence as Monique swung angrily on her heel and headed for the dressing room. McCulloch shouted after her: 'I should watch it choco, if my memory serves me right you'll soon be having a conducted tour of Holloway.' He turned towards Klein. 'Must be the nigger blood, makes them wild.'

Klein finished his champagne: 'I'd watch yourself Jock, if you weren't so quick on your feet you'd be in intensive care now.'

'It'll take more than some black bird to see me off.'

Klein sat in the Jaguar waiting for her to leave. When she drew level with the car he wound down his window. 'Get in, I'd like to talk to you.'

'*Merde!*'

'I don't know what it means, but it doesn't sound nice. Please get in.'

There was contempt in her voice: 'Looking for some *café noir*?'

'I don't want to lay a finger on you love, but I promise you, if you don't listen to what I've got to say you'll be in prison by this time tomorrow.'

She came round to the passenger door, opened it and sat in the front seat staring straight ahead through the windscreen.

He said, 'I'll keep it short. You got into this country on a false declaration, and you've worked without a permit. I don't know the ins and outs but I reckon they can deport you for that. Jock's a vindictive little bastard. He can't screw you in bed so he'll try and screw you some other way. Tomorrow morning the rozzers will be round at your place and you'll be in the nick.'

'Rozzers? Nick?'

'Gendarmerie, cherie, bogies, police. Nick is prison.'

Her chin dropped. 'I can't go back to Marseilles. I can't.'

'Spot of bother?'

She didn't speak.

''Nuff said. I've heard they don't mess about down there. All right, look. Don't go back to your place, not even for your clothes. I've got a flat –' he put up a hand to stifle her interruption, 'don't worry sweetheart, it's got two bedrooms, locks on the doors and I'm not in the habit of raping people, savvy? You stay there a couple of weeks and I'll see if I can get you a permit – a backdated one. I've got a few friends up at Westminster.'

'Westminster?'

'In the corridors of power my love. Anyway I'll fix your permit...'

'That's what Jock said.'

'Jock's all mouth and kilt.'

'Why?'

'Why what?'

'Why are you doing this for me? You don't know me.'

'Maybe it's because the little Scots git gets on my tits, anyway it doesn't matter.'

They drove in silence to the flat. When he had shown her her room, he took out his wallet, pulled out fifteen £10 notes and put them on the table. 'Few clothes, food and drink, okay? I'll be back from time to time.' He pointed to a door. 'My room, don't go into it, savvy?' She nodded.

Later he phoned Dudley. Three weeks after the night they'd met, he went back to the flat. She was in an armchair reading a magazine. He tossed an envelope to her. 'Your work permit. I've fixed a cabaret spot at the Starlight for you. You start Monday, ninety a week and your meals. You can stay here as long as it takes you to find yourself a flat.'

She got out of the chair and slowly began unbuttoning her blouse as Klein watched in silence. She was wearing no bra and her magnificent breasts were pointed and full. Her hair was like shiny black satin, her skin a rich mahogany. Her features were more European than African, speaking of the mixed blood the sailor from France had implanted in her veins.

'Now,' she said calmly, 'you'll want your bit of chocolate. Your reward.'

Klein picked up the blouse where she had tossed it carelessly on the sofa. 'Cover yourself. This town is full of whores, professionals and amateurs. I helped you because you weren't either. Don't make me change my mind.'

Two months later they became lovers. Klein returned to the flat, tired after an evening of haggling over a business deal. Monique was watching the late-night movie: 'Just improving my English,' she told Klein. He flopped down on the sofa and closed his eyes. Without asking she made him cocoa and sat down beside him. 'Tell me about yourself, Lewis.'

He started to talk and the words came as they had never done before. For the first time he was recounting his life, the hardships of youth and the battle to the top.

As the grey light of dawn seeped under the curtains she leaned across and kissed him. He kissed her back with a passion and fervour he did not think possible in himself. She led him to the bedroom – his room, the one she had been forbidden to enter – and they climbed into the bed and fell instantly asleep in each other's arms. When they awoke the sun had broken through the low cloud and they made love as the sunshine dappled the edge of the bedspread. Now Klein returned to the flat whenever possible. The days he was forced to spend for the sake of propriety at his home in Hampstead grew fewer and fewer. He saw his son David at weekends and the lad seemed happy. It had been over in bed with Miriam for years. First it was headaches, then migraine, then she became anaemic and lacked strength. She asked for and got a room of her own. For seven years Klein had been virtually celibate with the exception of one-night affairs. Until Monique.

She stood there, eying him quizzically. 'Do you want me to be worn out?'

He put his hands behind his head: 'All right, we'll make

up for it on Monday. Must have been that holiday, it's refreshed me.'

'Maybe we should go and live in Mauritius.'

'What? You must be joking. I'd snuff it without all this. Lousy weather, 'orrible people, strikes all the time, if it's not the villains after your money it's the rozzers after your hide. Look love, paradise is all right a couple of weeks of the year, but give me England any day of the week.'

She walked back to the bed, knelt down, and kissed him. 'You are one crazy man, Lewis, and I love you.'

He smacked her lightly on the bottom. 'I agree, and now bugger off and get changed or I'll drag you back in this bed and not let you out for a fortnight.'

He lay there listening to the sound of the filling bath and her singing. He remembered the first line. To think of that dirty little Scots git trying to get his hands on her. He shuddered. Jock hadn't given up either, started sniffing around her at the Starlight, spot of the old blackmail. Didn't tell me for a week, she was scared stiff, said he'd carve her if she told me. Cunt couldn't carve the Sunday joint. Well the little tartan laddie had a visit from Graham. Beat the shit out of him. He never learns, does Jock. Got to try and get back at me so he tries to buy old Manny's betting shops. Should've known he hadn't got the muscle. Now he goes round the pubs showing everybody his hands like he was Jesus Christ and it was the Second Coming.

He'll be quiet now though, and if he ever so much as whispers to Monique again it's a new pair of Gucci cement shoes and he fucking well knows it.

Klein steered the Jaguar out towards Hampstead. A van bearing the legend 'Lewis Klein Security Services' passed him on the opposite side of the road, and the driver, recognising Klein, gave him the thumbs-up sign. Klein pushed a cassette into the player and let the soothing spell of Dvořak work on him. Lewis Klein Security Services. He smiled. Come a long way, Lewis lad, a long way.

He remembered his boyhood. Poor Jews in a poor area

and more coming in from Germany and Austria, all scratching for a living. And the goys hating your guts when they had to hock the gold watch or the Sunday suit for a drink on Fridays. Two rooms over the shop and meals of sausage and soup, sausage and soup, then bread and margarine and tea. I still hate bloody margarine. Just a toddler when my old man went down Cable Street to fight Mosley's Blackshirts. Stupid old git. All he got was a broken nose from a copper's truncheon and a pair of busted specs for his trouble. If he'd have hit the Blackshirts as hard as he used to wallop me, Mosley would have packed it in!

Then the blitz and evacuation. Bit of fun at the time, away from the old man *and* the food was okay, first time I tasted butter in my life. And a bird. Screwed her at thirteen, she must have been at least seventeen, bush on her like a haystack. Eyes nearly popped when she saw my willy, don't think she'd ever seen a circumcised prick before.

All seems a blur now. Then the R.A.F., Padgate, exotic foreign posting! But learning a few dodges, wising up to what life was about. Few giggles – and a few punch-ups. A Yid's got to stick up for himself. Klein remembered that Catering Corps sergeant he'd whacked in Blackpool. Fighting Kike they called him after that.

The road was clearing and Klein pushed the Jaguar up to thirty-five. Army surplus was still thriving when he'd got out of the R.A.F. But to buy you needed money and he'd had about £4 7s 6d and a rail warrant. Four weeks later he'd robbed a sub-Post Office in Barnet, one-off job and the old woman screaming blue murder. But he hadn't been caught. That was the message, Everyone was on the make, Stalin, Churchill, everybody. Hitler got caught, that was his mistake. Moral? Don't get caught.

He bought five clapped-out Bedford three-tonners for £250 and flogged them the next day for £500. 'Double Your Money' he called it later in life after the popular TV quiz of the early 'sixties. In a year he'd made £20,000 – a fortune in the early 'fifties – and started putting his money about. Couple of haulage firms, nothing fancy, but they were still going strong now. When the government legalised off-course betting, Klein opened a string of shops. Competition was rough in those days, shops got set on fire, customers were 'persuaded' to take their mug money elsewhere. Klein knew the score. He got his own little gang and they gave as good as they got. But he was no Jack Spot boasting up West with two tarts on his arm. The bogies loved that. Quiet, was Klein, everyone said so. Polite, quietly spoken, always bought tickets to the police ball.

Protection rackets were popular, but short-lived. Everyone thought he was a little Al Capone. Strong-arm stuff, smash a few windows, bleed the shopkeepers white, then somebody got fed-up enough, broke enough or simply brave enough to spill it to the cops and then you were doing five in the Scrubs. Klein watched, studied and waited. There was a market, a need, but it had to be almost legit – legit enough for no one to feel threatened long enough to go running to his local Dixon of Dock Green.

He tried it out. For a fixed and relatively small sum each month paid to the newly-formed 'Lewis Klein Security Services' he guaranteed to keep any subscriber's premises crime-free. There was no coercion, and many shopkeepers, not believing their luck, refused to join when they realised that refusal didn't mean their windows would be broken, their premises looted.

Those who did got more than the two men, a van, an aging Alsation and a once-a-night inspection that they paid for. They got the Klein name, the reputation. The word went out. Bust a Klein-protected shop and you get hurt. It worked. You could have hung your gold watch on the shutters at closing time and it would have been there at opening time next morning. When the word got around, shopkeepers all over the East End flocked to join. The local police loved it, crime was down, and that was good for their figures. The only real test of the Klein crime-free guarantee came from a young up-and-coming cat burglar called Ian Lawrence. He climbed a skylight and cleaned out a Stepney jeweller to the tune of twenty grand. Klein let the newly-recruited Graham off the leash.

Graham found Lawrence trying to flog half his haul to a

terrified fence in the Blind Beggar. Expressing an interest, he took Lawrence into an alleyway behind the pub, took out a crowbar and broke both his legs.

He told Klein: 'He won't be climbing any more skylights, boss.'

The news went through the East End like a bush-fire and business boomed.

'Income £6,000 a month; expenditure, two men, one dog, one van, say £1,000 a month, net result, happiness,' beamed Klein, torturing Mr Micawber.

Klein always supported the forces of law and order. He did not approve of vandalism and petty crime. The local C.I.D. superintendent was a personal friend. Klein often lent him the villa he'd bought in 1967 a few miles outside Marbella, and the officer was a frequent recipient of goodwill at several West End clubs in which Klein had a stake.

He'd met Perry at a boxing charity dinner. They'd been seated together by chance and found they got on, this landed aristocrat entrepreneur and the East Ender. Their friendship had blossomed through a shared interest in boxing and each had come to respect the other's business acumen. And when, like a fading love affair, their friendship diminished, the business link and love of sport remained, a stronger hold than genuine affection.

Perry had introduced him to Archie at another dinner and he'd instantly distrusted the American. But distrust was a basis on which Klein could build, and build he had. The press was powerful, the press was useful, the press could be corrupted and manipulated – and Archie was the press. So with simple logic he cultivated Archie, drawing him into his circle of friends with a false display of friendship until Archie was firmly into the web of uneasy alliance, and knew like all the other Klein 'friends' that no one was safe from the long arm of Lewis Klein.

What no one, with the exception of the trusted Graham, knew, was that Klein had personally masterminded a third of the bank robberies that had taken place in London over the previous ten years. His methods were simple but effective. The gang was recruited, without the knowledge of each other, after their suitability for the particular role assigned to them had been established. They were only introduced to one another forty-eight hours before a raid, and kept together incommunicado. That way, Klein knew, no one could be an *agent provocateur*, or grass. The raids were carried out in the usual way. Fast, lots of noise, the men heavily armed, but with the minimum of unnecessary violence. No psychos went on Klein-inspired raids.

It was another Thought of Chairman Klein: 'Public don't mind you ripping off the banks. Robin Hood all over again, isn't it? They're always being told they can't have a loan or an overdraft so they don't mind us screwing the banks. But if you shoot some poor snotty-nosed cashier who's a year off his pension, or you cosh some young bobby, well, they get all maternal. The cops get a kick up the arse from the papers and next thing you know it's on Police Five and every little amateur detective in London is mugging up on Photofit pictures.'

And afterwards the Klein masterstroke. All the men hired for the raid accepted a one-year waiting period before their share was paid. That way no one suddenly came into money, started buying new cars, holidays in Majorca or fur coats for the old lady. No drinks all round in the East End pubs so the narks could go running to their paymaster bobbies at the Yard saying: 'Old Eddie's a bit flush. Perhaps he was on the Sydenham job.' And if the cops *did* get a name, when they went round and started tearing the cupboards down, well, there was nothing to find, was there? Within hours of a bank job a privately-hired courier would take a routine shipment – a locked leather briefcase chained to his wrist – to Zurich. There it would be handed to a cashier at a certain bank in the city's business district along with a wax-sealed envelope containing an account number. Two days later a registered letter containing a key to the briefcase would arrive at the bank and the money would be formally deposited.

And twelve months later each member of the gang would

enter any one of a number of designated betting shops in the Klein chain littered throughout east, north-east and south-east London. Here he would take a betting slip and instead of writing the name of a horse, would write the word 'Peacock' and hand it to a cashier wearing a white carnation. He would also hand over a £5 note. After the race he would return and hand over his copy of the slip to the same cashier. She would then hand him the amount of money he would have won had he placed £50 to win on the winning horse. This procedure would be repeated as many times as it took to pay out each member of the gang his share of the raid – including, for Klein was an exact man, interest calculated on each man's share at the rate paid by the Swiss bank.

If death preceded the pay-out, as had happened in one case, the widow or dependants received the money the same way if they were aware of the deceased's criminal activities, or as a 'gift' from the generous Mr Klein if they weren't.

Mr Klein never welches, the word went out.

He was a natural Conservative too – all for each man making his own way in life without help from the State, as he had done. He started working voluntarily for the Conservative Party, organising fund raising efforts which were, not surprisingly, very successful. He first met The Honourable Dudley Creighton in the late 'sixties when the then up-and-coming back bench M.P. had attended a fund-raising dinner for a no-hope candidate in Hackney. It was two years to the upset of 1970 but Klein liked what he saw. Naked ambition, talent, energy, a certain grasp of the practical realities of everyday life. Dudley had asked him, 'I hope we can rely on you for a donation, Mr Klein. Just because we are supposed to be the party of big business doesn't mean the small business man can't help too.'

Klein took out his chequebook. 'I'm hardly McAlpine's but how will twenty grand go down?' And he'd signed the cheque there and then. It was drawn on a Swiss bank and Dudley, for all his willingness for political compromise, may not have been as keen to receive it had he realised it represented a share of the sum taken by five armed men from

Barclay's Bank, Clapham High Street, the previous year. Klein, for his part, liked the irony. As he'd later said to Graham on those interminable evenings when he'd recounted his earlier days: 'Well it's the Conservative Party who believes in private enterprise, am I right?'

It had borne fruit too. A month later Dudley had invited Klein for drinks in the Members' Bar. They ate later at the Connaught and over brandy Klein had expressed his dismay at a G.L.C. plan to redevelop an area in which he had a haulage depot, rezoning it for non-industrial use. The plan had not quite been finalised. Dudley promised to speak to the Tory chairman of the relevant committee. A month later the plan was 'referred back for further discussion' and eventually forgotten.

But if Klein was prepared to sit down with kings then he'd also get his hands dirty with the knaves. True, Graham was his enforcer, but Klein didn't mind breaking an arm or two either. He was fearless and brutal – and, better still, everyone knew it.

There was a gym in Whitechapel which had a back room, padded and silent. There Klein had personally broken the fingers, and sometimes the arms as well, of people who had stood in his way. Like a spectre, his legend grew, some of the tales so weird and fanciful that even Klein laughed – but more importantly could disprove. He became larger than life. A godfather figure before the notorious film gave the word a bad odour. Any charity could touch Mr Klein for a score, maybe a ton. Tough, but fair, that's what they said about him. He started a stable of boxers, nothing fancy but good hitters, game fighters, gave as good as they got – and they got paid and he made sure they had somewhere to go before they got punchy. And one day, they all said it, one day he'd find a *real* fighter.

He'd had a word the Sweeney were after him, then a year later he got the all-clear.

'No evidence, see,' he said to Graham, 'our police can't work without evidence. Finest, most honest police in the world,' and he'd laugh and light another cigar.

I've got everything really, he mused as the big Jaguar turned up Hay Hill, leaving the Duck Pond on his left. He drove past The Spaniards and turned into Bishop's Avenue, where rows of mock Tudor houses lined the street. Businesses, no real aggravation from the filth, a world champion in the making, wife and kid, Monique, and the way the opinion polls are shaping up, we'll have Dudley in Number Ten and I'll get my knighthood. He felt the tingling sensation on his skin that he always experienced when he said the word to himself. 'Sir Lewis Klein.'

Then I'll knock off the bank jobs: you can never be too sure with the rozzers, all these bloody computers and their lads carrying guns like something out of Starsky and Hutch. Too risky. I'll get a proper place for Monique, somewhere up West, and try and get her some swanky singing dates. Perhaps Miriam will go and live with her sister at Frinton, and we'll get David into a good public school. Somewhere he'll get a bit of backbone, learn self-reliance and respect. He turned the Jaguar into the drive of the detached house and saw a small white face peep through the curtains. He waved a hand to his son.

Lewis my lad, to quote the wrong half of the Bible, your cup runneth over.

As the name of a night-club, thought Archie, in one of his more reflective moments, Animals reflects its patrons very accurately. The club was a plush jungle where the sleek well-groomed beasts of society prowled, went through their ritual mating dances and ripped with their gossip-sharpened claws at the weaker breeds who dared enter their territory.

And Archie loved it. Like an old lion he could sit back and watch contentedly, almost fatherly, as the young lions pursued their meaningless frolics. It was arguably *the* London night-club. Membership was two hundred guineas a year – Animals did not recognise, it seemed, decimal currency. But money alone was not an open sesame to this converted warehouse nestling on the banks of the Thames near Battersea Bridge. Members had to be approved by the club committee and they operated on an unwritten code of social in-ness known only to themselves. It was a social enclave of the rich and famous, the sons of the rich and famous, those who were famous but not rich, and those who were rich but not famous. A trip to the lavatory with its gold fittings and expensive soap could find one standing next to a rock star, an Arab sheikh, an oil financier or a European prince, all democratically peeing with their eyes respectfully to the front in the age-old male stance. It was a club where the real 'in' crowd could let their hair down far from the madding and maddening crowd of financial and social inferiors.

Archie often wondered why they'd approved his membership, ratting as he regularly did on the 'who's screwing whom' antics of the patrons. But deep down he knew. If he and his ilk had not been present then the club would have had no meaning. These people, he concluded, had to read about themselves before they were convinced they actually existed. What was the point of X turning up with Y's wife, or rock star A pointedly dancing with actress B until dawn, if they couldn't pick up their paper and read that they'd really done it? And more importantly, realising that others, included in their much-maligned public, had read it too. So they preened themselves before the old lion or his trusted spies. Boasting of their infidelities by the hands they put up to ward off the photographers lurking outside, and by the denials their tame press officers issued like toilet paper.

Just occasionally, some young buck would want to punch Archie on the nose, inflamed by family feeling and champagne at £25 a bottle. But Klein's men policed Animals, moving among the patrons as though they didn't exist. Hard men from a different world wading like trout fishermen through shoals of silver fish. They had orders to keep an eye out for Archie's welfare and their presence was usually enough. True, Archie had once been squirted with a soda siphon while dining with friends, by some young Etonian who felt his family name had been impugned by some reference to his father. The situation was momentarily tense.

The guests fell silent and the water dripped from the soaked shirt-front. Archie saw the Klein men moving like silent, deadly sharks towards the table. The boy could get hurt and Archie did not want that. He picked up a glass of Scotch and calmly poured it down his dinner shirt.

'There we are, Scotch and soda, my favourite drink. Now why not sit down and have one yourself.'

Everyone had laughed and the tension went. The boy laughed too, his pride restored, and sat down. Archie waved away with his eyes the two Klein men who were moving relentlessly in on the boy.

Archie sat there now, caressing the cool round base of the Dom Perignon bottle. Down from the raised dining area the couples cavorted in the dancing area. A Rod Stewart song thumped the music and the figures gyrated in the stabbing beams of coloured light. They wallowed in it like hippos at a mudbath, surrendering themselves to the sheer abandon. Music, deafening music, enveloped them, blocking out thought, conversation, sensation. It vibrated through the floor, their bodies, their minds. Lights, stabbing, flickering lights lifted them into another world of unreality. They were just figures – robots moving in time to the rhythm that possessed them.

In other times the sons and daughters of men of influence, the writers, musicians, politicians, adventurers, country's rulers, could never have come together like this. Now they elbowed and jostled each other on the crowded dance floor like football fans seeking a better view on the terraces. And afterwards these privileged dancers would go off and pee or powder their noses together like any bunch of kids at a Friday night palais dance.

Three figures emerged from the electric inferno. Perry had two girls on his arm and they all slumped into the seats. Archie raised a hand and a young, blonde-haired youth of about eighteen walked quickly to their table. He was dressed in satin boxer shorts, white ankle socks, white plimsolls, and nothing else. His torso was slim and hairless, his buttocks pert like an adolescent girl's. There was a hint of eyebrow pencil round the limpid blue eyes.

'Another please.'

'Certainly sir.'

Archie followed the boy with his gaze as the waiter headed for the bar.

'Fancy him sweetheart?' Perry's arm jerked Archie out of his thoughts.

'Not my type Perry. But seriously, what's wrong with this city? Every guy you meet is a faggot.

'Gay, my dear chap, gay. Faggot, poof, queer, nancy and all the other nasty epithets are out. Gay is good, gay is respectable. And your brand-new macho homosexual is quite likely to punch you in the eye if you say differently. And it's nothing compared with San Francisco. They should rename the place Gay City instead of Bay City.'

'So I've heard. Give me a good old-fashioned honest-to-God woman any day, hey Dawn?'

The red-haired girl opened one eye. 'If you say so, now let me sleep.'

It was 2 a.m. and the two girls were dancing together closely on the floor as Perry and Archie finished the champagne. Archie cocked a thumb towards the dancing pair. 'They sleeping together Perry? You've not landed me with a raving les have you? If I don't screw tonight I'll start chasing the waiters, so help me.'

'Don't think so, old love. Had a bit of a pash at school, I'm told, and they're a rum pair, but I don't think it's what you'd call an exclusive relationship.' He winked broadly. 'They're doing that to be outrageous.'

Archie looked back at the girls. Dawn had Wendy's face close to hers and was gently stroking her hair. Wendy had her two hands clasped tightly round Dawn's waist as they slowly rotated their pelvises against each other. Archie wanted very badly to go to bed with the red-haired girl, and if he was honest, at that moment he would very much have liked to have both of them in his bed at the same time.

Perry nudged him. There was a slight flush on the man's face: 'You getting turned on by that?'

Archie looked back at him calmly. 'I do believe I am.'

'But you're worried you're going to get landed with a frozen dyke as the Dutch say.' He laughed quickly at his own joke.

Archie felt a bead of perspiration break on his forehead. Perry saw the unnatural tension on the other man's face.

'You fancy that scene, seriously? You know, two onto one?'

Desire spread silently across Archie's face.

'All right my love, it's as good as organised. Back at my place suit you?'

'Fine, but what about you? Wendy's supposed to be with you. And anyway, how can you guarantee they'll agree? Might not be their scene.'

Perry laid his hand on Archie's arm. Archie could feel the heat coming off the other man. 'I can screw Wendy any time I want to. I'll rustle up something else. We'll have a little party. I don't think they'll perform cold, they're rather sensitive girls. Wouldn't like anyone to think they were weird or anything. Few drinks and some music'll warm them up.'

Forty-five minutes later, three car-loads of men and women made the short, high-speed breathalyser-dodging journey from Battersea Bridge to Belgravia. Soon the music was loud in the first-floor lounge with its leather furniture and Persian rugs. Stevie Wonder assailed them: 'You are the sunshine of my life, that's why I'll always stay around. You are the apple . . .' Couples were dancing closely in the semi-dark. Archie felt nervous. Goddam, I'm like a young virgin on his first date. He pulled at the Scotch to steady his nerves. He could see Perry talking earnestly to Wendy and Dawn, and saw Wendy throw back her head and give a peal of laughter. Dawn turned to him and gave him a long, slow wink.

He had a sudden urge to repay Perry for this favour. To give away something precious. Something which said how much he appreciated what was being done for him. Alcohol and desire made him feel warm and generous. He wanted to confide in his friend. I'll tell him about Dudley and his secretary. Archie realised he had become a little drunk.

Perry approached him, a girl hanging on each hand.

'Perry, can I have a quiet word with you? There's something I must tell you . . .'

Perry cut him short with a wave of a hand. 'Tomorrow Archie. In the meantime I'd like you to take care of these little ladies for me.'

But it was the 'little ladies' who took care of Archie.

In the large bedroom overlooking Eaton Square they quietly undressed him and then themselves. For a while the two girls danced together, silently in the moonlight, in a ghostly sexual ballet as Archie watched, transfixed, from the bed. Then they kissed and caressed each other, seemingly oblivious to his presence. Then they came for him and Archie felt a thrill almost akin to fear as the two walked determinedly to the bed like avenging night angels.

It lasted fifteen minutes.

He lay there, a mouth on his, a mouth on his prick, his two hands buried deep in the two heads of hair, one flame, one brunette. They slept together under the satin sheets in the circular bed, the girls cradled in his arms like daughters, their hair soft against his face.

I'll tell Perry, my friend, I'll tell Perry about Dudley. It will be his reward. Archie felt a tenderness for the world and the two girls who had given him such pleasure. He wished he could always sleep in this way, the two comforting soft bodies his guardians against the night. Watching them dress, bathe, kiss and touch each other. His eyes closed. I'll reward Perry my friend. I'll give him a bit of juice: he'd love to have something on Dudley to goad him with.

But Perry had already taken his reward. He pulled back from the fish-eye night lens inserted into a drilled hole between the two walls. His clothes were crumpled and awry, his face distorted and wet with perspiration. He slumped down next to the naked German girl.

'It was good?' Her accent was still harsh and the word came out 'gut'.

Perry nodded assent, his breath coming in rasped jerks.

He took the girl's hand and thrust it into his opened, disordered clothes.

'Now.'

And as the girl went mechanically, methodically to work, Perry closed his eyes and relived in his imagination the scene he had so recently witnessed in the next room.

The man who opened the flat door bore all the facial evidence of an unsuccessful career in boxing. His forehead was a mass of scar tissue and the nose was flattened from a series of breaks. His ears were bruised and flattened out of shape. His breath came harshly through the mouth.

'You managed to make it, then? I thought you'd crossed me off your visiting list.' The voice was laced with sarcasm and a sprinkling of petulance.

Graham pushed past the man and through the open door into the lounge dining room. He noticed the table was empty except for a pack of cards spilled carelessly across the polished surface like shed petals from a flower.

'Couldn't you even have laid the table, you lazy sod?'

The ex-boxer said, 'I thought as how you were cooking the dinner, you'd want to lay the table yourself.' He added, 'What kept you anyway, you said you'd be here at eight. Been running Klein's errands again? He treats you like a bloody servant.'

Graham took off the camelhair overcoat and hung it carefully on a hanger behind the entrance door. He eyed the other man, cruelty deep in the gaze. 'Mr Klein is my employer. I work for him. If he asks me to work overtime I do. Savvy?'

The ex-boxer managed a laugh, a sham defence under that wilting gaze. 'Christ, you're even beginning to talk like him. Savvy? Savvy?'

Graham turned on his heel and moved into the tiny kitchen. He took down a blue and white striped apron from a peg attached to the side of a working surface and slipped it over his head, tying the strings behind him.

'It'll have to be omelettes. I'm not in the mood for cooking anything fancy. 'Sides, I'm a bit pushed for time.'

Silence answered him. Graham took six eggs from a plastic carton in the refrigerator and broke them one by one into a bowl. He began to slice tomatoes taken from a basket in front of him. He pressed the switch of an electric mixer, thrust the bowl containing the eggs underneath it, and watched the whites and yolks froth together.

'Open the wine.' He heard the creak of an opening cupboard door and shortly afterwards the plonk of the withdrawn cork.

He felt a tap on his shoulder and the ex-boxer handed him a glass of red wine. Graham smelled it, wrinkling his nose, and sipped it apprehensively. He curled his lips in an expression of distaste.

'Where'd you buy this, sodding Algeria? It's bloody awful.'

'Down the off-licence. They said it'd be okay.'

Graham sneered. 'Well, they would, wouldn't they? What the fuck do they know about wine?'

'Cost me two quid.'

'Shouldn've bought a case, shouldn't you?' said Graham and turned to pour the omelette mixture into the hot copper pan. 'And get out of the kitchen, you know I don't like you in here when I'm cooking.'

The ex-boxer slunk out like a cowed dog. They ate in silence. Once, the older man put out a hand and tried to touch Graham's arm, but Graham pulled sharply away without a word.

'Why've you not been down the gym lately? You a bit tied up with Klein and this Tommy Booth business? Must be making a lot of extra work that, on top?'

Graham nodded assent, sipping reluctantly at the wine.

'We've got some new lads down the gym. Lovely lads, why don't . . .'

'Look,' Graham cut the older man short, 'I don't want to hear, savv . . . understand? I don't want to hear about your dirty exploits.'

The older man still tried to gain Graham's eyes. 'Sorry

Graham. It's just that you've not been around for so long. I thought perhaps . . . bit nervous, that's all. Talking twenty to the dozen was I?'

Graham looked at him with contempt in his heart, but hating himself more for the blackness. The need. God, he disgusts me. But Graham had telephoned as he knew he would. Four weeks and then it was too much. Then the journey, and the door, and that ravaged face and the kitchen. Like sad scars that no amount of sun can obliterate. Then the food and the cheap wine and the stupid conversation. I would be happy to kill him, thought Graham, and perhaps then?

Suddenly, with an abruptness that took even himself aback, Graham said, 'Don't knock Klein to me. I'd kill for Klein. I'd even fucking kill you.' It was like a statement about himself, re-establishing his masculinity.

The older man put out a hand tentatively, and touched Graham's arm as though it might burn him. 'I don't understand it either, Graham. I never have. It's just part of us.' Graham stared into the remains of the demolished omelette.

'How long have you got before you've got to go?'

'An hour.'

The older man got up and walked to a door. As he opened it Graham caught a glimpse of a yellow counterpane, like the symptom of a forgotten illness.

'It's up to you,' said the ex-boxer, went in and closed the door.

Graham downed the wine in one gulp, feeling its acidity bite at his tongue. The last time. I swear it's the last time. And as he walked to the bedroom door he repeated over and over in his brain like a Latin chant that could somehow save his soul from damnation: I'd kill for Klein.

Margot and Tommy had been making love for hours. It was the first time that Tommy had been to the Belgravia house. Dudley had been called away to Brussels and Margot felt that it would be safe. The moment he had walked into the house Tommy's face showed his approval. He loved her taste – the drawing room with its huge cream slubbed silk sofas and the heady perfume from the many baskets of flowers that seemed to fill every available surface. Most of all he loved her bedroom, the centrepiece of which was a vast four-poster bed covered with a Victorian lace counterpane on which were scattered large white silk pillows with the Creighton crest delicately embroidered on them. He had thrown Margot on to the bed, crushing her with his massive body.

Now, much later, Tommy arched his back, his hands deep in Margot's hair, moaning with sexual pleasure. He looked down at Margot, 'Christ, that was good – I love it when you do down on me.'

She sat upright in bed, her face flushed and an angry light in her eyes, and wedged herself against the pillows. 'Tommy I'm getting bloody well fed up with your selfishness. Why the hell don't you go down on me sometimes? Sex wasn't conceived for man's pleasure alone!' The words were out before she had time to stop them. 'Perhaps you should buy a book on the female anatomy.'

Anger flushed his face. 'Look, that's something I've never done before and I think it's a bit disgusting. It's not something they teach you at Plaistow comprehensive.'

She climbed out of bed. Cocky little bastard. 'Then they should have. Sex should be a two-way affair and you should make it your business to learn what gives a woman pleasure.'

He walked over and gripped her by the shoulders. 'I don't understand you sometimes! I thought you liked going down on me. Anyway, it's not a bloody competition is it? First prize for the best screw and points knocked off for mistakes. Okay, I'm sorry. Would you like me to do it now?'

'For Christ's sake Tommy, your timing's appalling.'

'God Margot, you're a bitch sometimes.'

She extended her hand placatingly.

'Tommy, I don't wish to be crude but that part of a woman's body is her most sensitive area, and likewise for a man. How can you square it with yourself to take pleasure from me and not return it?' Her voice was like a whiplash.

'Your stupid East End vernacular thinks that cunt is an obscene word, a dirty epithet to hurl at someone you don't like, which is probably' – her voice rose an octave – 'why you haven't the faintest idea what to do with one.'

'You bloody cow.'

'Little short on vocabulary aren't we Tommy? Reverting to type?' For a split second he was tempted to strike her, to slap that sneering inbuilt arrogance from her features. Instead he turned abruptly on his heel and walked to the bathroom. He locked the door and stepped into an ice-cold shower. Right you ace cow. We'll see if the next bird I come across thinks I'm such a bad lover!

Margot slumped heavily onto the bed, the anger still burning deep inside her. She hadn't meant to say those things to him. Her frustration wasn't about their sex life; she had no complaints whatsoever on that score. It was something much more complex than that. Margot was coming to depend on Tommy. She knew she was falling deeply in love with him, with his simplicity and his honesty. She had never in her life before met such an open and uncomplicated human being. But what was she to do? She was being tormented and torn apart by her commitment to her marriage and her love for a younger man. And she felt she was walking perilously near to destruction.

# *Chapter Six*

It was different, so different, from *watching* television. It all looked so natural then. Everyone sitting around chatting amiably; and the interviewer, at ease, putting his guests at ease and turning, swivelling in his chair, smiling to the camera and introducing the next item. Nobody'd told Tommy about the heat, the harsh lights, the make-up, the masses of wires and cameras moving across the floor – a jungle surrounding the clearing the viewer saw.

That's one part of my training, observed Tommy ruefully, that they missed out. His collar was biting into his neck, sawing a raw, red mark into the flesh. He could feel the perspiration trickling under his shirt and the make-up on his forehead and nose ('Too shiny,' the girl had said) itched unbearably. Beyond the arena of light he could see the ghostly figures of the technicians walking in the semi-darkness behind the cameras.

The fat man in the aubergine suit was smiling and asking Klein, 'So you're confident your boy can do it on Saturday, Lewis?'

Klein beamed broadly back at him. His hands were on the arms of the leather chair, relaxed, confident. A hand detached itself and patted Tommy's arm. 'Well, I'm biased Raymond, but in my hunble opinion, Tommy here is the best there is.'

'In Britain.' It was a statement not a question.

Klein laughed. 'I'm talking about the world, Raymond, the world.'

The fat man smiled, a sign that Klein could continue. Let the bastard hang himself.

'. . . of course we feel absolutely confident about Vincelli. But after that the Americans will have to take Tommy seriously. Roberts, or Kovacs, is going to have to come out of hiding and give Tommy a chance . . .'

'Lewis, you're not suggesting that either Roberts or Kovacs is frightened of meeting Tommy here?' He flashed a smile at Tommy. 'We all share your hopes for Saturday but isn't it stretching it a bit to suggest he's ready for someone like Kovacs? They're vastly more experienced men, Lewis.'

'Not a bit of it Raymond. This lad is the best, you mark my words, and he can see off the likes of Kovacs or Roberts any day of the week.'

The interviewer cocked his head. 'Tommy?'

This was the moment he'd been dreading. Apart from 'Hello', Klein had done all the talking up to now. Now it was his turn. All the TV interviews he'd done up to this point had been filmed, small crew and a chance to go through it again if he became flustered and messed up a reply. But this. Millions of people watching, live. If he fluffed it now? What if the words wouldn't come?

Then he found himself speaking, and it was as though he was listening to his voice from a long way away, detached, remote. Instinctively he remembered the advice Margot had given him after he'd muffed two answers during a filming session next to the pool. 'Keep your sentences short. Speak a fraction slower than you normally would. Keep to the point, don't try anything involved, and when you've said what you think is necessary, shut up!'

'Well Raymond. I'll leave claims like that to my manager here. But I will say that I intend to beat Vincelli, and beat him well. After that, who knows? I just take each fight as it comes.'

I said that? I said that? Confidence gripped Tommy but he successfully resisted the urge to say more.

Good lad, Tommy, good lad. Klein was pleased. Modest, but confident. Good image. They'll love you for that. Big test for you this was. You could have ballsed it up. It wouldn't have mattered. But you had to do it on your own. Test of nerve old son, and you came through.

'. . . but Lewis, seriously. Tommy *is* a relative newcomer to the professional fight game, how far are you suggesting he can go?' Raymond Bannerman raised an eyebrow and put his face into that well-known and well-practised expression of amused querulousness. 'To the world championship perhaps?' The question howevered in the air like a pheasant ripe for the gun.

Go on Lewis, make a tit of yourself on prime time TV, you little gangster. I know you from way back and I wouldn't give you the paper to wipe your arse on. You're bent, old son, a crook. If the cops in this city had any guts instead of safe deposit boxes, you'd have been behind bars years ago. Letting you near a lad like this, somebody should be ashamed. Go on, make yourself look a prize prick. Sing me the old refrain. Tell me how he's the next Great White Hope, the next Englishman, Briton, call it what you will, who's *really* going to make it. This is the one, is it Lewis? Tell me how he's going to be the heavyweight champion of the world and I'll try not to piss myself on the studio floor, laughing. I've seen it and heard it all before mate. I was covering boxing when you were in short trousers. From Hackney Town Hall to Madison Square Gardens I've seen the best there is. Joe Louis, Marciano, Patterson, Mildenberger, Ali – the bloody lot.

Before the war, that was the time. Always in the States the title fights were, and no bloody TV. Out on one of the Cunards, luxurious five days. Couple of weeks at the training camp, filing copy. Do the fight and then a nice pleasant booze-up in leisurely fashion with the rest of the Fleet Street lads coming back across the Atlantic. And damn me if there weren't newsreel cameras and blokes with microphones waiting to interview us when we got back. Now those really were the days. Now. Programme Wednesday. Out from Heathrow the next day to whatever godawful hole of the world they'd chosen this time. It'll be a floating raft on the Amazon next if the bright lads have their way. Do the commentary. After match stuff and then the next plane out. Takes some of the fun out of it. I've seen all your British white hopes, Lewis. Watched 'em bleed and suffer – and lose, pal, L-O-S-E. Cockell against Marciano. It was like putting Little Bo Peep in with Jack the Ripper. It hurt to watch. Marciano. Merciless, clubbing Cockell like some fighting animal. Butting, gouging. Poor old Don thought he'd come for a boxing match. They put him in with a killer.

We're losers, Lewis. Okay in our own backyards, left to scrap amongst ourselves, but the Yanks are in a different class, always have been. So tell me the old old story. If you want to make a fool of yourself I'm happy to oblige.

'You know Raymond, I honestly believe that given time and the right amount of experience, Tommy here,' he patted the boxer's arm again, 'can be the world heavyweight champion . . .'

A small, almost imperceptible smirk pulled at the corner of Bannerman's mouth. He did it, the daft sod. Oh boy is it going to be fun interviewing you when your precious lad gets seven kinds of shit knocked out of him. Lewis could feel the cynicism like radio waves emanating from the fat man, and thought he could spot a grin forming on the man's face. Yeh, smile you fat fucker, but you'll be the first in the ring with your arm round him and your microphone halfway down his throat when he wins. You sports journalists make me puke. Fat salaries, expense accounts, overweight and undertalented. You leech off the brilliance of others who have to sweat and graft, and you have the bloody nerve to criticise them. Klein remembered the words: 'Those who can, do. Those who can't, criticise.' That's you, you slob. Double chin, gut hanging over your trousers and you'll be stuck into the large gins when this is all over – at someone else's expense.

'Well Raymond, I can see that you're sceptical, and I wouldn't be surprised if some of the viewers shared that scepticism. But, you know, I'm patriotic and I'm not ashamed to admit it.'

Bannerman groaned inwardly. Patriotism, last refuge of a crook, in your case pal.

'I believe our boxers, our runners, our footballers, our

swimmers, are all just as good as any of those from any other country in the world . . . however,' Bannerman was getting the signal in his earphone to wind the programme up, '. . . if other countries care more for their sportsmen than we do, and if they choose to spend more on training facilities so that athletes can give their best . . . then, we must expect to finish second.'

'Thank y . . .'

'We arc lucky. Thanks to the backing of Sir Peregrine Hamilton, who believes in the future of British boxing and British boxers, Tommy here has the best training facilities money can buy. And may I say that when he fights on Saturday, he'll be fighting not only for himself but also for his country and all those athletes less fortunate than himself. Am I right Tommy?'

'I certainly will Mr Klein.'

Bannerman swivelled quickly to another camera. The red light was on.

'A patriotic note on which to finish there from Lewis Klein, manager of the heavyweight boxing hope, Tommy Booth, who meets the Italian champion Alberto Vincelli for the European title at Wembley on Saturday night. And remember, you can see the whole of that fight live, exclusively on BBC One at 9 p.m.'

Smile.

'Next week: ice-skating from Zurich, show-jumping from Hickstead and a look at Australia's youngest champion surfer.' Pause. 'From Raymond Bannerman's Sports Focus. Goodnight.'

Bannerman lopped a third off the tall glass of gin with one gulp, shoved a piece of ice noisily round his mouth and spat it equally noisily back into the glass.

'Lewis my dear fellow. Gin? Scotch? Brandy?'

'Brandy.' The fat man poured a generous helping.

'And Tommy?'

'Squash please.'

They stood drinking, not talking.

A girl with dark, thick hair and an ample bust approached them carrying a clipboard. Her eyes took in Tommy with something less than professional interest.

'Hi. Caroline Brown. Mr Bannerman's production assistant. I've got some Boy Scouts been brought into the studio by the public relations department. They heard you were in the studio Tommy, and they'd like to meet you.' Her eyes swivelled to Bannerman. 'May I borrow him Mr Bannerman?'

'Ask Tommy, not him.' Klein's words cut like a knife.

'Of course, how rude of me. Tommy?'

'Be delighted.'

She took him by the arm and led him out of the room. Klein turned to the TV man. 'Do me a favour Raymond. When you do your commentary on Saturday, make it a little fairer than when he fought Goettmann, will you?'

'Fairer?' The fat man looked contemptuous. 'Fairer to whom?'

'Fairer to Tommy. We had a video, seems like you thought Tommy was going to get a pasting. "Can Booth hold up under this onslaught? Is Booth going to be another in the long line of Panzer victims?" and other shit which I won't mention.'

Bannerman sneered: 'What do you expect me to say, "Let's hope little Tommy knocks out the big bad German"?'

Klein levelled a finger. 'You know what I mean, Bannerman. Let's have a little bit more enthusiasm for the British cause or you just might find ITV are getting preference in the dressing room afterwards.'

Bannerman's eyes, sunk in pouches of fat, flashed like green pebbles. Anger welled up in him. 'You fucking two-bit Al Capone, don't tell me how to do my job. I've been doing TV boxing commentaries since 1961 and before that radio and before that reporting for Syndicated International. My stuff's gone all round the world. And you're saying I try and pick the winner. Well sunshine, I've got news for you, ninety-nine times out of a hundred I *know* the fucking winner. I'm that good.' The fat man was breathing heavily, rattled and angry. 'And guess what Lewis, I wouldn't give a stuff for Tommy's chances against Vincelli.'

Klein smiled a tight, evil smile. 'Raymond, when you come on the box half the nation thinks it's watching the Muppets. You're a joke. You're only in this job because it's a bigger Mafia here than Palermo. So stow that shit.' Klein sipped at his brandy. 'You know as much about boxing as I do about flower arranging.'

Two passing directors heard the remark and laughed openly. Bannerman didn't win any popularity contests at Shepherds Bush. The fat man searched his mind for a reply. Then it came to hand quickly, easily like a gun from a greased holster.

'What do you know about the crucifixion, Lewis? Forget the flower arranging, I heard crucifying was up your street.'

Klein's eyes hardened. 'Care to explain, Raymond?'

Bannerman's hand went to the gin bottle and Klein noticed the slight tremble of the fingers. Safely around the glass again they steadied. He waved the glass casually, but the strain showed in his face.

'Well, a little dicky bird told me that the Scotsman, whatsisname, McCulloch, the one who got nailed up, that McCulloch and you weren't on good terms.'

'Wouldn't let him drink my piss if he was dying of thirst. What about it?'

Bannerman's eyes glowed like a fat schoolboy with a dirty secret. 'And that, well, you may not have actually wielded the hammer yourself, but you paid those who did.'

Klein put down the brandy glass and moved closer to Bannerman. The fat man thought Klein was going to strike him and instinctively raised an arm to his face in protection. But Klein merely put his arm round the fat man's shoulders. He could smell the expensive cologne working overtime. His voice was slow and measured, deceptively soft, each word coming out crisp and enunciated so there should be no mistake.

'Raymond I don't care what you think, or what you know. But remember this. If you ever repeat what you just said in front of witnesses or to anyone, and I get to hear of it – and I have many friends Raymond – I promise you you'll walk out of the Law Courts in the Strand without so much as a jock-strap to hold your dick up. Savvy?'

The cologne was fighting a desperate rearguard action against the waves of advancing sweat.

'You're a bastard, Lewis. A disgrace to the fight game.'

Lewis took his hand from the man's fleshy shoulders. The hand felt damp. 'Remember what I said, Raymond. Or I'll clean out your little piggy bank and the only ring you'll ever see is the one round the pan in the shithouse you'll be cleaning.'

The show's producer put a large hand on the back of each man: 'Good show, good show. Nice flag-waving finish. Doesn't hurt once in a while. Support the old country, eh?'

Lewis nodded. 'Right.'

Bannerman sunk his mouth sullenly into the gin and two rivulets formed on either side of his mouth. *I hope to Christ that Italian beats the shit out of Tommy Booth.*

The girl looked up at him. 'Thank you. That was kind. They'll remember it for a long time.'

Tommy shrugged. 'Glad to help.'

'Well,' the girl shrugged too, 'that's it. Back to the Green Room.' The sentence stopped, but the unspoken words lingered. The missing words seemed to say, 'If you want to. If you don't we can do . . . something else.'

It was like when you took a girl home after a dance and she stood awkwardly, her hands at her side and said, 'I suppose I'd better go in,' when what she meant was, 'Okay, kiss me.' These posh birds are no different. If anything they like it more. Christ, look at Margot. This is another one. All cut glass accent, silky scarves and soft skin, but she likes it like they all do.

'Why not show me round. I'd like to see how a telly studio works.' Relief flashed in her eyes. She just didn't want him to go. He was so like Brian it was uncanny. Not the looks, just the power, the strength. Caroline Brown felt a ripple of excitement. What is it about them? Maybe I just need a bit of rough now and then. All those eggheads at Oxford, it was like going to bed with the full set of *Encyclopaedia Britannica.* A year with Rodney and his boring Classics. He thought eroticism was giving me three halves of flat bitter, a lecture on Plato then shoving his hand up my skirt. Then it had to be a bricklayer, so help me. Brian Wilkinson. God my parents would have died. From Birmingham and he picked me up like I was some cheap tart in a pub in St Ives on holiday. Tall, tanned, hard as nails. Christ it was good. She glanced at Tommy and felt the sensation in her stomach like an old memory. Oh, you're cute.

Forty-five minutes later she swept an arm to take in a small carpeted room furnished with a small, littered desk, a chair and a potted plant and said: 'And last but not least the nerve centre of the whole BBC operation – my office.' He walked up to a green-baize noticeboard and pretended to read the jumble of notices pinned to it.

'Very nice. Now close the door.'

'What?'

'I said, close the door.'

He'd suspected from the start and the trip round the studio convinced him. Well, enough at least to make it worth taking a chance. The way she held her body, the times she 'accidentally' brushed against him and the too-quick 'sorry' which followed. He'd got the whole story too. The farm in Yorkshire, the years at Roedean, Oxford, then the BBC. And she fancies me? You've come a long way Tommy lad. He felt the power in his body. 'Treat 'em like shit.' And a gesture to Margot. See how much I feel for you?

Dumbly the girl closed the door.

'And lock it, we don't want someone to barge in.'

She was shaking. It was like the moment Brian had brushed deliberately against her in the crowded pub, and she'd felt the hard penis, tight and trapped in the denim. Oh God I want him.

'Now come here.'

She walked the few paces like an acquiescent schoolgirl.

'I don't know what you think you're doing.' the words came out flat and tinny, without conviction.

'I'm thinking,' said Tommy, taking her head in his hands, 'of fucking you.' He felt a tremendous secret thrill go through him as he dared say the word.

'How dare –' But the words were cut off as Tommy kissed her fiercely, crouching low, bending his body. She took his mouth like the sacrament. He pulled her down until they were both kneeling on the carpet. He slipped his hand round her back, tugged out her blouse and slid his hand under the silk to the strap of her bra. He fumbled vainly for the hook.

She tore her mouth free from his and said breathlessly: 'It's at the front.' He brought his hand round under the blouse. He felt the weight of her breast heavy and full, soft on his hand in the unwired cup. He gently unhooked the catch and her breasts fell deliciously downwards. He felt for the nipple and stroked it. She gave a low, soft moan. He felt her right hand move, hesitantly, pull back, then boldly grip his rapidly hardening penis.

He unzipped her trousers at the side and started to pull them down with both hands, over her buttocks, taking the tiny panties with them. She was stroking his hard penis now, eagerly, her moans coming faster and faster. He toppled them both gently sideways to the carpet and slid his fingers into her wet pubic hair. Jesus, she is hot for it! He worked his fingers up and down in the soft wet mound, and her body convulsed. She broke away from his mouth, gasping for air, moaning aloud. Images danced in her brain. The parked car, the steamed-up windows, the rain beating a tattoo on the roof and the sound of the waves thundering on the shore in front of them. Brian saying, 'You'll have to shift love, I'll never get it in.' Good, basic, honest. She gripped the nape of Tommy's neck: 'Stuff it in me. Please.'

He unzipped his trousers, pulled down his shorts and moved on to her. As he entered her she felt the fire steal into her body like a beautiful thief. The orgasm started immediately, building like thunder. She was weeping silently, great tears coursing down her cheeks. He was all I ever wanted. We should have stayed there forever. I didn't care about the accent, it was you who cared. You who mocked mine. We should have stayed. You and me and the sea forever. She was in the car now. Brian above her on the back seat, moving inside her, his curly hair rough on her face. The tears ran into her mouth and she tasted salt. I loved you. I really did.

Tommy moved mechanically. His face was in her hair. There it is love, what you've wanted from the moment you set eyes on me. He thought of Margot lying naked against the great soft pillows on her bed. It's sex not love, not affection. Just like Margot. He climaxed and felt no pleasure. He rolled off her and quickly dressed himself, his back to her. She lay there, eyes closed, the tear marks down her face. Her blouse and bra were up at her neck, her trousers at her knees. She looked exposed and ugly like a grotesque murder victim.

I'll work. I'll make you happy. It doesn't matter about our families. The train pulling out. Don't leave me Brian.

'Get dressed.' Tommy's words cut into the fog of her dream like a sea breeze.

She sat up and for a full second thought she was in the car with Brian. Tommy was looking at her and she saw the contempt in his eyes. Hastily she arranged her clothes while he looked away.

They stood like just-introduced strangers at a boring party. She coughed nervously: 'Look, this was all a bit silly. I mean, don't think I make a habit of seducing people in my office.'

'Forget it.'

'Look, I've got a flat in Baron's Court. I'll give you my phone number. Perhaps . . . ? That is, when you're not training you might like to come to dinner. My Stroganoff is rather good, I'm told.'

And what the hell, thought Tommy, is Stroganoff? 'Yeh.'

She took a felt-tipped pen and scrawled a seven-figure number. She folded the paper on which it was written and handed it to Tommy. He put it in his trouser pocket. 'My flat mate is hardly ever there.' There was silence.

'Well,' she smoothed down her hair, 'you'd better be off. I'm not sure,' she vainly tried to smooth her creased blouse, 'I'm not sure I should be seen like this. I'm off duty anyway, so I think I'd better pop off home.' She unlocked the door and reached up to kiss Tommy but he never moved.

'Well. Don't forget the Stroganoff.'

'No.'

'See you soon.'

'Yeh.'

'Bye.'

'Bye.'

She closed the door. He waited for a few moments and thought he heard the word 'Brian' and the sound of crying.

Tommy went through the deserted, unlit outer office and into the corridor. He took out the piece of paper and tore it slowly and deliberately into small pieces, letting them fall to the floor like a tiny snowstorm.

Which was where Caroline Brown saw them as she left hurriedly, still crying, five minutes later.

Vincelli was in the Marciano mould, as Bannerman never tired of telling his viewers. Stocky, iron-hard, craggy face, fists like hams and a seemingly indestructible energy source. What he knew about boxing you could write on the back of a postage stamp, but he could fight – in and out of the ring. He was famous for his bar-room brawls in Naples and his tactics were pure dockside. He hit hard and often, punched in flurries and kept coming. One of us has to give, was his message, and it ain't gonna be me.

For the first five rounds Tommy had hit him with every punch in the book. He'd stood off and danced and jabbed. Long straight rights jerked Vincelli's head like a marionette, but still he kept advancing. He'd corner Tommy, unleash an onslaught of blows, clubbing haymakers that hurt Tommy. He was getting disillusioned with the Italian; whatever he threw at him, the Italian shook his head like a dog and walked on for more. And Vincelli's punches were sapping his own energy. He could feel the tiredness in his arms. He'd never thrown as many punches in a fight before – professional or amateur. Fatigue was seeping into him.

Maxie was talking urgently. 'Keep out, Tommy, keep up the long range stuff, it's got to get to him sooner or later.' Maxie was lifting the elastic of the shorts, massaging the tight stomach muscles, talking at Tommy all the time, feeding him with confidence.

'I don't know, Maxie, he just keeps coming. He should have been down by now. It's uncanny.'

Maxie noticed the tinge of defeatism in the voice. Dangerous, corrosive. He grabbed Tommy's face and spun it to him. The cameras were on Vincelli's corner. Maxie's face changed. He was, in his bluff East End way, a psychiatrist as well as a trainer and he knew he had to get tough with Tommy for his own good.

'Okay you fucking little pansy. Shall I throw in the towel? I thought you said you wanted to be world champion. You'll meet tougher than this greaseball.'

'I wasn't quitting Maxie, it's just . . .'

'All right, forget the rule book, forget the jabs. Let him come in, mix it with him and work the bastard over street style. You're tougher than he is, you're better than he is. Get out there and prove it. Or would you prefer that fat slob Bannerman gloating all over you? Beaten by a fucking wop.'

Tommy felt anger rising in him. Anger at Maxie, anger at Margot, Klein, everyone around him. And slowly the anger intensified and concentrated like the flame of an oxyacetylene cutter until it was hard and sharp and pointed at one person – Vincelli. The tiny seeds of doubt in his own abilities were gone, banished quickly before they took root and flourished. Maxie had handled him just right.

At the bell Vincelli came out in his usual fashion, gloves up, head down, shoulders hunched, body in a low crouch. But the grey indomitable eyes were still impassive, inscrutable. Tommy let him come on and there was a faint flicker of surprise on the man's face behind the red gloves. But it was gone in a moment and he barnstormed in, pinning Tommy against the ropes. They traded punches viciously. A collective murmur went up from the crowd, part fear, part elation. Tommy was mixing it with the Eyetie and the last five men that had tried that ended up on the canvas.

But the lad had guts.

The tempo was furious. No one knew it except his own seconds, but Vincelli was almost at the end of his tether. He'd never met as accurate a puncher as Tommy in his career before and the head punches were taking their toll. He was operating on some psychological reserve tank of energy now and knew the clinches were his only chance. He was putting everything he had into the punches to Tommy's body.

Tommy felt the pain jarring through his body. He accepted it, it stung him to greater efforts, then it was filed in some forgotten part of his brain. Tommy was going for the head and the two men stood taking virtually free punches at each other. Tommy wasn't guarding his body and the Italian was sending pile-driver after pile-driver through. But his head was a sitting target, a human punchball, jerking back and forth from the blows. His mind felt muzzy and there was a slight blurring on the edge of his vision.

Dutch referee Alex Tietjens was watching them both closely. He loved the fight game and fighters and wanted no serious damage done in any fight he was overseeing. Leave that to those American refs, a man could die standing up in their rings and they'd still let the other guy keep on punching. But both fighters seemed okay on the face of it, and were capable of defending themselves and returning blows, which was the criterion. But for God's sakes, one of you lads has got to give.

Bang, bang, bang went Tommy's head punches, and right, left, right went Vincelli's head. Crash, crash, in came two lethal body punches. Lethal in a Naples bar against an untrained, unfit man, but not on the finely tuned fully fit body of a professional fighter. Neither man heard the bell, so engrossed were they in their maul and referee Tietjens leaped between them to pull them apart.

Tommy was breathing heavily, hurt and sore, but it was back. The feeling, the confidence. He said to Maxie between gasps of air: 'That-showed-him. Get-him-this-round. This-time.'

Vincelli was sitting like a hypnotised man, eyes glazed. The seconds looked anxiously down at the manager and shouted in Italian: 'Looks groggy.'

Signor Giuseppe Forelli leaned up. 'Give it another round. He's got the bastard on his last legs.' The Sicilian leaned back in his seat. Nobody told us the guy was this good. I've got Vincelli lined up for Kovacs in Philadelphia. Half a million bucks. Goddamn these English mother-fuckers. And goddamn Vincelli if he falls down on this. Forelli had once killed an American military policeman as a kid in Palermo when the policeman had caught him looting a PX. Just stuck a knife right in him. A kid of twelve. The policeman was so surprised he'd not even tried to protect himself. And there'd been others since them. It was a hard world he moved in. A world of money and deals and violence. He and Klein, had they known each other, would have respected each other. No one was throwing in the towel on a Forelli boxer – least of all Vincelli. Holy Mother and he is supposed to be like Marciano.

Vincelli was unaware of his second's plea. He was in the American bar in Victor Emmanuel Square, and he didn't feel well. His head didn't feel right. Too much to drink. Somebody was to blame. Somebody would pay. Somebody rang a bell and without knowing why he had got up from the bar stool. There was a crowd of people staring at him. Some wore all white, the others, he couldn't tell, they looked half-naked. He shouted to them: 'Stop staring at me you shits.' Then someone pushed him from behind, he tried to turn but he'd lost his balance, and the floor rushed up to meet him. It didn't hurt; it was very soft. He felt an overwhelming desire to sleep. It wouldn't hurt. I'll sleep for a while.

The Wembley crowd and millions of TV viewers saw it differently. It was to go down as one of the strangest moments in boxing history. Bannerman was saying during the interval: '. . . real humdinger that one. They can't keep that up. Something's got to give. Who can stand the pace the longest? That's the question now. Vincelli's a tough customer, he's got the know-how, the guts and the experience. But he's seven years older than Booth . . .

'Has the English boy got the legs, yes and the guts too? We'll soon see. Both corners are working frantically on their men. They've both taken a terrible pounding. The Italians are shouting to Forelli, Vincelli's manager. Never comes in the ring, Forelli. Forelli's shaking his head. Well, we don't know what that's about. Tommy's manager was telling me Tommy is in there fighting for Britain tonight and it must be said he's doing us proud. Good, brave show. And it's not over yet. He's mixed it with Vincelli which few men have dared to do, will it pay off? And they're out for round seven . . . oh . . . My goodness me! Vincelli is shouting, Vincelli is shouting something at the referee, or is it at Booth . . . oh my goodness he's staggering about, they'll have to stop it, the fight's over, they'll have to . . . Vincelli has fallen over. Vincelli has keeled over on his face. I have never seen anything like it. Vincelli's unconscious. What an end to a fight! Vincelli is out cold. He came out of his corner, he shouted something, stagged and just fell over right in front of me. Well, oh well. The referee has raised Tommy's hands – we've got a doctor in the ring – there's no elation. Tommy Booth has just become the heavyweight champion of Europe and you could hear a pin drop. I have never seen anything like this in all my years of watching boxing. Amazing. Vincelli is just flat out. Dead to the world. Tommy is bowing to the crowd and they're applauding him, but there's absolutely no elation here. Just look at Booth's face. Well. We can only hope it's nothing too serious . . . it was a game show . . . they're calling for a stretcher. THEY-ARE-CALLING-FOR-A-STRETCHER. My goodness, Vincelli is going to be stretchered out of this ring. Well he took some vicious punches from Booth. He's a tough cookie is Vincelli but the human body can only take so much. The referee is shaking his head sadly. I don't know. He's got a different view up there, but there seemed to be no indication that

Vincelli was on his way out. Alex Tietjens, one of the gentlemen of the fight game. He won't like what's happened. He won't like it a little bit. They're taking Vincelli out of the ring, they're not waiting for the stretcher. What an end to a title fight!

'Well ladies and gentlemen we have a new heavyweight champion of Europe, Tommy Booth from London's East End – and what will they call it, a knockout? I don't know. But that's it, it's all over in the seventh round. This is Raymond Bannerman wishing you goodnight. Good night.'

Tommy punched the switch and for the thirty-second time that morning the image of Vincelli staggered up in full colour. Tommy pressed another button, froze the picture and gazed at it intently as though searching for some clue. The door opened. It was Maxie.

'How is he?' Anxiety was etched into the words.

'He'll live.'

'Thank God.'

'After the op last night he had a comfortable night and the people up at the hospital said he'll be off the critical list tomorrow. He'll have a bit of paralysis, one side of the body – he won't fight no more, that's for certain sure.'

Tommy shook his head from side to side. 'Jeesus.'

'Strikes me he kept sticking his head where his fists should've been for too long.'

'What?' said Tommy. 'You're not suggesting he was punchy? He was the heavyweight champion of Europe. *I* put him in hospital. *I* did it. I nearly killed a man.'

'It wasn't your fault, son, accidents happen.'

'You're quite right Tommy. Absolutely one hundred per cent right. You did it, you're responsible.' Klein stood framed in the doorway. Tears pricked in Tommy's eyes as Klein went on mercilessly: 'And if your piss starts turning brown tomorrow from all those kidney punches he was giving you, he'll be to blame. But you're right. You might have killed him. It's your fault. Get used to it.'

He sat down next to Tommy, who stared ahead, blinking

back the tears. 'He didn't step in that ring with you because he liked the smell of your aftershave, son, he did it for £50,000 and a chance to look good in the States; they were lining him up for Kovacs and he had to show he was the right stuff, which was why he came here and defended. If the BBC hadn't done a deal with NBC he wouldn't have moved out of Naples, so don't fret over him. His seconds were trying to stop it, I saw them, but that bastard Forelli wouldn't let 'em. It's a risk he took. He's a professional with a bad manager. You're a professional with a good one.'

'Yeh,' said Tommy slowly, 'sometimes I'm not so sure I want to be a professional with either.'

Maxie's eyes flickered from Tommy to Klein. Klein's tone never altered an octave: 'Maybe you're right. Maybe the fight game isn't for you. Maybe all that stuff about "I'm going to be world champion Mr Klein" was just the ramblings of a big-headed kid. Go back to Plaistow, go back to Sylvia, go back to the high rise.' The soft voice was taunting now: 'Just think, no more getting up at five in the morning – and no more Margot.'

Tommy's eyes widened in surprise. 'I . . .'

'Forget it lad, I didn't come over here on the last banana boat. I know about you two. When it starts hitting your fighting there'll be trouble. But do you think she'd look at you twice if you were working on the road or at Fords on the assembly line?' He poked a finger at Tommy. 'You've grown up a bit lately; you *know* different. You have got talent, you can be the best. You don't want a council flat, two kids, a shagged-out wife and a beer gut when you're thirty – or do you?' Klein lifted Tommy's hands and balled them into fists. 'You can have everything in the world you've ever wanted – with these.'

Still no words came from Tommy.

'Get it right, lad. These Yanks will be trying to put *you* into intensive care, don't forget that. And they will if you start pulling punches. Okay, you hurt Vincelli, but he's been leading with his head too long. You did him a favour.'

'Favour? I nearly kill a man and I'm doing him a favour?'

'Right. He was a just-one-more-fight man, Vincelli. Should've retired at twenty-four. Now he's out, thanks to you. The next fight he could've got killed. You probably saved his life. Who knows what was burbling in that brain of his just waiting to go pop.'

Tommy said nothing.

'Well I won't waste any more words. The choice is yours. The press'll be here in an hour. I've got a nice little speech for you. Reserved, sorry, but still a fighter. It's up to you if you want to read it. If you don't, pack your bags and get the hell out.'

There was no decision to make. There hadn't really ever been one. Tommy knew what he wanted. A feeling, indefinable, but speaking of sadness and age touched him. 'I'll be there.'

'Good lad.' Maxie turned to him. 'After that I want you in the gym with the Texan and you have got my permission to knock the shit out of him.'

'The Texan! Christ Maxie, I'm red raw, I'm knackered. Why do you want me in the ring?'

Maxie brought his face very close up to Tommy's. 'It's called getting back on the horse Tommy.'

'Some bloody horse.' Tommy raised himself wearily to his feet. The image of the prone Vincelli was still frozen on the set, but Tommy realised that in his mind it was already fading, like an old photograph left for too long in the sunlight.

Tommy moved through the crowded room feeling no fear. He remembered his 'welcoming' party, his first introduction to social chit-chat and the moonlight walk with Margot. He'd been another person then. It was like remembering an old photograph of himself as a child: innocent, guileless, unknowing. So much had changed in him. He didn't know if he was better for it, or worse. But he thrilled to think he didn't care either way. Now he passed confidently from conversation to conversation like some visiting island ferry, stopping here, smiling, responding politely to the good wishes, not over-extending himself but moving on with an acceptable social excuse.

'It doesn't matter that you mean it,' Klein had said, 'or whether it's true, just so long as it comes out right. It's social intercourse.' Klein had laughed, '*Yes*, I did say social. Anyway these buggers are lying to each other, you, me and the general public every day of the week. They don't want real reasons, they don't want you to say, "Well I'm a bit bored now, must be off", they just want some bromide.'

So Tommy circulated in the best manner, glass of orange squash in his hand. Another Klein decision. 'I was wrong to let you risk even one glass of alcohol last time. Some snide bastard from the *Mail* did a bit of a knocking piece, nothing much, but it detracted from the image a bit. So it's squash for you my lad.'

Tommy didn't mind. He still didn't like champagne.

Bannerman was talking to the sports correspondent from one of the American wire services: 'Where are you staying over there, Hyatt Regency?'

The man nodded. 'Surprised they're letting me go really, but if it's a big American fighter they send their lads so I insisted it worked both ways. They bought it.'

Bannerman said, 'Forget the Regency. That's where the Klein circus is staying; you won't get a wink of sleep. Those Roberts people play rough. It'll be the old "Wakey-wakey" routine, all over again.'

'Oh shit,' said the wire service man, 'have they got any idea?'

Bannerman gurgled, part laughter, part wind and pulled at his champagne. 'Haven't the faintest. But if they're playing with the big boys they'll have to learn. If Roberts has his way Booth'll be getting in the ring in his nightgown.'

The other man nodded. 'They can be real sons of bitches.'

'You've worked for the U.P.I. for too long lad, you're beginning to talk like them.'

'Yeh, perhaps you're right. Anywhere where you're staying?'

'Hilton. I'll get my people to fix you up with a room.'

'Don't worry. I'll see to it.' See to it that my hotel isn't within half a mile of you. If I have to share another bar-room monologue on the merits and de-merits of Joe Louis and Mohammed Ali I'll throw myself off the godamn Golden Gate Bridge. He nodded across the room to where Tommy was circulating. 'What do you think? He got a chance?'

Bannerman was cautious. He'd let it be known among the rest of the sports boys, with a recklessness brought on by anger at Klein, that he didn't think Tommy stood a chance against Vincelli.

'Well, I confess I underestimated him somewhat. Mind you, I reckon Vincelli must have cracked before he even set foot in the ring, but –' he slid his tongue round his teeth, 'Roberts is a tough customer. Could go either way.'

The wire service man nodded. 'Know what you mean. He's got something, Booth. Bit of steel, hard to define. It's possible.' He stuck out a hand. 'Tommy, nice to see you. You know Ray Bannerman?'

'Yeh, nice to see you both.'

'Just talking about you Tommy.'

'Good I hope.'

'Of course,' said Bannerman, patting Tommy's arm, 'always good to see you son. Good party, thanks for the invite. Orange squash I see. Good lad.' Bannerman nodded with seeming innocence, 'How's Vincelli by the way?'

Tommy took it easily, riding it like a punch. 'Fine so I hear. Had a couple of letters from him. He's lost a bit of the use in his arm and leg, left side. Gets about though.'

'Must have hit him with some scorchers,' Bannerman was looking sad, concerned.

Tommy saw the wire service man – one reporter he did like – tense. Tommy could feel the needle from Bannerman. But Klein had briefed Tommy thoroughly.

'Yeh, but it's a risk he takes, isn't it? He's a professional, so am I. In many ways I probably did him a favour. Next bloke along, Kovacs say, would probably have killed him. I reckon he should be grateful. Must move on – enjoy yourselves. Might see you both in San Francisco.' He was gone.

'Cunt,' said Bannerman with feeling, when Tommy was out of earshot. The wire service man enjoyed the look of discomfort on Bannerman's face.

'Well up yours, Raymond my son. You asked for it.' He looked at Tommy's disappearing frame. 'That little bugger,' he said, almost to himself, 'is a bloody sight tougher than we gave him credit for.'

Tommy saw Margot sitting with a dark-haired woman he thought he recognised. He was constantly surprised at how much the sight of Margot affected him. She was simply the most beautiful woman he had ever seen. It seemed to him she changed her mood and style a hundred times a day. Sometimes, when he was making love to her and her face was shiny with perspiration, she looked like a fifteen-year-old schoolgirl: at other times, when she was photographing him or racing in the park with no make-up and her hair tousled, she looked like an enthusiastic young imp. And now, tonight, she was the sophisticated Lady Margot, his Margot with her jet black hair pulled away from her face in an elaborate knot on the top of her head, a few wisps of hair round her face, escaping from diamante combs. Her black silk jersey dress enhanced the womanly curves of her body.

He was shaken from his daydreaming.

'Tommy, how nice to see you darling.'

He could detect immediately that Margot was in a tricky mood. It was the first time they'd been together since that last, bitter row, and although Margot had telephoned him afterwards to make up, Tommy sensed that the angry words still hung there unspoken, between them. For his part, he was more than ready to forgive and forget, with the guilty memory of that BBC bird on his conscience.

Margot kissed him neutrally on the cheek and he smelled brandy. Although the glass in her hand contained champagne.

'Celia Fielding. Tommy Booth.'

'Nice to meet you, Tommy.'

'Miss Fielding.'

Tommy had seen her face a thousand times, in newspapers, magazines and advertisements and snuggling up to the heroes in a dozen films. She was beautiful.

'Looking forward to training, Tommy? This is your last night of freedom, I hear?'

The film star's voice was sheer silk, and yet Tommy was curiously unimpressed. She's a star. I've raved about her since I was sixteen years old. But she's just human. Celia Fielding took a sip from her champagne and Tommy saw Margot drain her glass and take another from a passing waiter.

'I never look forward to it, Miss Fielding, to be honest. It's hard work, but I know it's necessary if I'm to put on my best performance on the night. Just like you, I imagine. All those rehearsals so that when you actually perform before the camera – the one that really matters – you're in the best shape possible.'

'Quite so, Tommy,' she said kindly.

Well not quite so actually, my dear Celia, thought Margot, as well you bloody know. For the little sophisticate here doesn't seem to be aware that you can do twenty takes for one scene. I suppose he thinks you walk in, perform and. that's it. She felt the brandy coursing through her veins Half a bottle before she'd come to the party. Drunk hungrily, quickly, a manic desire to lay the foundations of inebriation. Now the champagne was trembling her nerves with its silver fingers. Why was she getting drunk tonight? She looked across at Tommy and Celia. They were talking as though she wasn't there. My God he's quite the little socialite now. The last time he was terrified, running away from the first people who spoke to him. Running to me in the moonlight like a frightened child. And now he's managing very nicely without me. I'm the one who's frightened. Frightened of him, frightened of myself. I'm in love with him. An East End boxer and I'm in love with him, it's crazy. She swallowed more champagne. I want him more than anyone I've ever known. Crazy.

'Excuse me a moment.' She went to the drinks table and

downed three glasses of champagne in quick succession. I want to be drunk. To blot out the fear, the elation.

They were still talking. Celia had thrown her head back and was laughing. They'd been joined by Johanneson, the closed circuit TV magnate. He was saying: 'Very good, Tommy, very good. Must remember that.' She rejoined the group and gripped Tommy's arm. The feel of the muscle sent a tremble through her. Dammit, I'm not sixteen years old. He could feel the sharp nails through his jacket. 'Come on Tommy, I know Celia and Mr Johanneson won't mind. You promised to talk to Mrs Arlington, remember?'

As they moved away Tommy whispered, 'I didn't need any rescuing, I was doing all right.'

'You certainly were,' there was acid in her tone. 'Not the little wallflower any longer are we?' He caught the slight slur in her voice.

'You told me not to worry about them and you were right.' His voice was harsh and defensive. He was stone cold sober and he suspected she was a little drunk. There was a wildness to her eyes he'd never seen before.

'Yes I did,' she softened her tone by an effort of will, 'you're quite right.'

He looked at her uneasily. 'You okay?'

'I'm fine, don't worry about me.'

He saw Klein waving to him, and waved back.

Margot said, 'How is the illustrious Mr Klein?'

'He's okay.'

'And Maxie?'

'Fine.'

'Is that all you ever say?'

He remained silent. 'And how is the lovely Graham – and don't say fine.'

'He's okay.'

A desire to hurt rose in her, to stab at the thing she loved, claw at the affection until it bled.

'I should watch yourself there Tommy – don't turn your back on Graham.'

'What are you talking about Margot?'

'Well I have seen him looking at you on several occasions in a way which suggested it wasn't totally professional.'

Anger tightened in Tommy. 'You saying he's queer? I don't believe it. He's as hard as nails. Pull the other one.'

'Well Tommy, I wouldn't expect you to understand but they're the classic closet queen type, all public school and rugby club backslapping – or in Graham's case, comprehensive school and betting shop eye punching. Anyway, I think he fancies you.'

'Jealous?'

'Of Graham being a faggot? Course not, Toots. Why should I be?'

'You know what I mean.'

Grham moved through the crowd, feeling the proximity of the bodies and hating them. Sometimes I think I am Klein's messenger boy. Bring this, drive me there, now it was 'Fetch Tommy I want to talk to him'. But the secret knowledge of his own violence stirred within him and sent back his pride. Then it came like a waterspout from the heaving sea of conversation. The words, isolated, thrown up from the storm, floating clear and defined '. . . Graham being a faggot . . .'

His secret shame flooded through him. The dark knowledge opened like a picture book before him. The voice was Lady Margot's. Bitch! She knew and had dared to speak the words aloud. The shame bowed him like a crippled man. But slowly the violence in him took hold and made a secret vow. She would suffer for the words she had spoken, must suffer, must be made to realise that he, Graham, was a man, a whole man. He would make her rue the day she had challenged his manhood. He polished the hard evil secret deep within him.

'Lady Margot, Tommy.' They whirled and if he had doubted the evidence of his ears, their faces told the story. 'Sorry to interrupt your conversation. Tommy, Mr Klein wants a word with you. That was why he waved just now.'

'Sorry, I'll be right over.'

Graham melted silently back into the crowd.

Tommy's face was flushed red. 'Think he heard?'

'Maybe. Who cares?'

'I do.'

'Go Tommy, your lord and master has commanded.' She bowed slightly and with undue formality, 'I'll look forward to seeing you later.'

It was over an hour and a half later when he met her in the corridor, a full glass of champagne in her hand. She had been drinking steadily and knew now she was irretrievably drunk. She had fought the battle and lost. She wanted him, she was afraid of losing him, and hated herself for the fear that made her attack the one thing she loved.

'Hi. Where've you been?'

'Talking to Perry.' The slur was more pronounced now, and the wild look in her eyes had changed to a mere inability to focus.

'What's he doing?'

Oh my God, I can't tell him. Two hours ago I would have flung it in his face, but now? 'Playing cards.' She laughed mirthlessly. 'A private game in one of the bedrooms. He wanted me to join in, but I told him I wanted to look for you.'

He spread his arms. 'Here I am. At your command.'

'Good.' She linked her arm with his, feeling the power of him close to her: 'I would like a conducted tour of the Perry mansion, hall, stately home or whatever he calls it.' They marched up the main staircase, turned left down a long corridor and Tommy intoned in the voice of a guide: 'On your left we have the Green Room which was once the Red Room before they got the decorators in.'

Margot giggled. She paused in front of a door. 'What's in here?'

'Haven't the faintest.'

'Let's see.' The door opened with a slight creak and they were in a darkened room with ghostly white drapes covering the furniture. She closed the door. 'Looks like nothing very much.'

She looked at him in the half light, towering, massive. She came close and put her head softly against his chest.

'Oh Tommy I love you so much.' She felt calm, at peace. She was drunk but in her drunkenness she had arrived at a kind of decision about herself and her feelings. 'Make love to me.' Her mouth was on his, and he tasted brandy.

He pulled away. 'Christ Margot, we can't; not in here.'

'Why not?'

'We just can't. I've got to be back at the party.'

'Please Tommy, please.' Her hand was stroking him urgently but he felt no arousal. She lost her balance slightly and almost stumbled but he managed to hold her. Her body was tight against him now: 'Please Tommy.'

He realised with a shudder of disgust that she was very drunk. He pulled her face away and gripped her by the shoulders. 'Stop it Margot, stop it. You're drunk for God's sake. We can't do it.' He looked about him helplessly in the semi-darkness: 'We can't, you're in no fit state.'

His hand found the light switch and they were bathed in the unforgiving glare of a naked bulb. Her face was deathly white, eyes red-rimmed. In an instant she saw herself as she really was, a drunken woman, pawing at a man, begging him for sex. A bitter reversal of their relationship only weeks before. A shudder of disgust ran through her, but anger hardened inside her. She had only wanted the man she loved and he had spurned her without tact or dignity. She smoothed down her dress.

'Of course, quite right. I am a little drunk. Happens to all of us once in a while. I'm so sorry to have embarrassed you.'

'Margot,' he put out a hand.

She took his hand. 'I've got a great idea. Let's go and play poker with Perry.' Don't, her conscience screamed, don't do it to him, it could mean the end. But the devil imp, fuelled on jealousy and rejection, spurred her on.

He groaned. 'Margot, I don't play poker, and I can't stay away from the party for too long.'

'You'll bring me luck. Just one hand.'

'Okay. Five minutes that's all.'

Five minutes is all it'll take, my little sophisticate, and the evil part of her drove on relentlessly.

'Come on.' She took his hand.

In the private wing of the hall she led him to a small anteroom, and he could hear men's and women's voices coming from the next room. Margot turned to him and there was something indefinably evil in her gaze. 'They're playing in there.'

She opened the door and at first he could see nothing. The only illumination came from a small red bulb, and several joss stick tapers which glowed in the darkness. There was an overpowering smell of incense. He followed Margot inside like a blind man. No one could possibly play cards in this light. Then his eyes accustomed themselves to the gloom and his whole body tensed. A figure was kneeling on the bed. A grotesque woman. Acres of podgy white flesh, rouged cheeks, hideous curly wig, black bra, corset, suspenders and stockings.

Then a voice came from the apparition, deep and masculine: 'Margot, come to join the party after all – and Tommy! What a surprise.'

'Perry,' he said incredulously, 'Perry?'

'A little harmless fun my dear chap, don't be shocked.'

Tommy recoiled in horror as he took in the scene. The room was larger than it first appeared, and bodies were littered around the floor. Music was coming from somewhere in the darkened recesses of the room. A naked blonde girl of no more than twenty was draped at Perry's legs, stroking the white flesh. A black girl, naked to the waist and wearing deep red leather trousers lounged sideways next to Perry. She had a rolled banknote and was inhaling from a small mound of white powder on the back of a tiny silver spoon. Bottles were littered about the floor, and he could see two women locked in a drunken embrace. Cigarettes glowed in the darkness and as his eyes accustomed themselves he could see the cigarettes being passed from hand to hand.

Apart from Perry and Tommy there wasn't another man in sight.

It's a dream, thought Tommy, a bad dream, a nightmare.

A woman approached them. She was naked, a half-empty bottle of Veuve Cliquot in her hand. She put an arm round Margot and kissed her fully on the lips. 'Darling,' she said at last, 'how sweet of you to return.' She pushed past towards Tommy. 'Guest of honour. Welcome.' She pointed over her shoulder and Tommy saw a glimpse of light from another room and heard the splash of water and a woman's cry: 'Come and join us.' The woman moved away, and lay on the bed. Perry detached himself and bounced obscenely towards him. He took Tommy's hand in a damp embrace: 'Don't look so shocked Tommy love, we're all friends here and we're just having a bit of fun.'

Tommy's mouth worked but no sounds came.

'I know what you're thinking, what's old Perry doing dressed up like Charley's Aunt? Just a bit of fun old love, you've heard of drag artistes, pantomime dames – that's all old Perry's doing.'

Margot turned drunkenly. 'Come on Tommy. You're not in training yet. Is he Perry?'

The man giggled obscenely. 'Tonight anything – but anything – is yours for the asking.' He giggled again. What say you to a little show for starters, Tommy?'

'Perry . . . I'm not sure I . . .'

Like a lamb to the slaughter he was led tamely into the bathroom. It was carpeted from floor to ceiling in deep purple. Across the ceiling a giant mirror picked up the naked figures below as they cavorted in the deep suds of an enormous circular bath sunk in the floor.

Perry said, 'I believe you've met Celia – perhaps not quite so intimately.'

The film star in the bath waved: 'Hi Tommy, coming in for a paddle? The other two ladies are Joan and Diane. Say hello girls.' The two redheads shouted 'Lo lover' and 'Come on in'.

Perry turned: 'You're very welcome Tommy, they're the best Mayfair can provide; apart from the warm water each of those little girls is costing me £300 just for the night.'

'They're . . . prostitutes?'

'Harsh word Tommy, too clinical, but you're right in one.' Perry lurched towards the tub and refilled the champagne glasses.

Celia Fielding called: 'Hope you're not going to monopolise him Margot darling. There's enough to go round.'

Tommy felt the room reeling, his senses bombarded with the new sensations. He felt two hands on his shoulders and a musky scent. A dark voice said: 'Tommy, I give the best head, and for you it would be a pleasure.' He was aware of Perry sliding like some overweight sea creature into the suds while the two call girls went professionally to work. Celia Fielding, star of stage, screen and TV looked on with rapt attention.

He turned to the black girl: 'Take your hands off me.'

Her face clouded: 'Sorry lover, didn't realise you were gay.'

He brushed angrily past her. Margot was standing at the entrance to the giant bathroom. She put a hand out to him her love and hate merging and clashing like a tidal race. 'Come on Tommy, you're a big boy now. You can say all the rude words you want.'

Then he was pushing away, and running, running, out of the private quarters, his mouth tasting of bile.

Klein found him in a corridor, white-faced and shaking. Klein smelled trouble. Bloody Margot, she had a hand in this, he'd swear. God damn that woman.

'You all right son? You look as though you'd seen a ghost.' Maxie hovered in the distance, looking akward and uncomfortable in the dinner suit he'd been made to wear. He smiled reassuringly at Tommy.

'I'm okay. Bit tired. I'll go to bed.'

'Why not? Been a long night. I'll make your apologies.'

Tommy trudged away, heavy with loss of innocence.

Sleep was a long time coming.

Margot awoke slowly, the taste of sour booze in her mouth. She turned to the warm body next to her to kiss Tommy into wakefulness.

The redhead nestled in her arm moaned softly in her sleep, snuggled closer and put a hand on Margot's breast. The events of the previous night hit Margot like an express train and jolted her awake with horror, her head thumping.

She roughly shifted the sleeping woman and picked her way through a heap of sleeping snoring bodies to find her clothes. She dressed numbly like an automaton. It was 5 a.m.

She unlocked the Porsche, found a pad and pen and scribbled a note. She popped it under the door of Tommy's room and went to her quarters, the hangover gripping her remorselessly. She took a long, warm, perfumed bath, cleaned her teeth, rinsed with mouthwash, took two sleeping pills and swam into blessed unconsciousness.

Tommy saw the note as soon as he awoke. It said: '*Tommy. Sometimes we do things of which we are not proud. We do not know why we do them, but they seem to be part of being alive. Last night was such a thing. If you have never done anything for which you are ashamed, then you will not understand. If you have, you will. We will never speak of it again. I love you. Margot.*' Tommy folded the note carefully and put it in his pocket.

'*If you have never done anything for which you are ashamed . . .*' He thought of the girl at the BBC, brutal, quick, casual. Done to humiliate who? Margot? The girl, what was her name, Carol, Caroline? What had it done to her? The weeping as the door closed behind him.

Last night is over. It belongs to the past.

She was kneeling, looking at a flower, touching it gently with her fingertips, feeling the soft velvety touch of the petals, its radiant yellow dazzling her eyes. She didn't hear the footsteps on the dewy lawn.

'Margot.'

She stood up slowly. 'Tommy.'

He leaned down and kissed her softly under her right ear, his hand touching and lifting her hair. No words were needed.

They looked at each other for a full ten seconds and she felt the same intensity of light, colour and touch she had experienced with the flower just seconds before.

She said: 'We must get away Tommy. Just for a while. You and I, no one else, no boxing, no training, no Perrys or Kleins. Just you and me.'

'I want that very much.'

Everything seemed so clear in her mind, as harmonious as an ordered universe, serene and at one with itself.

She said, 'We'll go to Venice.'

He felt the harmony, the peace, the ease. He said, 'Perfect.'

'We'll see the most marvellous things, and we'll see ourselves. You know what I mean?'

A year before he would have laughed at such a conversation, sniggered with embarrassment. Now he understood.

He said: 'I know.'

They held each other close in the early light, the bird calls clear and true like a perfectly formed note from a clarinet. Neither wanted to break the spell.

At length he said: 'You're not going to like this Margot, but I'll have to ask Klein.'

She traced a figure eight on the back of his hand with her fingertips and smiled. 'I know.'

'It will have to be after Roberts.'

They were magicians in an enchanted, far-away land.

She said: 'It doesn't matter when, just that we get away. Soon if we can.'

Never had Tommy felt such power in words. 'We will go to Venice, you and I and it will be perfect.'

She closed her eyes and held the image of Tommy's limpid blue eyes. Perfect.

# *Chapter Seven*

The Alitalia DC-9 scudded low into the approach for Marco Polo airport across the Venice lagoon. Margot and Tommy had window and centre seats on the right-hand side of the plane and could see the haunting, beautiful city below them, grey in the February light. The canals, the alleys, the small squares just charcoal marks on the toy city.

Like a child, Tommy had his nose pressed against the perspex inner window.

'It's fabulous, just stuck out there in the water.'

'It's beautiful, Tommy, wait until you really see it.'

The water rushed up to meet them, but at the last second water touched land and the plane jolted onto the runway. A small man in a leather overcoat and carrying a shoulder bag was waiting to meet them as they cleared customs. He doffed a small trilby hat and offered: 'I am Signor Faraglioni of the Cavalletto.'

Fifty feet from the airport entrance a long, sleek, varnished-wood launch with open cockpit, covered area and open rear seat, bobbed on the water at the quayside. The man took their luggage and helped them into the boat where a stocky man, his face like teak, sat idly drumming his fingers on the launch steering wheel. The man in the leather coat said, 'The launch will take us to the landing stage at Harry's Bar, not far from the Piazza. It's just a short walk from there. A porter will take your luggage.'

The launch burbled into life. The man at the wheel untied the mooring rope from the gnarled twisted larch pole driven into the sea bed and bently backed the boat out from the quay. He turned it round and when it cleared the channel leading into the airport he pushed the throttle forward, the bow lifted and the boat surged forward through the avenue of larch poles that marked the navigable channel across the lagoon.

Margot and Tommy sat on the open bench at the rear of the launch and Margot quickly unslung a Leica camera and shot three frames of Tommy as he peered round the curved glass panel protecting him from the spray, only to be splashed by spume rising from the bow wave.

Across the lagoon, Venice, timeless, beautiful, waited for them, low in the twilight. Margot's idea had paid off. After Tommy's win against Roberts, she had suggested to Klein that the boy looked jaded. A diet of training, fighting, life at Perry's – and a string of clichéd homilies from Klein, though she didn't mention those – seemed to have dulled him. Something to lift himself out of the world in which he was immersed, that was what Tommy needed, she decided. Something to stimulate his mind as well as his body. He'd been reading like never before. He seemed hungry for words, ideas, new horizons that the printed page could offer him.

Margot didn't have to sense the growing hostility of Klein. He was not a subtle man. He resented her growing influence on Tommy, the way she was changing his mind, opening it to the promise of better things. But culture was a dirty word with Klein. He agreed with Goering, 'When I hear the word culture I reach for my revolver.' Well damn him. Tommy was worth more than Klein could give him. She wanted him to be champ as much as any of them did, and she was sure he could do it. But what then? A life of stultifying TV soap operas, tabloid girlie newspapers, cheap paperbacks and soft porn movies. Was that to be Tommy's cultural future? Success to the Kleins of this world was a 26-inch colour television, a Rolls Royce and a house in Chigwell with a cocktail cabinet hidden in a mock globe. Well Tommy could have the house and the TV and as many damn cocktail cabinets as he wanted. But he'd have more too. A mind that understood something of the world he lived in, its history, its art, its . . . yes, its culture too. More than his background, education or aspirations could ever have promised him.

Already he was going through the classics like they were Len Deighton spy stories. He had a natural understanding, raw, untutored, but uncluttered by a need to impress or take stances. He was learning, naturally, easily, without guile – like a child. She'd given him a simple introductory book on the history of art and Tommy had been fascinated. One night he'd taken it to bed with him and read it secretly with a torch under the bedclothes long after lights out, like a schoolboy with a dirty magazine.

The next morning he was dull and sluggish in training. Maxie found the book in Tommy's training bag and showed it to Klein: 'To Tommy with love – Margot' read the inscription on the fly-leaf. Klein challenged Tommy.

'You doing a bit of reading in bed last night, son?'

Tommy's sheepish grin told its own story.

Klein's voice cut like a razor blade: 'Listen son and listen good. If you want to be Michaelsoddingangelo it's okay by me. But not on my time, or Perry's. You're fighting that nigger from Oakland next month and when he gets you in a clinch on the ropes and starts butting the shit out of you, what are you going to do, hit him with a fucking Canaletto?' He gripped Tommy's wrist viciously. 'Look sunshine. If you want to screw a bit of upper class crumpet, fine, as long as it doesn't interfere with your boxing. Savvy?'

There was a sullen defiance in Tommy's eyes. 'What's the objection to me improving my education?'

Klein jabbed a forefinger at the training ring. 'That's the only education you need. That's where you learn to beat Roberts and the best in the world.' He pointed to Maxie, who stood uneasily watching the conversation. 'And him and me are your fucking professors. So don't forget it.'

Tommy stood silent and sullen, and Klein could feel the resentment. Resentment would make their relationship harder. Counterproductive. The fighter would work against him, there'd be an unconscious resistance to ideas, suggestions.

He broke into a smile and patted Tommy on the back,

then Klein spread his arms wide. 'Tommy my son, have I ever let you down?'

'No, never Mr Klein.'

'Haven't I always made sure you had the best?'

'Course you have Mr Klein.'

'And have I ever tried to stop you doing anything you wanted?'

'No.'

'Then look, Tommy. I just want to help make you the world champion. And believe me, you won't do it with bags under your eyes wandering round the ring half-asleep, whether it's *War and Peace* you've been reading or *Playboy*.'

Tommy grinned. 'Guess you're right.'

'You better believe I'm right. When you've beaten Roberts you'll be ranked Number Six. Then you can visit all the art galleries in Europe if you like or lock yourself in a room for a month with a million old masters.'

So Tommy put away his books and trained with renewed determination.

Klein had been right. It was straying from the path. Roberts was the target. He had to take Roberts. And take him he did over seven gruelling, bruising, jarring rounds in San Francisco's Cow Palace with Roberts's supporters crossing the Bay in their thousands to shout on their man.

Tough, was Roberts. The Oakland cops once beat him senseless with billy clubs after a bar-room brawl and a week later he was back in the ring. He ran on Panther money and was on the Klan death list come the white revolution. Tommy was just another white sonuvabitch and a Limey s.o.b. at that to be whupped and sent home. They tried the works on the Tommy party. His fourth floor hotel suite at the Hyatt Regency was the target. Constant phone calls twenty-four hours a day, phoney orders for room service, constant interruptions and a stream of cars parading up and down throughout the night before the fight, lights flashing, horns going.

But Tommy stayed cold as ice in his suite bedroom. Curtains tightly drawn, phone disconnected, cotton wool in his ears, sleeping soundly and effortlessly as always. Klein and Maxie stood guard in the lounge outside, sleeping in relays and shooing away the unwanted callers, 'reporters', 'TV men' and confused waiters delivering the umpteenth steak sandwich and cola 'ordered' by Suite Four.

Klein warned Tommy. The ref was a 'homer'. Word was that the Panthers had promised him trouble if the Limey sneaked it. Klein told Tommy calmly and quietly: 'Watch your punches, anything remotely out of the way and he'll be just looking for an excuse to disqualify you. Keep your head up and try not to clinch too much. Roberts could stick a meat axe through your head tonight and this ref wouldn't see it. It can't go the distance, I don't rate your chances if it does. Make it clean, don't rush it, but work him over from the start. There's no time for games; you've seen what those cunts have been up to all weekend. If they'd had their way you'd be stepping in that ring a sleepless wreck, so show 'em Tommy. Show these nigger Yanks where to get off the tram.'

It washed over Tommy like a wave on the skin of a seal. He was breathing, relaxing and thinking. Gearing his mind for the contest. Another obstacle in my path. The atmosphere was poison. Fear, hatred hung in the air like humidity. Only Tommy seemed unaffected. It was a battle from the bell. No dancing, no feinting, no sizing up the opposition. Two men each determined to crush the other into oblivion. By the third Tommy had cut the American over the eye, but Tommy had an ominous swelling over his right eyebrow.

In the fourth Tommy connected with a searing punch just above the waistline of the American's red satin shorts and heard the gasp of pain. To his amazement the referee parted the boxers and made great show of warning Tommy about low punching. Klein shouted to Maxie above the din of the crowd: 'If he's got balls there he's a fucking freak.'

Tommy set his face grimly. Okay, I'll beat the both of you. His eye was closing and he wanted no opportunity for the referee to stop the fight. He knew that Roberts could bleed to death there in the ring but the fight would still be allowed to go the distance. But blood was now streaming from the American's cut and he was having difficulty seeing out of the eye. At every opportunity he dabbed at the cut with his glove to try and clear the blood.

At the end of the sixth, Klein whispered urgently to Tommy: 'When he dabs that eye again, try a jab. He's leaving his chin open a bit.'

Within thirty seconds of the re-start all the work of the American's corner came to nought as a right hand from Tommy opened up the greased cut with a spurt of thick, red blood. Instinctively Roberts sent up his glove to clear the eye and Tommy saw the gap. A straight right went through the gap like a striking viper. The chin jerked back and Roberts's arms flung wide, momentarily failing to obey either brain or instinct. Tommy threw in a left-right-left-right-left combination in a blur of punches. He thrilled to them. Devastating in their accuracy, ferocious in their power. Each landed like a guided missile flush on the American's chin. Roberts lost his legs. He stumbled backwards against the ropes, then down, sideways onto the canvas, an arm clinging hopelessly for support to a rope. The referee waited for three long illegal seconds before starting his count, his mind on his two young daughters and the threats of the Panthers. He could have counted to fifty and it wouldn't have saved Roberts.

The referee lifted Tommy's arm reluctantly aloft as though it were a great weight. A full beer can sailed out from the blackness and landed with a dull thud in the ring. It was no time for bowing. Tommy got out of the ring quickly and raced to the dressing room flanked by Klein and Maxie. A gob of spittle hit him in the face as they ran the gauntlet of jeering, hissing Roberts supporters. Thirty minutes later their black limousine was heading south for San Francisco International Airport and a TWA domestic night flight to New York. Klein, who knew a thing or two about violence, didn't think it wise to wait for the 1 p.m. London flight the next day. Doctors ordered Roberts hospitalised with a broken jaw and referee Dave Benneker decided to move his family to Portland, Oregon where his brother-in-law was a sheriff's deputy.

Klein had the sense to honour his promise.

'You still want to go poncing off round Venice with Margot?'

'You bet, Mr Klein.'

'All right. Come and see me tomorrow and I'll give you some readies.'

'You don't have to do that Mr Klein. Your cheque goes in regular each month. I've got more of the stuff than I know what to do with.'

'Just a little thank you for the Roberts fight, Tommy. You're a good lad and you've worked hard. Have a good time. And don't go cross-eyed staring at all those paintings.'

'Thanks Mr Klein, I won't.'

Klein's conversation with Margot was more to the point.

'Okay, Margot, listen to me. That little sod's quite hooked on you one way or the other. But you're a married woman – a very well-known married woman at that and he's the clean white hope. So it's two rooms in Venice, right, and they don't adjoin. I don't give a damn which one you sleep in but ruffle the bedclothes of the other, savvy? Tommy's face is famous and you're hardly anonymous, so no hand holding in public and the like. I don't want some crafty little tourist ringing up the *Daily Express* or the News of the Screws when he gets back. You're working, right? And I want a damn good portfolio of pictures when you get back.'

Margot mock-saluted with an open palm. 'Sir.'

Klein spoke evenly. 'I don't know what all this Eliza Doolittle stuff with Tommy is about, Margot. But just you remember this. The only thing that makes that kid different from a thousand others is that he is a world class fighter. Take that away from him and he's just another East End kid you or your old man wouldn't piss on if he was on fire. Now I'm all for education and people bettering themselves – including Tommy. But remember, he's successful because he doesn't mind battering another human being into a pulp, cut down to basics. Now if I understand art and culture and the like, it's all about beauty and appreciating the finer things of life. Am I right?'

Margot cocked her head arrogantly as though seriously pondering the question. 'I've heard it put more subtly Lewis, but yes, in a shorthand kind of way you could say that was what it was about.'

Klein smiled, and it was as though someone had opened a window on a frosty day. 'Well then, Margot. If Tommy gets too full of culture he might lose a little of his ruthless edge. I mean he might begin to look on the guy in the other corner as a fellow human being with whom he shares a great cultural heritage.' The voice was heavy with sarcasm: 'Which may make him less than keen to scramble the bastard's brains.' He paused. 'And I would not like that, Margot. I would not like that at all. Savvy?'

Margot held his stare.

'*Oui*,' she said mockingly. '*Je comprends*.' And indeed she understood only too well the veiled threat in those cold grey eyes. Before she left the room she turned to Klein and said sharply, 'Don't threaten me, Lewis. Remember me? I do just as I like.

Graham, who had observed the whole conversation in silence, watched her leave the room and moved closer to his boss, like a dog expecting a command. 'Mr Klein?'

Klein sat with his fingers sunk into his furrowed forehead, eyes closed. He remained motionless for a full minute. She was going to screw the whole thing up. She was already pulling Tommy away from him and Maxie. She'd blow it; the championship, maybe even her old man's chances if the press got wind of her and Tommy. Stupid fucking bitch. He leaned back and looked at Graham.

'She's going to ruin him, Graham. She's going to turn him into a bloody pansy traipsing around art galleries.' Graham winced.

'She's got to be stopped, Graham.'

'How Mr Klein?'

Klein looked silently at Graham and Grahem knew. He felt his heart pounding. This was the moment. The moment that would wipe out the memories of the Borstal, the blonde boy, the boxer and the yellow counterpane; his revenge for Margot's taunting words. The words came back and he uttered them like a litany: 'I'd kill for you Mr Klein.'

'How d'you fancy a trip to Venice, Graham?'

And now Margot and Tommy lay in the large double bed feeling the gentle kiss of the white linen on their bodies as a shaft of sharp winter sunlight knifed through a gap in the shutters. Margot slid out of bed, padded naked to the window and threw open the shutters. The crisp cold air cascaded onto her skin and she darted back to the safety and warmth of the large bed. She awoke Tommy with a soft, full kiss as the sunlight bathed the room. Below their window gondolas, parked like taxis, bobbed gently on the green aquatic forecourt of their hotel.

Tommy rolled over and took her, half-asleep as he was, his climax bringing him awake then wafting him slowly back to sleep.

She was dressed when he awoke. A dark blue silk blouse, black tailored trousers and a long black leather blazer, single-breasted.

He pulled her down to the bed and kissed her. 'Time is it?'

'Nine. I'm going back to my room before the maid gets there. We've got to observe the proprieties. I'll see you in the lounge in forty-five minutes.'

He rubbed sleep from his eyes and sat up in bed. Her eyes took in the muscled, supremely fit body.

'Any chance of a cup of tea and some bacon and eggs?'

'Darling, this is Venice, not East Ham. We'll eat breakfast Italian style. I know a beautiful little place just a couple of minutes walk away. First we'll do some sightseeing.'

'What's an Italian breakfast?'

'You'll see.' She kissed him on the neck, murmured 'I love you,' and was gone.

In her own room she pulled back the cover of her bed, sat

heavily on it, dimpled the pillows, and hated Klein for his pretences.

They stood in the Piazza San Marco in the crisp winter sunshine, with the Campanile towering over three hundred feet above them. The square was virtually empty of tables and chairs, the patrons of the smart cafés and tea shops preferring to take their capuccino indoors. But the ubiquitous, overfed inhabitants of the square – the Venice pigeons – strutted and swaggered arrogantly, outnumbering the strollers who fed them overpriced corn from the street vendors.

Tommy looked up. 'It doesn't look all that old to me.'

'It's not. The old one fell down in 1901 or 1902 – I can't remember which, so they rebuilt it, *com'era, dov'era.*'

'What's that?'

'As it was, where it was.'

Margot pointed across the square from the bell tower. 'That's the Torre dell'Orologio, which is clock tower to you. The two men on either side of the bell, with the hammers, are Moors. Each hour those statues come alive and strike the time.'

Tommy looked up. 'They look like the Jolly Green Giant to me.'

Margot gave him a withering look. 'You'd look green too if you'd been up there in all weathers for five hundred years. Come on, we'll work up an appetite for breakfast and assure our sex lives for at least a year at the same time.'

'What?'

'All will be explained, Tommy.'

They entered the clock tower through a small metal door in a narrow alley off the square. Margot handed the man behind the desk a 500 lire note and took a 100 lire coin in change. They started climbing the 136 spiral staircase steps to the top.

When they emerged through the military-style metal hatch set in the roof, only two German tourists were there, posing and reposing for pictures. Margot and Tommy climbed the ten steps to the bell and its flanking Moors. The sheepskin garment each was 'wearing' failed to cover the generous penis and testicles the sculptor had given each man. Margot unslung a Nikon.

'Now the legend has it Tommy – and who are we to doubt? – that if you stroke the private parts of the Moors you are assured of sexual potency for a year.'

Tommy grinned. 'I didn't think we were doing too badly.'

She wagged an admonishing finger. 'Don't scoff.' Her hand went out and traced the genitalia of one of the Moors. 'Now you.'

Tommy laughed and stroked the statue's penis. Margot shot two frames. 'Blackmail. Send a million pounds by return post or I'll send this to the world's press!' They sat with the bell behind then, looking out across the Piazza and the Basilica of St Mark, to the Piazzetta, the Doge's Palace, across the Canale di San Marco at the end of the Grand Canal to the tiny island of St Giorgio Maggiore. The water glistened in the sunshine and the air tasted fresh in their lungs after the gloom of a damp English winter.

'Come on, breakfast.'

Margot found the bar on the Calle Largo San Marzo on the way to the Accademia bridge spanning the Grand Canal. The bar was every bit as much a work of art as the ancient buildings, palaces and museums with which it shared the city. It was small, and immaculately clean. There were no seats or chairs; patrons stood at the right-angled stainless steel counter sipping their espresso, drinking early glasses of white wine and reading *Il Gazettino*, the local Venice paper. The floor was marble; the ceiling inlaid with mahogany. A gleaming Gaggia coffee machine burbled happily at one end of the bar, at the other sat a refrigerated cabinet with meat and cheese in one section, chocolate in the other. Behind the middle-aged woman who was serving, a dishwashing machine sat flush into the wall.

But the real delight was the shelves which held the sparkling glasses and the bottles of liquor of every variety from Teachers whisky to Galliani. Each was set behind its own nave of carved and polished wood, two pillars which rose and met in a curved piece of inlaid wood like the entrance to a small Norman church.

It seemed to Margot, as when she had first set eyes on it five years before, to marry modernity, the old values, beauty and efficiency in a stunning example of good design.

The woman said, '*Buongiorno.*'

'*Buongiorno. Due cappuccine, per favore.*'

The woman turned to the Gaggia machine. Tommy wātched, fascinated, like a small boy in a toy store. Margot took a paper napkin from a glass tumbler, lifted up the clear plastic lid of a container loaded with croissants and handed one to Tommy. She took another napkin and repeated the process.

'They're delicious. Bite into the middle. They've got apple in them.'

The woman behind the counter took the cups, half full with pungent black coffee, and filled the cups from a jug of hot milk, swirling the jug as she did so, and making the milk froth into a creamy layer at the top of the cup. She took a shaker from under the counter and dusted the frothy milk with powdered chocolate. Then she pushed a lidded stainless-steel sugar container with a long spoon protruding from it along the counter towards them.

'*Due Cappuccine.*'

'*Grazie.*'

'*Prego.*'

Tommy sipped at the froth, inclined the cup and felt the milk and coffee combine on his tongue with the hint of chocolate.

'It's certainly different from bacon and eggs. And I can't say I remember the last time I ate breakfast standing up.'

Margot laughed. 'Remember for future reference darling. Here you don't have a choice, but if you do and you sit down to be served, the price goes up accordingly.'

Tommy bit deep into the croissant and felt the apple, sharp on his tongue. He said through the mouthful, 'I think we can both just about manage to afford to sit down.' He demolished three more croissants and another two cappuccine before his hunger was assuaged. They strolled through the Campo di San Maurizio across the Rio di Santissimo, where they paused on the tiny humped bridge, then turned left through the Campo Morosinia into the Campo San Vidal. A glass-fronted cabin nestled against a church wall and a woman was selling flowers to a family. Tommy darted from Margot's side into the cabin. He emerged with a bunch of freesias wrapped in delicate tissue. He bowed and handed them to Margot.

'Present.'

'That's kind of you, you're beginning to turn into a romantic Italian. What did you say to her?'

Tommy extended his forefinger. 'I didn't, just pointed and handed her a large note. It's all Monopoly money to me, she probably charged me fifty quid.'

They laughed together, feeling the exhilaration of the surprisingly warm sun on their faces. In front of them lay the Ponte dell'Accademia. They climbed the arched bridge to its centre and leaned on the thick wooden rail. Beneath them the traffic of Venice scuttled along the Grand Canal. Vaporettos, the work-horse water buses of Venice, nosed in and out of the landing stage 'stop' below them to the left; water-taxis, sleek and brown, surged past like thoroughbreds as they overtook the more cumbersome vaporettos and the numerous working barges and gondolas carrying the food and supplies vital to a living city.

Margot pointed. 'The Grand Canal bears gradually right and the next bridge up is the Rialto, that's got shops on it and is quite the tourist attraction. Then it turns back and the only other bridge after that is the Ponte deli Scalgi. The Canal is like an inverted S running through the city.

'Suppose you want to cross over and you're not near a bridge? Must mean a bloody long walk.'

Margot shook her head. 'Clever people, these Chinese. Gondolas aren't just for the tourists. There are crossing points all along the canal. Two men in old gondolas. They pack as many people as they can into the boat and ferry them across. Costs about 100 lira each and cheap at the price when you think what they'd spend in shoe leather.'

They came down from the bridge to the Galleria dell' Accademia e di Belle Arti which gave the bridge its name. They paid their 200 lira and walked into the cool marble entrance hall. Before they climbed the stone stairs which flanked them Margot said, 'Word of warning, Tommy. Don't try and do it all. Just pick some pictures you like and spend a while looking at them. Work by some of the finest artists in the world is here, and certainly the best work ever done of Venice. Titian, Canaletto, Tintoretto, their best work is in here. It's like a feast.' She handed him the guide. 'See you back here in a couple of hours.'

'Aren't we walking round together?'

'I prefer to enjoy my art alone – and so will you.'

He wandered through the long corridors hung with paintings and into the large high-ceilinged rooms hung with massive masterpieces. In Room Ten he stood in awe at Veronese's 'Feast at the House of Levi'. He remembered what Margot had told him of the painting. It had been originally titled 'The Last Supper' but the Vatican were angry at it. They ticked Veronese off for including 'dogs, buffoons, drunken Germans, dwarfs and other absurdities'. They gave him three months to change it. He didn't bother, just re-titled it instead. Tommy laughed. Showed how much they knew about art.

On another wall he stood transfixed before Titian's 'Transport of the Body of St Mark'. He moved on and marvelled while looking at Bellini's 'Procession Around the Piazza Bearing the Cross' at just how little the Piazza San Marco had changed. Margot was waiting outside when he finally tore himself away.

'Sorry. I got carried away and forgot the time. It's fascinating.'

She smiled in genuine pleasure. 'See what I mean?'

They re-crossed the Accademia bridge and lunched on *pasta e brodo*, *vitello milanese* and salad washed down with a jug of dry white wine in a small trattoria off the Campo San Angelo. As Tommy took a mouthful of veal, Margot said, 'I've got a great idea for this afternoon.'

'Yeh,' he said through the food, 'what?'

She leaned across and whispered in his ear.

He laughed and almost choked on the veal. He honestly thought she was joking.

But Margot smiled secretly back at him.

They hired the gondola on the Rio di San Marina near the church of San Giovanni Crisostano. The gondolier, in his black shirt and trousers, was leaning idly against the silver grey prow of his black-painted gondola. There were few tourists about and business was slack. The traditional straw hat with its blue headband and tailpiece was slung carelessly on a chair propped in the bows. When Margot approached he quickly put the hat on. There was some shoulder shrugging but eventually the man took the proffered 10,000 lira note and helped them into the boat. They sat on the centre cushioned bench with its collapsible canopy, facing forward. The gondolier went to his oar at the stern and expertly propelled them out into the cool green water of the canal.

Tommy thought it was magical. They glided under bridges, under lines of washing strung from house to house along the dark watery canyons that criss-crossed the city.

Margot moved to the prow of the gondola and shot frame after frame as they moved silently on. Once she shouted briskly in Italian and the gondolier slipped deftly forward and plonked his straw hat on Tommy's head. More pictures. After twenty minutes they found themselves in a small canal off the Rio dei Barcaiali. Margot was back in the centre bench and spoke quickly over her shoulder to the gondolier. Though Tommy could not understand Italian, he could hear the puzzlement in the man's reply. The man steered the gondola to a small empty landing stage which was no more than a wooden board extending from a tiny, narrow passage. He tied up, came forward and spoke again to Margot. Tommy sat like a deaf person, isolated by his inability to understand the exchange.

The gondolier pointed to the strip of blue sky between the

towering walls. Margot smiled again, spoke a few words and proffered an unspecified denomination note. The gondolier broke into an understanding smile, ushered the bewildered Tommy to the front of the boat and began to erect the collapsible wet weather shelter over the centre bench. He then skipped jauntily off the boat and, whistling happily, walked off down the alley.

Tommy said, 'Can I ask what all that was about?'

Margot pulled back the flap of the shelter, turned and said: 'Come into my parlour, said the spider to the fly.'

Tommy felt his heart race: 'Christ, you weren't serious at lunchtime were you?'

Margot disappeared wordlessly into the shelter. Tommy looked around him wildly. The windows of the houses flanking the canal seemed to peer down at him. God Almighty, it'll be like doing it in the street. But he could feel the blood rushing to his loins, the familiar herald of lust trumpeting his passion. She must have undressed in seconds. When he climbed into the shelter, and when his eyes became accustomed to the gloom, she was naked. Her clothes were folded neatly into a bundle tucked under the bench with her cameras.

'Hello Tommy.'

'Margot,' he found his breath coming in gasps, 'I never dreamt you were serious.'

She took his right hand and placed it on her left breast. He could feel the nipple firm and erect. In the half-light he could see her lips, moist and slightly parted. Waiting. He kissed her hungrily and she turned so his body was half across her. He took her head with his left hand. In the confined space he felt her legs open and he thrust his right hand into the soft mound of her pubis. He felt the wet, warm welcome on his fingers and thrust them deep into her. She convulsed at his attack, impaled on his searching hand. Her left hand found his penis, stroking the imprisoned strength. She found the zip and eased it down, her hand plunging, searching. With a gasp Tommy felt her nails on him, her hand enclosing. She eased her mouth from his and whispered urgently in his ear. 'Sit up.'

Tommy leaned back in the seat, freeing Margot from his crushing embrace. She got to her feet in a crouch, her head brushing the ceiling of the shelter, and lowered herself onto Tommy with a small cry. He plunged into the soft, welcoming secret caverns of her body. Her hands were on his shoulders, her head tossed back. She began to move rhythmically back and forward, up and down like a child on a rocking horse. Tommy felt an orgasm racing through him like a rip tide and a cold wave of nausea as he repressed it with sheer effort of will.

The gondola began to sway gently with the motion. He heard the 'put-put' of a small launch and an American voice say, 'She was in Paris and he was in Rome, so it seemed logical . . .'

The undulating motion began to be racked like a sobbing body with vibrations that threatened to destroy its rhythm. Margot's body began to jerk, sideways, forwards, without patterns. She was like some devil dancer being exorcised of her evil spirits in a grotesque tribal ceremony. Her head bobbed from side to side, eyes closed, a low moan coming from her empty mouth. Her nails cut through the cloth of Tommy's jacket, stabbing into the flesh. She jerked violently, a series of animal noises tore from her throat and the gondola rocked. Then her body went limp and she slumped forward, her wet face against his cheek. Strands of hair, matted with perspiration, clung to her forehead. She whispered over and over: 'Oh Tommy. Tommy.' They stayed that way for what seemed an eternity, his prick still hard, unresolved, deadly deep within her.

Then, very gently, he lifted her limp body from his and laid her across the pillows. She watched the blonde head move down from her throat, pausing to tease her nipples with his tongue, brushing his cheek across the smooth skin of her stomach. Slowly, he parted her legs and ran his tongue along the inside of her thighs. Her fingers moved blindly over his face, feeling his eyes, his nose, his brow – those familiar contours that she had come to love so much. A shudder ran through her as Tommy's tongue neared the centre of her being. He opened her legs wider and probed deep inside her, licking, nibbling and sucking until he brought Margot to her climax, her fingers entwined in his hair as she sought to draw him deeper and deeper inside her.

After a few minutes, Tommy raised his head to hers, unable to conceal the rather cheeky look of pride on his face. Margot, her eyes still soft and hazy with pleasure, smiled lazily down at him, her glowing face reward enough for this ultimate act of love.

After an age she rolled away from him and slumped to the carpet floor of the gondola. Tommy looked past his stiff prick at Margot. The sheer sensuality of the moment rippled through him. He felt an enormous dangerous power akin to the power when he hit an opponent and saw the surprised, dazed look in their eyes. He reached out his left hand and his finger slid softly into her mouth. She shifted slightly, took his finger, kissed and sucked it gently. Then she put his hand on her hair, shifted slightly and her tongue began to trace a wet line around the tip of his penis. Suddenly, angrily, he leaned forward and gripped her head in both hands. Mechanically he pulled and pushed at her, feeling the soft grip on his prick and the tiny, beautiful pain of her teeth biting him. His back arched as he climaxed. Uncontrollable, a release of energy, power, that tossed him, drained, back into the seat.

They were dressed and sitting in the prow of the gondola when the gondolier returned. He lowered the shelter without a word and began to propel them down the canal. He dropped them near the Teatro La Fenice. As he helped Margot out of the boat he took her hand, kissed it, and spoke softly to her in Italian. As they walked down the Calle Verona Tommy said, 'What did he say to you just now?'

Margot laughed, 'Well to paraphrase it and strip it of a lot of the glamour contained in the original Italian, he more or less said he'd like to do with me what we just did back in the gondola. Oh, and he says you're a very lucky man.'

They were passing a tiny alley and Tommy took Margot by the arm and dragged her quickly several yards into the gloom. He kissed her violently, crushed her body against his.

She felt the strength of his loins against her. He crushed a breast under his massive fist.

'Let's go back to the hotel – now.'

Tony Duggan leaned on the counter at La Reserve Wine Bar in Fleet Street, a bottle of the house wine in front of him. Long day, long, long day. Get out of practice out in the provinces.

Couple in the Kings and Keys before lunch, couple of bottles with Archie in El Vino's, then down to Scribes, with that mob from the *Express*. The Golf Club? Did we go there? Of course, large ports, whose idea was that? Get out of practice, no danger. He thrust a hand into his wallet and felt the few crumpled remaining notes. You can get through a few bob up here, thank God I've got a return ticket. He looked at his watch. Nine thirty. I'll get the ten o'clock. Kath'll go up the pole when she sees me in this state. It's why I bloody moved to Brighton in the first place. They're all bastards up here, drunken piss-artists. Two hundred quid. Two hundred lousy quid. I give Archie a knockout bloody story like that. Next Prime Minister screwing his secretary and all I get is two hundred sodding quid to keep my mouth shut. Thinks 'cause I'm out in the provinces I'm a woolly back. Couple of hundred, two bottles of champagne and I'm sorted out. American cunt.

He took another swig of the wine. I should've stayed, sod Kath. It's all Mickey Mouse down there, this is where it counts.

A blurred figure came up to the bar and he tried hard to get it into focus. His heart leaped. 'Jimmy. Jimmy Donaldson. You old bastard. How are you?'

'Tony? Nice to see you, mate. Where have you been? Heard you took redundo?'

'Right. Opted for the easy life. Brighton *Argus* now.'

'Best thing mate. Wish I'd got the guts to pack it in. Sod this for a game of soldiers.'

'Come off it Jimmy, you love it.'

'Like a pain in the fucking head.' He settled himself onto

the stool next to Duggan, pouring wine from the bottle he'd just bought into Tony's glass. 'What brings you up here?'

'Bit of business. You still freelancing?'

'Nah, *Globe* made me an offer I couldn't refuse.'

Donaldson took a sip of his wine. 'This business anything I can help out with?'

'Bit private really.'

'You know me,' Donaldson crossed his heart, 'won't go any further.'

Duggan drained half his wine. 'More than my life's worth Jimmy.'

'Right, not another word.'

They started to talk over old times. They'd been at the Spaghetti House siege together, and Balcombe Street.

Duggan looked at his watch: 'Oh fuck it, missed another train. Same again, Jimmy?'

'Why not?' He was with Archie Taylor at lunchtime, I saw him. Archie doesn't entertain for the fun of it. What the hell's he got that Archie would bring him up all the way from Brighton for?

Duggan staggered back with the bottle. 'See that Jimmy, a fucking stagger. That's what happens when you get out of practice.'

'Yeh. How's Archie Taylor these days? Haven't seen him in a month of Sundays. You used to be mates, didn't you?'

'Mates. He can go and fuck himself as far as I'm concerned.'

Donaldson moved in for the kill. 'Well he pays sod all, I know that. He robs his contacts blind. I sometimes wonder he doesn't pocket half the cash himself.'

'You wouldn't believe the half, Jimmy.'

'Yeh.' Donaldson could feel the resentment there, just waiting for a bit of encouragement to spill out.

'Oh I can't talk about it. S'posed to be a bloody secret.'

'Up to you mate, forget it if you want.'

But Duggan was drunk, very drunk. He felt cheated, used, a discarded Fleet Street man going to seed in the provinces. Archie was using him and he resented it. It was a good story,

I deserve some recognition. Two hundred sodding quid. Everyone knows he's got a budget of £30,000 a year for informants. He could have bunged me a grand.

'Look Jimmy, promise me you won't whisper a word?'

'Sure.'

Duggan began to speak and when he finished he felt better that he'd confided in someone. Jimmy was one of the lads, he was out on the road, he knew what it felt like to get your feet wet, he didn't pick up telephones like Archie sodding Taylor.

The next day Tony Duggan stayed in bed until 3 p.m. with a crippling hangover. When he staggered down to his sullen wife he could not remember anything after leaving Scribes at six o'clock. He couldn't remember the Golf Club or Peter Evans or La Reserve, the meeting with Jimmy Donaldson, the train ride home or the 1 a.m. drunken row with his wife at Brighton station.

But he had an awful, awful feeling that he'd made some incredible mistake.

The Monarch Airlines BAC 1-11 reached Venice at 3 p.m. local time after a one-hour stop at Bologna on its journey from Luton Airport. Among the passengers met by the Pegasus Holidays representative that Friday afternoon was Graham. He had booked in his own name at a travel agent in North London a week earlier. There had been some umming and aaghing and telephoning because it was a late booking and a single room was required. But eventually he was found a room at the Grand Hotel Luna in the Calle Larga dell'Ascensione a few yards from the Piazza San Marco. He paid the £123.60, which included insurance and single room supplement, in cash.

Klein had been clear about it. 'It's all straight and above board. You're taking a small holiday – and Venice will suit your "investment" interests, after all. When the shit hits the fan you're my man there to look after Tommy, all right, so the press won't think there's anything dodgy going on between him and Margot. If you bump into them in the street, have a chat; Tommy won't mind and Margot'll just think you're there to keep an eye on her. But don't go out of your way to meet them. If they don't know you're there so much the better. But if you spend all your time skulking in the hotel it'll look suspicious. Tourists don't do that. We're not going to start fucking around with false passports and stuff. It gets James Bond and blows up in your face.' He crushed out the ash of a thick cigar. 'She's bound to go out on her own some time. If she doesn't, use your initiative. But make sure nobody sees you. Don't go berserk, but a bit of disguise won't hurt when you actually do the job. After it's done, throw her cameras in the canal. It's a local lad, right? Pretty girl, expensive cameras. He thinks he'll have a bit of naughty then have it away with the cameras. She panics, he sticks her. Simple.'

'It's done Mr Klein.'

'Don't forget, Tommy's going to take it hard, so get him back on the first plane, we don't want him blabbing to the press. It was a picture assignment and you were there as well. We don't want any muck splashing on Dudley. A dead wife won't hurt him – might even help. But a wife who was screwing a boxer, that's another matter.'

'Don't worry Mr Klein, I can handle it.'

He lay on his bed now in Room 129 on floor 2A, smoking and thinking. First the knife, then a stake of the Cavaletto. If she didn't come out, then a phone call or something to get her away from Tommy. Graham felt the burden of responsibility on him but welcomed it like a weightlifter challenging his personal best. I am a man. And I will kill for Klein.

That evening, as Graham sat eating his room service pasta and drinking Chianti from a large flask he'd bought in a local wine shop, unknown to him Margot and Tommy passed under his bedroom window as they strolled down the narrow Calle Vallareso to Harry's Bar.

Harry's Bar was a Venice institution and the prices reflected it. There were two vacant bar stools as a couple headed for the tables laid for dinner and Margot and

Tommy sat down. They drank Campari and soda followed by Moët and Chandon served by the glass. Narrow, cylindrical glasses with the engraved motif of a waiter serving drinks.

'What's so famous about it?' Tommy asked.

'It's famous because it's famous because it's famous,' Margot replied. 'They say Hemingway used to drink here, and Orson Welles. Now they say anybody who is anybody comes here to look at all the other anybodies.'

Tommy sipped at the champagne. He still didn't like the taste, but it signalled success and he drank doggedly from the glass.

'Can you see anyone famous?'

Margot pretended to look around the bar. 'Oh yes. Two very famous people.'

Tommy swivelled his head. 'Who? Where?'

She prodded him in the chest. 'You and me. The future world champion and one hell of a photographer and sometime wife of Britain's next Prime Minister.'

They paid the astronomical bill and walked back – under Graham's bedroom window – on their journey back across the Square. They had dinner at the Ristorante Al Columbo in the Corte del Teatro. Margot ordered *zuppa all vongole*, *fritto misto*, salad and a bottle of Soave. Tommy heard the word *zuppa* and said, 'If that sounds like I think it sounds, I'm not really in the mood for soup.'

'It's not really soup, it's clams in white wine sauce. You'll love it.'

As Tommy spooned the last of the liquid under the mound of clam shells, a girl carrying a camera with flash attachment stopped at their table. She raised her camera until Margot addressed her sharply in Italian, then lowered it sulkily and moved to the next table.

'Table photographers,' said Margot. 'They're the bloody plague of Italy and the Côte d'Azur. I don't know why they let them in. They're just a damn nuisance.'

Tommy surveyed the barren clams before him. 'She's just trying to make a living – like all of us, I suppose.'

Margot laughed. 'I suppose you're right. I just don't think it's a good idea for someone to have a negative of us having an intimate little dinner.' A white-coated waiter deftly removed the bowls and brought a serving table to theirs. As he spooned the mound of small fried fish and shellfish from the serving dish to their plates, Margot deftly dressed their salads from the containers of oil and vinegar. The waiter put down the filled plates and Tommy hungrily shovelled a forkful to his mouth. Margot sipped her chilled wine and said, 'I'm going to leave you for a while tomorrow afternoon. I want to do some shots up in the ghetto area.'

'Ghetto? You mean like ghettos in America?'

'Not exactly. This ghetto was where the Venetian Jews used to live. Remember *Merchant of Venice*, Shylock and all that?'

Tommy nodded, his mouth full of food.

'In the sixteenth century the Venetian senate restricted the Jews to an area completely surrounded by canals up in the Cannaregio district. They say it's probably where the word ghetto came from. There were lots of foundries there and they think the word could have come from *gettare*, which means to cast in metal.'

'What's so interesting about it now?'

'Nothing especially. It's just that now it's the poorest quarter of Venice. I've got an idea for a picture series on the two sides of the world's famous cities. On the one you have the Eiffel Towers, the Big Bens and the famous landmarks. On the other the sights most tourists never see. The slums, the poor kids, that kind of thing.'

'Sounds a great idea, when do you plan to go?'

'Round tea-time. There's a beautiful light just before the twilight. Very sharp, very clear, and I want to shoot some colour.'

Tommy swallowed a mouthful of seafood. 'I've seen all the poverty I want to see. I don't think it's beautiful, whatever the light.'

'*Touché*,' Margot dipped her fork in acknowledgement. 'Very perceptive of you to make that point. I wasn't suggesting that poverty was attractive in whatever light. But some of the world's best photographers have debated along those lines for years. Does photography beautify poverty, violence and the like by turning them into an art form which people admire? But . . .' she left the sentence unfinished.

Back at the hotel they lay with the shutters open as the moonlight bathed them in its blue glow. They made love, slowly, tenderly, luxuriously. They climaxed miraculously together and fell asleep entwined in each other's arms.

Graham ate breakfast in the hotel dining room, went back to his room and put a pair of horn-rimmed glasses into his pocket. He turned up his coat collar and put on a shabby hat that shadowed his face. He walked towards the Rialto bridge until he found the shop he was looking for. In the window was an astonishing selection of knives, everything from tiny penknives to giant hunting knives. He slipped on the spectacles with their thick lenses. 'The eyes,' Klein had told him, 'it's the eyes that identify you.'

He wandered round the shop until he found the knife he wanted. A narrow-bladed stiletto. Graham gingerly tested the edge with the tip of his thumb. Razor sharp. He deliberately moved on. He picked up three penknives, a small hunting knife, then the stiletto and laid them on the counter. The shopkeeper wrapped them in a bundle of thick brown paper and said cheerfully, 'English? American?'

'Deutsch,' said Graham sullenly, 'Deutsch.'

The man scribbled a figure on a piece of paper and Graham handed him several notes. The man said '*Danke schön*,' but Graham just nodded and left the shop. Damn Germans, thought the man; had a bellyful of them in 1944. Barbarians, no manners and no style.

Back in his hotel room Graham unpacked the stiletto and slipped it into the small leather sheath, then put the clothed knife into his overcoat pocket. He stationed himself on a corner across from the Cavaletto, pretending to read a copy of *Die Welt* he'd bought from a news stand. At one o'clock he went for lunch, figuring that Margot and Tommy would be doing the same. He resumed his watch at two-thirty and at four saw Margot and Tommy come out of an alleyway leading from the Piazza and walk towards the hotel. On the steps they spoke and parted. Margot, cameras swinging from her neck and shoulders, turned and headed off in the direction of the Calle dei Fabbri. Unable to believe his luck, Graham adjusted the spectacles, folded away his newspaper and followed at a distance of fifty yards. Margot reached the Grand Canal at the Riva del Carbon and bought a ticket at the vaporetto station at the Pontile Carbon. He waited three minutes until a vaporetto nosed in to the landing stage, darted forward and bought a ticket all the way to Fondamenta di Santa Lucia, at the end of the canal, to be on the safe side. Margot was among the first on the boat and went to the stern. Graham hugged the wall of the wheelhouse. As the boat went under the Rialto bridge he saw Margot take a seat offered her by a young national serviceman. As the vaporetto came into the Pontile San Marcuola, he saw her stand up and move to the exit point in the centre of the boat. The blue-jacketed attendant deftly lopped the rope over the mooring post and, as the boat eased against the landing stage, slid back the metal railing.

A stream of people stepped off the boat onto the landing stage. Graham waited until the very last second and then slipped off before the joining passengers started to swarm aboard. Margot was about forty feet ahead of him, striding purposefully. She walked towards the curving Rio Terra San Leonardo – a filled-in canal made into a pedestrian thoroughfare, wide and spacious. She crossed the Rio di San Girolama into the Fundamenta Ormesini. A group of men were loading a barge and Margot worked quickly, shooting frame after frame of the working men. They spot, ted her, whistled and waved. She waved back, then walked along the side of this wide, functional canal and turned right into the Calle della Malvasia. A group of children, brown and ragged, were playing football with coats for goalposts, and she snapped them as they played, oblivious to her, immersed in their game. For an hour Graham shadowed her as the soft winter light began to fade. He fingered the knife in his overcoat pocket.

It had to be somewhere quiet.

Margot dangled her tired feet over the canal edge, her eyes darting left to look back the way she had come. The man in the spectacles and the hat was following her, she felt sure. Ever since she'd stepped off the vaporetto she'd noticed him. At first he was just another man in the crowd. Then she slowed her pace but he made no effort to pass her.

What was his damn game? There was something about him; some hardly discernible familiarity. Her curiosity was larger, at that moment, than her growing fear. It was getting dark now and Margot saw out of the corner of her eye the flicker of a movement from a shop doorway down the canal from where she had walked. The light was failing quickly. Great pools of darkness spilled out like inkstains. She shivered unconsciously. The tiny alleyway, the small squares lying deep in shadow that had seemed so charming, now menaced her with their darkness. She got up quickly and began to walk rapidly down the canal side.

She looked briefly at her map as she walked, then over her shoulder. There was no sign of the man. Ahead of her a woman with a bag of shopping turned right into an alley flanked by doors. She looked at her map again. It had to take her through the Fondamenta della Misericordia. If the man didn't see her, it would be a useful short cut.

She turned quickly into the alley and trod in the reassuring ringing footsteps of the woman ahead of her. But fifty yards ahead the woman stopped, inserted a key into a metal door and was gone. The silence hung emptily around her. She paused. Then she heard the almost imperceptible footfalls coming behind her. Panic rose in her throat and she broke into a run. Her cameras were swinging wildly, and still running, she managed to tuck one, the Leica, inside her leather jacket still on its neck strap. She zipped up the coat to stop the camera bouncing and felt it tight against her breast.

Incredibly, she felt an obscene thrill deep within her as the fear gripped her and her body urged her on. For a wild, insane moment she thought she was going to climax as her knees turned to water. Thirty feet on the alley divided and she plunged thoughtlessly to the right. The alley curved right and began to taper. To her horror, ahead of her she saw the alley end at the murky waters of a canal. Trapped.

She tried to scream but no sound came. She backed against the damp wall and edged backwards until her feet were a foot from the canal edge. Through the gloom she could see the figure of a man walking softly, softly, towards her. The perspiration streamed from her body despite the damp and the dark. She looked wildly at the forbidding canal with its floating carpet of refuse and even in her terror rejected the thought of escape that way. Ten feet away the man halted. Margot said in Italian, the words dry and rasping, 'What do you want?' As though he had not heard, the man said in accented English, 'Put down your cameras, I want your cameras.'

Relief washed over her. The cameras. Of course. Thousands of pounds worth of cameras round the neck of a woman walking alone in the dark, deserted streets of the poorer quarter. She unslung the two Nikons, one with its telephoto lens, and put them down in front of her. The Leica beneath her jacket seemed part of her body, solid and reassuring over her pounding heart.

'Take them. You can have them,' she said in Italian.

Again the man seemed not to have heard. 'Now move across the alley away from the cameras.' The voice, the strange accent, something moved – almost recognition – in Margot's brain, but fear swamped it. She went sideways, crab-like across the alley, until her palm touched the damp, mossy wall.

The man moved forward and picked up the cameras in both hands. With first one then another underarm sweep he swung the cameras into the canal. There were two heavy splashes in quick succession, then silence. The man put his hand in his overcoat pocket and Margot saw the dull gleam of the knife.

She gagged and fought back the nausea.

'Oh Jesus Christ in Heaven you're going to kill me.'

She watched fascinated, mesmerised like a rabbit before a cobra as the man moved closer. Graham could only see the whiteness of her face. He gripped the stiletto like an avenging phallus. The power. His whole life had been leading up to this moment. The act of finality. The ultimate step into the ultimate depravity. The blade was flat, his wrist straight. He aimed for the heart, a short thrust and serpent swift. He said: 'Die you bitch!'

The shock as the blade hit the Leica jarred Graham's arm to the shoulder. The point snapped on impact and the stiletto dropped from his grasp. The camera jolted bruisingly into Margot's breast and the pain jarred her into animal action. With a cry of terror she brought up her right knee, aiming for the groin. There was a gurgling scream of pain as the bone crushed into Graham's testicles. Then she was running, running, fear at her heels down the alley. The sound of her heart pumping echoed in her ears. She ran for her life, sucking in searing lungsful of air, her chest heaving with the strain.

Suddenly she burst out onto a lighted canal bank. In front of her a young man in a small launch and smoking a cigarette looked up from the wheel where he sat. She rushed to the canal edge, her words coming in gasps punctuated by her laboured breathing. She spoke in English and the man shrugged his shoulders. With a supreme effort of will she remembered her Italian.

'Want to hire – your boat. San Marco. Piazza.'

The man laughed in puzzlement. 'It's not a water taxi, it's a working boat.' He picked up an empty balsa wood crate. 'Look, I've been carrying fish all day,' he pinched his nostrils with two fingers.

'I don't care.' She took two 10,000 lira notes from her jacket pocket, leaned down and thrust them into the man's hand.

He shrugged. 'Piazza here we come.' She jumped down into the boat and he fired the engine into life. As they headed down the Rio della Misericordia for the Rio di Noale and the Grand Canal, Margot looked back at the alley exit. There in the shadows, almost invisible now because of the darkness, a figure stood crouched in pain. A wave of fear and cold passed through her, sending a shiver that racked her from head to toe. The boatman saw her looking back and said in his thick Venetian accent, 'What's wrong? Have a fight with your old man?' She nodded dumbly.

Tommy was in the bath reading a copy of Venice's English language newspaper, *The American*. He called out, 'Successful?'

There was no reply. Margot peeled off her clothes, walked into the bathroom and slid naked into the bath. She slumped back, white-faced and shivering.

'What the hell is wrong?' He saw the ugly, purple bruise under her breast. 'What happened, Margot?'

She let the warmth work on the shock before she spoke, 'Someone tried to kill me.'

'Christ!' Tommy sat bolt upright, sending a mini tidal wave down the long bath. 'We'll call the police.'

Margot said quickly, 'No police. We don't want the press to get wind of this.' She closed her eyes. 'Please Tommy, I'd just like a large, large brandy and the chance to think.'

He got out of the bath, poured the drink and came back. Margot downed half the contents at one gulp and felt the alcohol like oil on a troubled sea, calming her jagged nerves.

'Tell me what happened.'

Slowly Margot recounted the details as Tommy gripped her hand. She omitted one detail and she didn't even really know why, for it was emblazoned on her mind. Before the blur of the stiletto there had been that voice. That voice which had said, in English – London Cockney English – 'Die, you bitch!'

So she couldn't leave her would-be killer behind in Venice when they flew out. He'd be in London. Waiting.

As she climbed wearily into bed, her body fatigued from

the shock, exertion and the alcohol, she lifted a book from the pillow. A book Tommy must have bought that day and been reading on the bed. She saw the cover, and an ironical expression flitted over her pallid face.

It was Thomas Mann's *Death in Venice*.

# *Chapter Eight*

Archie was already at the table in a discreet corner of the restaurant, toying with a Campari and soda. He saw Margot enter the restaurant, and waved as the head waiter ushered her to the columnist's table. They greeted each other, studied the menu, made small talk, and ordered.

'Well how super of you, Archie darling,' said Margot, 'I haven't been here in an age. I do believe they've decorated.'

Archie sipped his drink. 'They have. it's the only place, too, in walking distance of my office with passable food. Plus,' he made a writing gesture, 'in their wisdom my lords and masters allow me to sign.'

'Now you've spoiled it, Archie. There I was thinking I was to have a mysterious *tête à tête* with my favourite newspaperman in some secluded restaurant, and all the time I'm just another name on your expense account.' The waiter placed a chilled glass of Punt e Mes in front of her.

His face clouded. 'If you must know Margot, this *is* business. Of sorts,' he added half-heartedly.

'I'm intrigued.'

Archie toyed with his drink. 'Look, I don't quite know how to put this. I'm a friend of you both – Dudley and yourself. I adore you both.'

'And we you Archie. Go on.' Her heart began to pound.

'He is going to make a splendid Prime Minister.'

'Hear, Hear.'

'I would hate anything to come out that would spoil his chances.'

'Archie darling, this sounds like some blackmail scene, is this where you produce the compromising photographs?' She laughed.

He banged the glass down on the table. 'It's no laughing matter, Margot.'

'Yes?' He knows about Venice. Damn, he knows. Before, people could have speculated about Tommy and me. Klein knows, he's no fool. But the press? I never dreamed. How *could* he know about Venice? And if he did, separate rooms. We were discreet, discreet. But we were there alone. Damn me.

'Yes, Archie, say it or you'll burst.'

'Margot, you know what an affair could do to Dudley's chances – particularly an affair with someone like . . .'

She cut him short. 'Well done Archie. So your little spies found out about Venice. My, my, quite the international network you run, isn't it? I promise you something. You can't prove one single thing. One word, just one word, and you'll get the biggest libel writ you've ever seen.'

He fell silent as the waiter put two plates of giant prawns, a bowl of mayonnaise, and two finger bowls containing lukewarm water and a slice of lemon, in front of them.

'Venice?' hissed Archie, 'Venice? I haven't the faintest idea what you're talking about. Margot this is serious for God's sake.'

The wine waiter appeared, poured an inch of the white wine into Archie's glass, and when the columnist brusquely waved aside the tasting ceremony, quickly filled first Margot's then Archie's glass. She picked up the glass, took a sip of the wine and realised her hand was trembling.

'Go on.'

'This is difficult for me, so I'll take the bull by the horns. Dudley . . . Dudley is having an affair and Fleet Street knows about it. I've been sitting on it for months out of friendship, thinking I was the only one with it. But my source leaked. The *Globe* knows, I got the word from a friend. They've got a picture. I'm going to look sick if they use it, given that I knew first.'

Her mind was cold as ice. Not me and Tommy. Dudley and . . . Dudley and who?

'Who is it Archie?'

The columnist hastily swallowed a half-chewed prawn. 'You're not going to like this Margot.'

'Who?'

'Emily Carstairs.'

She didn't waste words on anger. The bloody fool. The bloody fool. He's almost got the key to Number Ten in his pocket and he's risking it all on humping that little mouse.

'Evidence Archie?'

'I know you're angry, Margot.'

'Archie, I know men. They all like screwing something on the side. So, believe it or not, do some women.' She let the words hang in the air. The cunning little bitch, why couldn't she be content with screwing his mind? But maybe it was him, not her.

Archie haltingly told her the story.

'And what do you think the *Globe* has got?'

'A telelens shot of Dudley leaving her place down on the coast. They're embracing,' the words came out with distaste.

'Good God.' She was not thinking of her husband's infidelity but of the possible political repercussions.

'But,' Archie added, 'it's all been done on a need-to-know basis at the *Globe*, I gather. A trusted staffman took the picture and did the devving and printing himself. The pictures and negs are in the chairman's safe. Only he, the editor, the reporter who came in with the tip and the photographer himself, know.'

'So?'

'So I'm sure they'd forget it if Dudley called off this affair.'

She studied him. He had a furtive look, a man with a mission too big for him, trying to stave off the fateful moment.

'Archie, given that it's all on a "need-to-know" basis, you seem to have learned an awful lot. Come clean for Christ's sake.'

He grinned sheeplishly and drank some of his wine. 'Okay I'll level with you. The chairman of the *Globe* group is a personal friend of my chairman. He felt it was above newspaper rivalry. National importance.'

A flicker of alarm crossed Margot's face. 'Are Intelligence in on this?'

Archie shook his head happily. 'There've been no approaches. With a wife like you they probably didn't think he'd be making field trips.'

She got back on course. 'And of course you'd told your chairman, who no doubt is a personal friend of yours.' Her voice was bitter.

'I had to Margot,' his voice was desperate, 'I had to cover myself for just such an eventuality. My job wouldn't have been worth that much,' he clicked his fingers.

'Sure.'

'It's not all bad. It's just the two papers. Both the *Globe* and my mob want this pack of pinkoes out of Downing Street, and they want Dudley in. They've been hammering away at the government for months. Just when it looks as though it's bearing fruit they're presented with this. They could hardly ignore it, now could they?'

'Will they use it?'

He lowered his voice again. 'That's where you come in.'

'Putting it at its simplest, I'm an envoy. Get Dudley to end it, and the pictures will be destroyed with the negatives? Now it *is* beginning to sound like some silly blackmail film.'

He gripped her hand. 'I'm serious Margot.'

'And if someone talks?'

'All the participants in this sorry affair will be well looked after. Promotions, better jobs, higher expenses, so on and so forth. And if they do get drunk and shoot their mouths off, without evidence it's just scuttlebut.' He squeezed her hand. 'You do want him to be P.M. don't you?'

'Yes,' she said sincerely, 'he's a good man, an honest man. But the British public make me sick. So he's humping little Emily, so what? Kennedy was screwing everything in the White House I'm told, and he had his finger on the button.'

Archie motioned a waiter to take away the virtually untouched food.

'It's not the sex Margot, honestly. I think that had it been some discreet Ambassador's wife they wouldn't have blinked an eyelid.'

'Or me and Tommy Booth?'

Archie winked, and it seemed out of context, out of mood. 'Don't worry,' he said cheerily, 'the thought has occurred to not a few of us about you and friend Tommy. But we'd have trouble proving it since you have such a legitimate excuse for spending so much time with him. By the way, guilty conscience about Venice?'

'No. But why is Emily such a big deal then? She's discreet.'

'Because, my dear political innocent, people are fed up with powers behind the throne. After that stuff with Marcia and Harold the great British public has had its fill of kitchen cabinets. But they'd have taken it from Dudley because they think he's his own man.'

'And so?'

'And so they'd have put up with Emily. But, and it's a big one. If they thought for one minute he was screwing her as well, that would be it. They vote for him, not her.'

'Are you sure? Do you think people care any more about sex in politics?'

'You better believe it.' Archie broke off a piece of bread roll and nibbled nervously like a rodent, 'We have got a man down in Sussex now. He's been there three weeks trying to get the same picture the *Globe* has got. And if we and the *Globe* used it Dudley is dead, D-E-A-D. We don't have a Bible belt here, but we've got what I'd call a Mary Whitehouse belt. Dudley being unfaithful to Lady Margot, beautiful, kind Lady Margot. Emily Carstairs trying to usurp power through the bedroom. My God they'd close their eyes, think of God and chastity and vote Labour in their millions.'

He paused. 'Do you want that?'

She shook her head wearily. 'No.'

'Then stop it Margot. You've got a month. That's my message.'

'After that?'

'They'll use it. Both papers simultaneously, matter of national importance, public's right to know, distasteful, regrettable, etcetera, etcetera.'

'How will they know he's given her up? Suppose he lies?'

'She resigns,' said Archie flatly. 'She finds a pressing need to work elsewhere. It's an amicable split, she's well qualified, she wishes him well for the election and rides off into the sunset or Oxford or wherever she chooses.'

'And if he ditches her, then brings her back?'

Archie's voice was cold. 'My people would feel cheated and would launch the biggest campaign of innuendo you've ever seen. If they so much as touched each other after that some hairy mob of paparazzi would pounce.'

They ate the rest of the food in silence. Archie ordered cognac and they sat back in their chairs.

'Aren't you just the teeny-weeniest bit jealous, Margot?'

She eyed him. This was his fun now. Reward for the unpleasant task he'd been lumbered with.

'A little I suppose. That tiny, untrained corner of me that is possessive; that won't accept you can't own someone. But only that.'

'And why will you do this for him? It won't be pleasant for you. He's cheating on you after all.'

'Because I want him to be Prime Minister. Believe me, not because I want to be the First Lady of Downing Street, which I have a horrible feeling is how Dudley sees me, but because he will be good at that job. He is a good man. Sometime's he's weak – hence Emily Carstairs I suppose – but essentially he is honest. And if that sounds too Boy's Own for you, I'm sorry, but it's true.'

'Sounds very loyal.'

'Where my husband is concerned,' said Margot carefully, 'that is just what I am.'

Archie nodded.

'To be honest, my American friend, there are not many things in my life that I can remember doing for any other than an ulterior motive. But this, believe it or not, is one of them.'

Archie lifted the cognac. 'Here's to your success.'

*

Margot sat across the dining room table from Dudley. She sipped her glass of Chablis and contemplated how she was to broach the delicate subject of Fleet Street versus Emily Carstairs and Dudley Creighton, the possible future Prime Minister of England. Would he understand that she was not nagging him for his infidelity but only trying to protect him? She felt a great surge of maternal love for Dudley at this moment. Poor Dudley, he'd feel like some schoolboy, caught looking at dirty pictures. Would it shatter his confidence and self esteem when he needed it most? A wild thought prodded her. Maybe after all he needed Emily more than Margot imagined, needed her political fuel and intellectual expertise. As she needed Tommy's strength and love. Well, better get it over with.

'Dudley darling, I'm afraid I've something to tell you that isn't very pleasant.'

Dudley looked up and smilingly said to Margot, 'What is it, Margot? I know, Porsche's brought out a new model and you want it. Okay darling it's yours.'

'Dudley don't be flippant. I saw Archie Taylor today and he tells me the whole of Fleet Street knows about your affair with Emily Carstairs, and are planning to expose you.'

There was a momentary hesitation while Dudley contemplated denying the story. Blood drained visibly from his face.

'Oh my God Margot, what am I to do? Will you ever forgive me?'

'There's nothing to forgive Dudley. Let's not lose sight of the important issues. We must secure your position in Number Ten.'

'Margot you're mad. How can you possibly do that now? My political career is finished. The British people will not accept infidelity in Downing Street.'

Margot outlined Fleet Street's terms as Archie had explained them, but she could see that Dudley didn't believe the scandal could remain hushed up for long.

As they went to bed that night like conspirators, Dudley looked a beaten man, but Margot went to sleep with one thought pounding in her brain, and the same thought was there when she woke up. Klein. Klein could stop it. Klein could do it. She had seen him manipulate the press before. She knew he could do it again. She hated him, but she had something to trade and Klein always liked to trade. He had power and friends in the strangest places. She'd seen him deal with the press before; they seemed to eat out of his hand. It was the only way to prevent Dudley destroying his career. They had to stop the pictures being used – and convince Dudley he was out of danger.

Klein beamed an insincere welcome. If Graham had done his job properly Margot wouldn't be walking into this office. But Klein never dwelt on past mistakes: he used them to plan for the future.

'What can I do for you Margot?'

She told him, without hesitancy, without hedging, and he listened quietly, not interrupting.

At last she stopped, and he said, 'Pretty pickle.'

'Yes.'

'And you think I can use my influence to stop the pictures being used?'

'I hope.'

He said, innocently, 'I have some friends.'

'Or,' Margot said bluntly, 'you could get someone to break into the safe and destroy the pictures.'

Klein looked genuinely shocked. 'Margot you amaze me. That is called breaking and entering, burglary, theft, or whatever category our overworked police force charge you with these days. It changes so much I lose track.'

'Lewis. If those pictures are used Dudley is out and so is your knighthood.'

He looked quizzical. 'Knighthood? Last thing on my mind. Wouldn't mind one, I confess, and Dudley is a friend. But there'll be a lot of influences when he gets to Number Ten. There'll be no guarantee I'd be on the list.'

'Do this for me and I promise you I will use every power of influence I have over Dudley – which believe me is considerable – to ensure you get the knighthood you so obviously want.'

Klein pressed a buzzer on his desk. 'Come in a minute, Graham.'

Graham was wearing a neat dark, three-piece suit with white shirt and dark striped tie. It was the first time he'd been this close to Margot since that moment in the dark Venetian alley when the stiletto had plunged into the solid body of the Leica. Klein had taken it remarkably well. 'She'll be on her guard now. You're sure she had no idea it was anyone other than a local?' 'I said nothing,' Graham had lied. But he had said, 'Die You Bitch' and those words moved his destiny and must seal her fate. For he would live in fear of the day she would put the words to the face.

'What can I do for you Mr Klein?'

Margot felt a cold wave of fear pass over her. Graham? Could it be possible? Klein was a ruthless man. If he thought I was having too much influence on Tommy, he was capable of anything. She looked at Graham, callous and unruffled. Surely he would have given some reaction. It couldn't be true. She was being paranoid.

'Any friends in the safe-cracking business, Graham?'

He looked uneasily at Margot.

Klein said, 'You're among friends, Graham, speak freely.'

'One or two,' he said reluctantly.

'Klein spread his hands. 'There you are Margot. Good as settled.'

She rose and went to the door. She put her hand on the handle and turned. 'If there is any comeback I would deny everything, you know that?'

'Naturally,' said Klein.

'And, Lewis,' she added menacingly, 'everything has to be destroyed. No happy souvenirs for anyone. If I have reason to believe that one negative remains, the Home Secretary will get a detailed memo which would make life most uncomfortable for you.'

He smiled. 'Girl after my own heart.'

She closed the door softly behind her.

*

He told Graham everything.

'She's fucking stupid. They'll have two sets of negatives, bound to. They're not daft. Busting that safe would be a sheer waste of time.'

'So what do we do?'

'I know Dudley, and Margot's right. If anybody confronted him he'd lose his nerve and his performance would go to pieces. Then he'd go stubborn and insist on keeping Emily on, even if he stopped screwing her. And according to our lady visitor that's not enough for the papers. They want her head on a plate to make sure Dudley stays Mr Clean.'

Graham didn't interrupt. This was the way his boss worked. Moving towards his point by a process of rambling rationalisation.

'But, my son, if the said Miss Carstairs was to die in a tragic accident, honour would be satisfied. No Emily, no shame, Dudley in Number Ten and all's right with the world.'

Graham felt he could safely speak. 'They'd still have the pictures, though.'

'Yes, but they'd never use them. A dead girl, her brilliant young life snuffed out like a candle, and they're gonna show her snogging with Dudley? No way. That would be the end of it. Buried with her.' He sat down and was all business. 'Find out everything you can about her. What she drives, does she swim, fish, ice skate, the lot. It's got to be an accident and we've got a month. Savvy?'

'Okay Mr Klein, I'll get right on it.'

'And Graham,' said Klein, dangerously, 'I want to approve this one. It seems your own little schemes don't work out too well. I trusted you with the last lot and you botched it. Luckily for you it might just have turned out for the best. If she hadn't come to us with this who knows what might have happened. As it is, we've got a chance to get him out off this mess. We can deal with Margot later if the need arises. Get on it.'

Graham left the office.

Klein pounded the desk. Damn Dudley! Why do men like him jeopardise everything they've worked for for a bit of skirt? Well we'll have to watch out for that knighthood; might not be even as surefire a bet as we thought. But I'll get it somehow! Damn it, I deserve it!

Graham walked quickly in the falling rain to the local public library, a faint memory stirring in his brain. After half an hour in the reading room he found it in a three-week-old copy of the *Sunday Telegraph* Colour Magazine. A full colour picture of Emily Carstairs in jumpsuit and red crash helmet, parachute strapped to her back, leaping into space: 'The Freefalling Political Dynamo.' Graham made copious notes.

Outside the rain was still falling as he went into a steamed-up telephone kiosk. He dialled a number, inserted a coin; it slid through but the second time he got the connection.

'Alan O'Brien?'

'I'll get 'im.' The phone clattered down. There were hollow shouts in the background then the sound of footsteps.

'Alan. Graham. Wanna see you tonight. The George, you know where, nine o'clock.'

The man's voice rasped in a thick Irish accent, 'I'm busy. Some other time.'

'Alan,' said Graham softly, 'it was a personal request from Mr Klein.'

The phone went dead.

They drank lukewarm, flat halves of bitter and spoke above the noise of the jukebox.

'So what you doing now?'

'Going straight,' said the Irishman with emphasis, 'sausages, would you believe? I make sausages.'

'Miss the paras?'

'Best outfit in the world, mate. They'd piss through the IRA if the government would let 'em get on wi' it.'

'Heard you got one?'

'Too fucking right I did.' He gripped an imaginary rifle. 'Down the Ardoyne, early hours. Saw thc fucker creeping across the rooftops, think he was setting something up, we were a bit early. Crack, right through the fucking chest, you'd have thought he'd been hit by a train,' a look of grim satisfaction spread across the Irishman's face.

'How come they kicked you out then?' There was a sneer on Graham's face.

The Irishman snarled: 'Seems I didn't read him his little warning first. And afterwards they reckoned he wasn't carrying. Fucking boyos had it away with the Armalite like as not. I can tell a Provie with a Widow Maker from a civvy with his hands in his pockets.' He pulled at the beer. 'And what was he doing on the roof, eh, cleaning the chimneys?'

'But they didn't see it that way.'

'Well,' said the Irishman grudgingly, 'there'd been a bit of bother before that. Few complaints, you know. But the cunts are too soft. If it was the Jerries or the Russians they'd bulldoze the fucking Creggan, the Bogside, the Ardoyne, the whole fucking works. Flush 'em out then we could pick 'em off.'

Graham ordered large Scotches. He took an envelope out of his pocket and handed it to O'Brien. The Irishman greedily counted out the £100.

'Christ, Graham, you're a mate. From Mr Klein?'

'Purpose of the visit, Alan. Never forgets his own, Mr Klein.'

'I'm straight,' said the Irishman defensively.

'Sure you are. Tell me, do any parachuting now?'

'Whenever I can, which isn't often. Costs a packet. Greatest sensation in the world though.' A faraway look came into his eyes. 'Totally silent, floating through the air. Ground below you, fucking marvellous.'

Graham ordered more Scotch and gently primed O'Brien for details of parachuting, mentally noting them. The Irishman was getting drunk and recounting details of his military and civilian jumps.

'. . . so this wee girl, she'd done a few jumps mind you, freefall, the works, and she's given the instructor all this ass. And he says, "Eh lassie, any more from you and I'll supaglue yer pins".' The Irishman convulsed.

'Don't get it,' said Graham sourly.

The Irishman coughed and wiped his mouth, 'Well I told you. First jumps you go out on a static line – in case you forget to pull your cord,' he laughed again. 'When they think you're up to it you go out on your own. You've got an altimeter on the front of your chute. You watch the altimeter and pull the cord.'

'And?'

'The ripcord, laddie, is a piece of wire with an alloy handle. The wire runs to four stainless steel pins – this is most of the civvy chutes I'm talking about anyway – the pins are set into four cones. You pull the handle, Bob's your uncle, out comes the pins, out comes your chute – you hope.'

'And the supaglue?' Graham was all ears.

'Standard civvy parachuting joke is "I'll supaglue your pins". Meaning, this glue is famous, it bonds in seconds and an elephant couldn't break the seal. Blob of glue on the pin when you're packing the chute, pop it in the cone. You pull the cord, pin won't come out of the cone. Pack won't open. Bingo.'

'You're dead?' said Graham excitedly.

'Not quite,' said the Irishman. 'You've got a reserve chute round your middle to open when you've got over the shock of your main chute failing.'

'And how's the emergency chute fixed?'

'Same way,' said O'Brien, 'one ripcord, two pins in two cones.'

Graham forced a laugh. 'And if some bastard superglued one of those?'

'Yippee,' said the Irishman, making a plunging motion with his flattened hand, 'strawberry jam. Get it now?'

'Yes,' said Graham, 'I get it now.'

They drank until closing time. Outside the pub Graham said quietly: 'Alan, just one thing. If ever you have occasion over the next couple of months to remember this occasion. Don't.'

'Why should I?'

'No reason. Just remember not to. The R.U.C. still haven't solved that Dungannon Post Office job from 1978. We would hate to help them with their inquiries.'

'We were all pissed Graham, I swear it. They'd just got three of our lads with a lorry bomb; we thought, what the fuck, spoils of war. It was only a couple of thousand. I've got a wife and kiddie now.'

'Forget it Paddy. And forget tonight.'

'It's a promise Graham. Cross my heart and hope –'

'Don't hope that Paddy.'

Graham turned and walked away, his heart singing with triumph after a successful evening. Klein would be pleased. This wouldn't go wrong.

Graham turned the rented Ford Escort off the country lane near the perimeter of the airfield, switched off the engine and settled down to wait for darkness. Three telephone calls was all it had taken to locate the right one. Would Miss Carstairs be there tomorrow? Going up at three, they'd said. Never misses a Saturday if she can help. No message. The research had paid off. Graham uncrumpled the *Sunday Telegraph* cutting. The tiny picture, one of half a dozen, a grey metal locker, 'Emily Carstairs' stencilled on the door.

Dusk closed over the downs and Graham waited, patiently, stoically. Klein had accepted the risk. If the parachute was intact after impact they might find the tiny traces of glue. But she might come down in a lake or river and anyway Graham would be on hand to try and get to the chute before anyone else. It had to look like an accident but if it wasn't, only one person would suspect – Margot. And she was implicated. The drop was scheduled for the airport itself, a quiet country runway with just four planes and not scheduled for use other than the plane carrying the jumpers. So Graham was to stay in the vicinity and try to be first to the body. Risks, risks all the way but Klein had weighed them and found them to be worth it.

Night came down like a blanket. Graham locked the car and checked the contents of his overcoat's large outside pockets. He vaulted the low perimeter fence and padded silently towards the cluster of buildings several hundred yards away across the runway tarmac. The only lights came from the clubhouse, separated by a parking area from the other buildings. Voices echoed from the clubhouse and there was the sound of clinking glasses. Graham carefully went to the rear of the buildings, away from the parked cars. He took a short jemmy from his pocket, reached up, prised open a window and lifted the catch. He put a hand on the sill and lifted himself onto the window ledge. He reached an arm through and unlatched the main window, swung it open and slid through, landing silently on the balls of his feet. His body tingled and his jaw ached from the tension. He took out the flashlight, switched it on and was careful to keep the hooded beam pointing downwards. He quickly found the locker, fourth along. The stencilling had been done, paint fresh and new. He took out a long thin spike of metal and inserted it into the lock.

Five minutes later he put the tube of glue back in his pocket and quietly closed the locker door. He felt an enormous thrill going through him.

He shut off the flashlight, climbed out of the window and pulled them both shut. The noise rasped out in the darkness. He stood for a full minute, heart pounding, but the only noise was the sound of cheerful voices from the clubhouse. A man's voice started singing off-key. He loped across the tarmac in a crouch, started the car and drove slowly back to London. This was no time to get a speeding ticket.

He set his alarm for ten and got a good night's sleep.

The instructor made a random check of the chutes, missing out Emily's. She repacked hers after each jump and she was good and careful. He gave her another warning about delaying the opening. Twice in the last month she'd gone over the recommended time, bravado, foolishness, he didn't know which, but he whispered a quiet aside to her so the other two jumpers couldn't hear: 'No Red Devil stunts, okay?'

She smiled and nodded. The instructor, who was also flying the aeroplane, the other two jumpers, both men, and Emily climbed into the small Cessna 172. They got clearance from the 'tower' and took off heading east. It was cramped in the plane and Emily longed for the jump. She spent all her life in a world of people, ideas, intellectual action, power and the pursuit and use of it. Judging, calculating how men would react on given situations. It could be a dirty world. But when she launched herself into the air it was into another dimension and it cleansed her. With some people it was the sea. Once they were on the ocean they took on another outlook – part, as they were, of a different environment with different rules for survival.

With Emily it was the sky; the cool, clean air rushing against her face beneath the goggles. As she guided her body aerodynamically like a bird then felt that sharp tug and the incredible floating sensation, she was detached from the world of people. Free for those short moments to hang suspended in another world surrounded by the magical silence.

Roy Webber turned from the controls. 'Four thousand, we're a bit off but the wind should take you over. Watch the power lines.'

The three pupils smiled. Standard instructions, but they all knew how to control a chute and the lines were a full mile from the landing zone.

'Okay, Emily. First,' He shouted and added a thumbs-up in case his words were lost.

She opened the door and put a foot on the wing joist as the slipstream buffeted her face and upper body.

Graham watched the plane circling high in the clear blue sky. A tiny red figure detached itself. He did not know whether she was a lone jumper or, if not, whether she would be first out. He held his body rigid, heart pounding. Emily let herself fall backwards and felt the cold slap of air on her face, exhilarating and alive. She righted herself, spread her arms and legs and got her balance.

Out at four thousand, ten second free fall. She was counting in her mind, a glance at the altimeter. So good. So clean. The ground was a patchwork quilt below her. Life bubbled inside her.

Ten. Altimeter check. Now. Remember the instructor's

warning. She tugged the handle firmly. Nothing. Her heart jolted as the body pumped adrenalin into her veins. Don't panic. First time. Reserve chute. The ground seemed all around her now.

Her hand went for the reserve chute around her belly. She tugged firmly. A cry came from her lips and was snatched away. She tugged again. God have mercy. She fainted and her eyes rolled upwards in their sockets, her head fell forward and her crumpled body hurtled to its death.

The instructor was looking sideways as he banked the plane and keeping an eye on his watch, nine, ten. Open Emily. Come on you little bitch. Come on. 'Come on,' he was shouting now and the other jumpers were looking at him with alarm, 'you're cutting it fine. Open your bloody chute. For Chrissake open it.' The voice was a scream.

As the body impacted into the electric high tension cables that looped across the fields there was a massive shower of sparks, followed seconds later by a sheet of flame as the body dragged the wires to the ground.

Graham watched the display of death with fascinated horror. He revved his car and sped off in the direction he'd seen the body come down.

He saw the fire, stopped his car and ran across the field. A farm labourer, white-faced and shaking, rushed up to him. 'The power lines are down, you'll kill yourself.' Graham stopped and looked. A large red bundle was burning fiercely, and the grass all round was alight. Severed lines snapped and spat like live snakes. There was a strange, sweet smell which clawed at the throat. He could feel the nausea rising unwillingly within him. He heard the sound of a klaxon far away. He edged closer. It was a funeral pyre. Nothing would be left. He turned and ran back across the field. The farmhand was kneeling, his head between his knees, retching heavily. Graham slid the Escort away in a shower of mud from the rear wheels. Ten miles nearer London he found a public telephone kiosk, dialled a number and put in a coin. He said, 'A job well done boss.'

Instructor Roy Webber set down the Cessna heavily and taxied to a stop in front of the clubhouse. His face was a mask of grey, his knees weak. The two other jumpers clambered, shaken, out of the Cessna. A man in a blazer bearing an R.A.F. badge said, 'Good God, Roy what happened?' The instructor ignored him. He looked around at the knot of spectators. 'Anybody see her trying to pull the cord?' There were shaking heads. The ex-R.A.F. man said, 'It was too far away.' He repeated, 'What happened, Roy?'

'Ground fixation,' he stamped the ground, 'bloody ground fixation. I've warned her about it. I told her, before she went up, I told her. Leaving it late. I warned her a . . .'

He turned and vomited near the wheels of the Cessna.

Tommy was working up a sweat on the punchbag, his facial muscles contorted with effort.

Margot stood with Klein in the corner of the gym. He said softly, 'You heard the inquest verdict. She became hypnotised with the ground. It can happen. It's tragic, but being a practical man it does solve some of our problems, does it not?'

'Lewis, if I thought for one moment . . .'

'I can do lots of things, Margot, but I cannot persuade people to jump out of aeroplanes, forget to pull their rip-cords and burn themselves to a frazzle and black out half of Shoreham, now can I?'

She winced. But there was something else.

'Lewis, when I was in Venice, someone tried to kill me.'

It was a creditable bit of acting on his part, all the better for its show of indifference towards her and concern for his protégé. 'Tommy wasn't involved? I can't have that kid hurt.'

'Tommy wasn't involved, just me.'

'Vicious these Italians, always were.'

'He wasn't Italian. He spoke English. With a London accent.'

Oh Graham, it's a good job for you the Emily thing went right or you would be suffering from a severe earache.

'How do you know?'

'He spoke to me. He's a Cockney.'

'Let's not beat about the bush Margot, are you suggesting it has anything to do with me?'

'I'm suggesting nothing. But hear me out Lewis. I've spoken with Tommy. I understand he may have a slim chance of getting a crack at the title?'

'We're working on it. It's a long shot but the champ's been bled white. He wants to get his hands on some real money that his nigger brothers can't steal. There's some offshore bank in the Cayman Islands. A bank here could make the transfer but only if he earned it here for tax purposes – I don't know the ins and outs. But if the TV stuff works out all right he just might agree to get on a plane and give Tommy a chance.'

'He's come a long way very quickly.'

'So have we both. Make your point, Margot.'

'My point is, at his next fight Tommy very much wants me to be there, front row, where he can see me. Gives him encouragement.'

'So?'

'So if something happens to me, if I should slip in the shower or be mugged in Harrods, or my brakes fail or the million and one things that can happen to a girl in this wicked city, Tommy won't fight.'

Klein's eyes flashed to the sweating boxer.

'He won't fight?' Anger crept into his tone. 'I tell him when he fights, not you.'

'He won't, Lewis. He knows someone tried to kill me in Venice. If I die he's never going to set foot in that ring again, he's promised me.'

'And what if bubonic plague sweeps Belgravia and Knightsbridge?' Klein's mouth was curled in a sneer.

'Your problem. He's not stupid, Lewis, just because he's a boxer. He knows there's something strange going on and he has promised if I am killed he won't fight. I've told him that he is my insurance policy, and he doesn't know why, but he's promised.'

'And do you think I couldn't persuade him if you *were* unfortunate enough to have an accident?'

'You couldn't bank on it, Lewis.'

They fell silent and the only noise was the whoomph, whoomph as Tommy punished the bag.

Klein said, 'Spoken to Archie?'

'Yes,' said Margot glumly, 'it's over. Not the way they wanted it, but it's over.'

'How'd Dudley take it?'

'Bad, but he's getting over it. He knows nothing of course. Oh, Lewis. I kept my part of the bargain even though you, technically speaking, didn't have to keep yours. Barring mishaps you are on the list. Maybe six months or so but you can start planning your day trip to the Palace.'

'How kind.'

'You're evil, Lewis. Tommy should have nothing to do with you.'

'The world is evil, Margot,' he said evenly, 'I didn't make it that way, I just try and survive in it. And I wasn't,' he added bitterly, 'born with your built-in advantages.'

She half turned to go. 'Remember. If they are your dogs, call them off, or you'll lose everything.'

He watched her go, noting academically that she was a very beautiful woman. I have time Margot. I can wait. All things come to him who waits. He wrapped the cliché around him like a protective cloak.

# *Chapter Nine*

Klein put down the telephone and leaned back in his chair. He closed his eyes and pressed his fingertips together like a clergyman at prayer.

'What did he say, Mr Klein?' There was anxiety in Tommy's voice.

Klein stayed silent.

'Was it yes?'

'Tommy,' said Klein quietly, eyes still closed, 'in six weeks time you will be given the opportunity to fight for the heavyweight championship of the world.'

Tommy sprang to his feet, voice high-pitched: 'He agreed! He bought the deal!'

Klein opened his eyes and his face became a picture of sheer, unreserved delight. 'Lock, stock and bloody barrel.'

'Fantastic!' Tommy smashed his fist into his palm. 'Fantastic. I just can't bloody believe it.'

Klein swung his chair. He was smiling so much it hurt. 'Believe it Tommy. His tax lawyers have worked him out a nice little package. The TV rights are the clincher; world-wide and it brings the receipts up to a million and a half U.S. dollars. He gets two thirds after the normal deductions, because he is the champ. And *you*,' he pointed at the flushed, excited face of Tommy, 'should step out of that ring a quarter of a million pounds better off.'

Tommy shook his head in disbelief.

Klein said with a laugh: 'Don't order your luxury launch yet. There's *my* little slice for a start; Perry has to have his return on investment, there's Maxie, all the odds and sods, and not forgetting our gallant friends from the Inland

Revenue to satisfy. But,' he grinned broadly, 'there should be a little left over to stick in the bank.'

Tommy shook his head again. 'I just can't bloody believe it.'

Klein came from behind his desk. 'And that's just the start, son. You're going to beat Lucius. Beat him!' His voice rose. 'After that *you're* the champ, *you* get the big purses.' There was a faraway look in Klein's eyes. 'The first British heavyweight champion of the world. Do you realise what that will mean, Tommy? Your future will be assured. You will be rich. You will be a national hero. You'll go down in history. Every door will be open to you.'

Tommy's head swirled with the possibilities. A whole world seemed in his grasp.

Klein sat on the edge of his desk, as if savouring the future. Lewis Klein, manager of the heavyweight champion of the world. Sir Lewis Klein. A long way, Lewis lad.

Tommy said sharply, 'Let's win it first.'

As if suddenly awakened from a dream, Klein's face cleared and it read business. 'Too right son,' he said briskly, 'too damn right. You're going to train harder than you've ever trained in your life. Lucius is the best you'll ever meet, make no mistake about that. BUT YOU ARE BETTER! Understand me? You can beat him.'

Confidence welled up in Tommy: 'I understand. I can beat him.'

'You bet your sweet arse,' said Klein thickly, and there was a choke in his voice.

He went back to his desk. Six weeks. Six weeks to make you an even better and fitter fighter than you already are. By God that Lucius is going to think he's got lead in his boots.

'When will it be announced? Formally, I mean.'

'Kennedy's the promoter. That was him I was talking to on the phone. He's in New York. Should get the thing finalised by tomorrow and they'll announce it first from Lucius's camp. Mid-afternoon tomorrow here, I expect. Then, my son, you are going to be one big celebrity.'

Tommy stood up to leave, still shaken by the news.

'Just one thing, son,' Klein did his best to keep his voice casual. 'I was having a chat with Margot recently, and she said something that puzzled me.' Klein tried hard to look puzzled.

'She rambled on something about, "If she gets killed in a car crash, you won't fight", maybe I've got it wrong. Seems she's paranoid someone's trying to kill her. Though what the hell it has to do with you I can't fathom. Can you?'

Tommy said defensively, 'Somebody did try to kill her, in Venice. I saw her afterwards. She wasn't making it up. I know her.'

'You'll never know her son, never. Never in a million years. You're from different planets. You could be the richest man in the world and you'd still be like chalk and cheese. And the biggest gulf? Well, you just can't conceive of the fact that she is out to screw you just as you were out to screw those birds you picked up at the palais as a teenager.' Klein kept cool. 'But what's all this about you refusing to fight if she gets hurt?'

Sheepishly Tommy said, 'Well, I did say that because I thought . . . I thought, that's what she wanted me to say. But it's not really true.'

Klein resisted the temptation to smile. Margot, I think someone just tore up your insurance policy.

Tommy looked at Klein. The things he had heard about this man, the rumours, the lies? They couldn't be true. Couldn't.

'No,' said Tommy, 'it's not that I *wouldn't* fight if something happened to Margot, It's just that, well, *if* anything happened to her, I *couldn't* fight.'

Klein's face went pale. 'Couldn't you?'

'No,' said Tommy, 'I just know, 'that I couldn't fight if anything happened to Margot.'

Josiah Ezekiel Lucius draped himself across the leather sofa of the hotel suite like a grizzly bear at grips with his prey. To say he was a massive man was a massive understatement.

He was six feet four of solid muscle and bone. His shoulders and arms, the powerhouse of his armoury, dominated his body, framing the broad chest and tapered, muscled waist. He moved with astonishing grace for a big man, a cat-like quality about his poise and balance. To look at him was to look at sheer menace. His head was shaved and oiled to billiard ball smoothness, giving the effect of a dangerous, black cannon ball waiting to be fired.

His face was sullen and set, scarred by years of fighting in the ring and years of fighting outside it. But it was the eyes that spoke of danger. Hooded and immobile, deep brown pupils and the whites flecked with yellow, they peered out at a hostile world.

The closest confidante, the most confident interviewer had wilted under the unblinking stare.

And if the looks were not sufficient to convince of the menace a glance at his short life history was.

He was twenty-seven years old and had been champion for two years. He was born the fifth and youngest son of a poor Philadelphia family and christened Josiah Ezekiel; names plucked from the Bible for this most unpeaceful of men. His childhood followed the classic ghetto pattern. A harassed undernourished mother too tired to cope with this last, unwanted, un-needed child; an unemployed alcoholic father who simply didn't care to.

His schooling was intermittent. He learned to read and write but only just. Whatever knowledge Josiah Ezekiel Lucius acquired was street knowledge, hard learned. How to survive in the ghetto, where everyone from the cop on the street to the slum landlord is against you. He learned how to steal a six-pack from the liquor store; how to run faster than the ageing cop who chased you; how to rifle an unlocked car in twenty seconds or roll a drunk lurching down a quiet alley to urinate. He graduated at fourteen years old to a juvenile detention facility where he learned how to hate.

At seventeen he took a variety of jobs, packer in a warehouse, errand boy, soda jerk, until he was drafted. Already he was the toughest kid in the neighbourhood, black or white, proving it in a dozen and more fierce fist and boot fights. Taunted, he volunteered for the Marine Corps and to his delight was accepted. He relished the hard physical exercise, the open air life and the equality between black and white under the harsh discipline.

Insulted by a white marine in a bar on the Pacific island of Guam, Lucius started a brawl. Two passing M.Ps knocked both protagonists unconscious with their billy clubs and hauled them away in a jeep. It was to be the turning point in Lucius's life. An officer told the two offenders: 'If you want to fight you can do it in the ring. We're looking for champions in the Marine Corps.' The two men donned gloves and the officer said: 'Now sort your differences out like men – in a fair fight.'

It was hardly that. Gloves or no gloves, Lucius had the man on the canvas in thirty seconds, and the Marines had a boxer on their team. Back in San Diego Lucius was coached and trained until he delighted the elite corps by k.o.'ing the Navy champion in two rounds.

At twenty-three, with thirty amateur fights behind him, he left the Marines after an incident in which an Alabaman NCO had his jaw broken in two places after a racial remark.

For a year Lucius drifted through the south-western United States, taking odd jobs, until he walked into a small bar in Tucson, Arizona and met a thin, small man with a shock of red hair called Patrick Joseph Maguire. Maguire was from Brooklyn, New York, and had grown up wondering why his family was the only one on the block that celebrated Christmas. He'd run two no-account boxers until he moved west with his capital tucked in a money belt close to his body.

His capital was now a bar with six stools, five tables and assorted glasses and bottles. It wasn't the better part of Tucson and he was looking for someone who could persuade the customers not to rearrange the furniture every Saturday night. 'Joe' Lucius seemed like the man. Maguire's judgement proved right. A look from the Philadelphia boy and argumentative drunks had a habit of quickly patching up their quarrels without resort to violence. And on the odd occasions when Joe had to go into action Maguire watched him with a practised eye, and liked what he saw. He persuaded Lucius to spar and it was enough to launch the second boxing managerial career of the New York Irishman.

In two years Lucius became the sensation of the boxing world, starved for personalities after the likes of Ali, Frazier, Norton and Foreman had quit the ring. Lucius was the typical American Negro boxer. Rough and tough, he punished his opponents, clubbing them brutally. He reminded critics of Sonny Liston in his heyday.

Behind the hooded eyes, a potential killer. He seemed to feel no pain, and with an almost sadistic streak would sometimes ease off when an opponent was ready for the *coup de grâce*, the more to prolong the agony. The TV boys loved him. No two minute knock-outs with Lucius, not that s.o.b., they'd brag as they planned their advertising slots; he'd kept 'em up past the tenth and threw in a lot of blood for good measure.

Before each fight he went on a spartan routine, living like a monk – an image accentuated by the hooded garb he always seemed to wear outside the ring during training – up in the Adirondack mountains of New York state. Few penetrated the Lucius camp, only selected journalists and TV men at selected times, and rumours grew of secret seances and raw flesh eating which added to the mystical, menacing quality of Lucius.

He won and successfully defended the title in the space of eight months. Then something happened to Lucius. He woke up and realised he was a rich man and had done nothing else with his money but buy his mother a new home and pay the clinic fees for his father.

He was like a child given eight weeks' accumulated pocket money. He rowed with Maguire, who wanted him to fight again, and the Irishman went quietly back to his bar in Tucson. Lucius then set out to show the world he was no longer the Philadelphia ghetto kid. He took long holidays, touring the world; gazing open-mouthed at the Taj Mahal, the Eiffel Tower, the Acropolis and the other picture post-card wonders of the world like a child. And always the big Polaroid hanging from his massive fist. In four months he met, proposed, married and was separated from a beautiful black New York model. She repaid his brief generosity by sueing him for half his wealth. He flirted with the Black Muslims and gave a reported donation of a million dollars to their funds. Wherever there were nightclubs there was 'Joe' Lucius, one or more pretty girls draped like rag dolls on his tree-trunk arms. He drank champagne like Schlitz. And all the while the patient Maguire sat back and served beer, polished glasses and waited.

And one day the phone rang. The Inland Revenue Service was pursuing Lucius more implacably than any opponent had ever dared. Accountants were pushing figures in front of him that could have been the checkout list at a supermarket for all he knew. He was being asked to sign cheques. So he turned to the only man in whom he had ever really put trust and not been disappointed, Paddy Maguire.

Maguire flew back to New York and locked himself in a room with two accountants and a mountain of papers and a lot of hot, strong coffee. Twelve hours later he emerged with the verdict.

'Not good, Joe. You've earned, but you've spent. Especially that damned fool thing with the Muslims. Sarah's going to screw you for every dime, the bitch, and the IRS want a big, big slice and they ain't going to take no for an answer. You need a fight Joe, and a good one.'

The black man inclined his head in the suggestion of a nod. 'Who?'

It didn't catch Maguire on the hop. He'd been preparing for just such an eventuality for weeks.

He said slowly, 'You've got a choice.' He had to let it look like Lucius's decision. 'Kovacs, Roberts maybe. They're not big numbers but it'll pay your tax.'

'Anybody else?'

'Limey guy. European champion,' he jerked his thumb

towards the room from which he'd come. 'They reckon they could do a deal if you fought over there.'

Lucius's eyes became even more hooded. 'I don't throw no fights.' There was thunder in the face.

Only Maguire could have got away with it. 'Not that kind of deal you dumb sonofabitch, a financial deal, a tax deal. You fight in Europe, one of those fancy London banks pays you, all the money goes to the Bahamas or the Caymans or somewhere. You pay the British tax people, the IRS here don't get a bite. I don't know the dollar signs but they reckon they can swing it so you get to keep a large slice.'

'How much?'

'Hard to say, but we ain't had a Limey fight for the title for years. Good TV. There's Limeys all over the world, I'm an Irishman and I know. Australia, Canada, New Zealand, Africa, they're like flies. Worldwide TV should net you half, maybe three quarters of a million bucks, maybe more.'

The black face was impassive but the lips moved. He said, 'I'll take it.'

That had been a week earlier. Now Lucius lay on the sofa listening to the finalised deal. When Maguire had finished Lucius said, 'What's the rundown on Booth?'

Maguire flicked open a typed sheet: 'Came up the hard way, but quick. Young, strong, taken punishment, can punch.' His eye scanned the sheet. 'Nearly killed some Eyetalian. Ambitious, shrewd manager. He's a Cockney. Know what a Cockney is?'

Lucius attempted to smile and his face seemed to shift like a mountain before an avalanche. 'Sure. I seen Mary Poppins. They talk like they was being strangled.'

Maguire laughed. 'The English aren't my favourite people either.' He threw down the sheet. 'Don't worry Joe. I don't think he'll be a problem. If I did I wouldn't be taking you over there.'

'Should be nice,' said Lucius languidly, 'I can see the Queen.'

'Look. You've not fought in a year. You've screwed and

drunk yourself round the world. That takes its toll. We're going upstate tomorrow and we're staying there till we board that plane at JFK. It's the whole works for you, you're going to hate me but I'm going to sweat that booze out of you. This guy might be better than we think, and we're not taking any chances. From what I hear of the way things are going in England they must have a few hungry fighters there too. Don't get careless.'

Lucius stared out from behind the rawhide inscrutable mask. 'Patrick, I'm going to whup that white motherfucker, but good.'

Maguire crinkled his lined face into a smile. 'And this white mother is going to make sure you do just that.'

They sat in Tommy's quarters as the summer dusk settled gently on the countryside.

Tommy stroked her hand gently. 'I don't know how you even got in here. According to Klein I was to live the life of a monk. I'm glad you did, but how?'

'Threatened to scream – and also promised on my honour,' Margot crossed her heart, 'that I would do nothing an elder sister wouldn't do. *I* also want you to win that fight.'

'Just seven days. I can hardly believe it.'

'How do you feel?'

'I've never been fitter, but it's not just the fitness. I *know* in my heart I can do it. If I was honest, I've always known. Deep down I've always known I could do it if I got the chance.'

'I'm sure you can.'

There was a pause and they could hear the wood pigeons cooing from across the lake.

'And afterwards?'

'You'll be a busy man. A celebrity.'

'I won't be too busy for you.'

'That's nice.'

He gripped her hand. 'Leave him Margot. After the election, leave him.'

'Tommy I can't, you *know* I can't, the scandal would

destroy us both, particularly if they suspected something had been going on before.'

'You could. You *could.* People do it all the time now, no one's shocked any more. For a bit perhaps, but it soon dies down.'

'You've never seen the press *really* in action.'

'I'd be rich, Margot. We could go anywhere in the world we liked.'

'Like Venice?'

'You're still worried?'

'Yes, yes, you could say I was still worried. It isn't every day someone tries to kill you.'

'But why, why Margot? Why would anyone want to kill you?'

Margot leaned back on the sofa. 'I don't know. Unless it has something to do with you and me.'

'I don't understand. I just don't. Only a handful of people can possibly know and they wouldn't . . . Margot, you can't think it was Perry or anyone.'

She put her face deep in her hands and the words came out muffled: 'I don't know Tommy, I honestly don't. Maybe I got it wrong, maybe it was some Italian maniac, but I could swear he spoke English. I'm sure. But I was frightened. I don't know . . . maybe I'm becoming paranoid. But Tommy, promise me – if anything happens to me, don't fight.'

Tommy was baffled. 'I've promised. I mean, I don't think I *could* ever fight again if anything happened to you, but *why*? *Why*? Nothing makes sense.'

'Just promise.'

'I promise.' He kissed her softly on the lips.

She said: 'I'm trying very hard to remember my vow.'

'And afterwards, is there a promise you can make?'

'Tommy, we're not children.'

'I . . .'

'Don't interrupt, just listen, please. For the first year we're going to have to be discreet, a damn sight more discreet than we've been up to now. After that, if all goes well and Dudley is secure I'll announce a trial separation.'

'Margot . . .'

Her voice was harsh. 'It's the only way. Dudley is a fine man and I'm not going wilfully to make it any worse for him than I can help. After that, who knows, maybe it will work for us. We have a lot in common, but we have a lot that separates us. Remember that.'

'No blue blood in my veins.'

She put two fingers to his lips. 'Don't, Tommy. I don't have to tell you what I feel for you. But we're grown-ups, let's not play games. If you care for me as much as you say, you'll wait. Remember if you . . . *when* you become champion you'll be able to pick and choose from a thousand girls. Give it a thought.'

'I don't want a thousand girls, I want you.'

'And I want you too. Remember when we first made love, I said: "You're a fine man Tommy", and I meant it and still do. If we rush it or do it wrong we'll regret it for the rest of our lives.'

He kissed her. 'I'll wait, and I'll win for you on Saturday.'

She left the room quietly as the night began to enter.

Tommy forked back the last of his steak and placed his knife and fork carefully across the empty plate. Klein, Perry and Maxie still ate, noisily. Klein said through a mouthful of food: 'Video for half an hour. Then bed.'

'Okay.'

Tommy stood up and walked to a telephone on a polished oak sideboard. He punched out a number from memory.

Klein watched him uneasily. 'Who you calling?'

The answer went into the mouthpiece: 'Margot? Tommy. Great. You? Good. Good trip home? Great. Thing I forgot to mention, stupid, should've been the first thing.' Tommy swivelled so he was facing the three eating men: 'The fight. You've got a ticket? Oh good. Front row, fantastic. Now remember, Margot, I want you to be there, you're my mascot, my lucky charm.' Tommy's voice was strained, nervous. Little Rock Hudson, thought Klein, put up to it by that bitch. Come on, lad, play out the show, I'm getting the message.

'You miss the bus to Wembley, I'm sitting in my dressing room until you get there.' Tommy's eyes bored into Klein's, and the manager knew Tommy meant business. He looked hurriedly away.

'So don't forget, I want a wave as soon as I get in the ring. You too. Take care of yourself.'

Tommy came back to the table and picked up the half-empty glass of orange juice.

Klein pointed a finger at him. 'That's the last one. You ask my permission to phone. Next time you see or speak to Margot is at the fight – *after* the fight. All she gets at the ring-side is a little wave. Savvy?'

'I savvy.' Tommy looked at Perry, who was more interested in his *filet mignon* and Beaujolais Villages: 'I just hope she gets there on time.'

Stupid little sod can't even pick out the right villain. If he wasn't the best boxer in the world I would be tempted to hand him over to Graham. 'She'll be on time Tommy,' said Klein evenly, 'I'll make sure of it.'

It was a warm, June night, soft and limpid with a touch of humidity, but a sky clear and dark blue, twinkling with summer stars. Normally it would have been a night for sitting outside a country pub drinking and laughing with friends, or perhaps just leaning outside the front door talking to a neighbour. A night of contentment, time to feel the warm air on your face and savour the evening fragrance. Evenings like this were rare enough not to be wasted huddling round a glowing TV set.

But all over Britain, this night, millions of families were doing just that; perspiring slightly behind closed doors. In pub and club bars, sweating, jostling customers elevated their eyes to the giant colour televisions. Hundreds of thousands of drinking extensions had been granted for the occasion, so that the dreaded cry of 'Time, gentlemen please' would not disturb the big night. Night shifts at factories all over the nation reported mass absenteeism, and everyone who had to be out or working strove desperately to make some private arrangement to be near a television set. By mid-evening electricity generating stations monitored a massive upsurge in demand for supply as sets throughout the country were switched on.

And all over the world from the Pacific coast of Canada to the Mid-levels of Hongkong, in towns drenched with tropical rainfall and baked at all times of day and night by hot sun, men who hadn't set foot for years in 'U.K.' as they quaintly called it, turned on their sets and thought of England.

With less fervour, more cynicism, but no less interest millions of Americans turned on their sets at lunch or tea-time and settled back with a cold beer.

At 10 p.m. Greenwich Mean Time, Tommy Booth (Great Britain) would meet Josiah Lucius (United States of America) for the heavyweight championship of the world.

Wembley Stadium, the archaic but fadingly majestic showpiece of British stadia, was to be the host. And already one hundred thousand people were in its seats and tiered stands, eyes riveted on a tiny square patch of light in the centre of what was normally the playing arena. Without binoculars they would see only tiny matchstick men, and would have got a better view, plus the benefits of commentary and playbacks, had they stayed home in front of their televisions. But they wanted to be there; had paid black market prices, bargained, hustled, begged, borrowed and in some cases stolen, to get a ticket. They wanted to smell the atmosphere, feel it; to be able to say in years to come: 'I was there the night Tommy Booth fought Lucius.' Or, dare it be said, let alone thought, perhaps one day: 'I was there the night Tommy Booth won the world title.' And here they were, and no one could rob them of this moment. They had only one envy, and that was reserved for the four thousand élite who sat in the rows of chairs which fanned out from the ringside onto the covered playing area. Those tickets had been changing hands for as much as

£1,500, and title jostled celebrity, fame rubbed shoulders with wealth for this fight of the century.

The special covering, which was to have shielded the ring in case of rain, had been removed. There was not a cloud in sight and the Met. men promised no rain until dawn. For once everyone believed the Met. men. God had smiled on this June evening. The postage stamp ring, a blaze of light, sat empty like a Shakespearean stage waiting for the actors to give it life.

Dudley kissed Margot gently on the forehead – 'I'll no doubt be asleep when you get in, if you're definitely going to the reception.'

'I promised.'

'Of course. I'll take supper at the club after the meeting and have an early night.'

Margot wrapped the towel around her, her body fresh and alive from the fragrant perfumed bath. She said, 'You must be the only man in Britain who's not going to see the fight.'

'Politics darling. Election in a month, it's important we work. But I certainly wish the lad luck.'

'Don't work too hard.

'I seem to have had so much to do since Emily . . .'

She took his hand. 'You promised not to brood. Win the election darling. For the country and all of us. Emily wouldn't have wanted you so distracted.'

'Of course, of course. What time is the car coming to pick you up?'

Margot took an onyx hairbrush from the dressing table and curled it through her hair. 'Seven, Klein said. He's sending Graham. It seemed rather early to me, but there'll be an awful lot of traffic.'

'You're not doing pictures tonight?'

'No. Jostling and pushing with a lot of Fleet Street men is not my forte. For the moment I've done my little bit towards Tommy's career. They're hoping to produce a soft-back scrapbook on him next month. It was to be before his next fight but I understand the Lucius deal came up rather quickly.'

'I'm sure it'll be marvellous darling,' he kissed her again on the forehead. 'I must be off.' She heard the front door slam behind him.

She took a red gown from her wardrobe and laid it on the bed. She unwrapped the long bath towel from her body, put on her knickers and bra, arranged her hair and made up quickly but expertly.

A faint muffled noise came from the small, unused service kitchen directly below her room. She listened but there was nothing. A trace of fear touched her and she went to the bedroom door, listened; but there was only silence. She shouted, 'Dudley, darling. Did you come back for something?'

Silence greeted her.

She went uneasily back to her room and slipped into the red dress. She took the gold embossed ticket from a drawer of her dressing table and popped it into her handbag. She took a light fur from her wardrobe and looked at her watch. Seven o'clock. She turned off the lights, closed the bedroom door, walked along the long landing and down the sweeping curved stairs.

It echoed like a pistol shot. The sound of a heavy heel on the tiled floor of the hall. She froze in horror, hand clutched to the balustrade. There was someone in the house. She edged her way slowly down the stairs. The front door was thirty feet away. If she could only get to the door. It was the alleyway in Venice; she could feel the dampness, smell the canal. Her right foot touched the tile of the hall and clanged eerily. Graham was due at seven. If she could get to the door. The things she had thought about Graham, her mind reeled. Now he was the one who could save her. Please, Graham. She was praying. Please. She took a pace down the hall, and a figure moved in the shadows.

Her stomach was hollow and blood pounded in her ears. She felt dizzy and sick. Where was Graham? Where was Graham?

The figure detached itself from the shadows and she gave a cry of relief.

'Graham, thank God, thank God. God I was terrified, I thought it was an intruder.'

Her relief turned to anger. 'What sort of silly game was that? I suppose Dudley let you in? Don't you ever do that again. And don't remain in my house without making your presence known. I will not permit it. Now let's get on our way.'

Graham moved forward a pace, a tight smile on his lips, his cheeks bloodless. 'I made a mistake in Venice, Margot. You made a fool of me. You called me names – you told Tommy I was a pervert, turned him against me. You and Tommy were laughing at me. But it won't happen again.'

'It's all in your imagination, Graham.'

The voice. That voice. 'Die you bitch.' It flooded back. All the time it *was* Graham, Graham. Then Klein? It must be Klein. But she had warned him, he wouldn't dare. Her mind raced as the icy tide of fear began its numbing journey through her veins. An invisible hand clutched at her throat and no sounds would come. Graham was inching forward, almost imperceptibly, the glinting knife as if by magic in his hand.

'No cameras to save you tonight, eh Margot?'

Scream. The brain commanded, scream, but the voice would not obey.

'You'll wish,' he said flatly, 'I had done it in Venice. I'm going to make you suffer.'

He was an arm's length from her now and the right hand darted forward like a striking snake. She felt a blow like that from a fist in her side, and a dull pain. He pulled back and smiled.

She found herself speaking, as if her brain had taken direct command, the general going to the front line in time of dire crisis.

'You fool. You're killing yourself as well as me.'

He laughed, but there was a hint of unease in the eyes. It was a strange thing for a woman facing death to say.

'Klein will kill you for this.' She gambled. Klein doesn't know. It's just Graham.

'Klein will never know; you were dead when I arrived, which will be,' he looked at his watch, 'in about thirty minutes' time. The front door was open, I found you in the hall. My car is having a puncture repaired ten minutes walk away and I am with it. I have two witnesses to confirm it.' He smiled confidently. 'I think Mr Klein would approve, anyway.'

She shook her head and a fire leaped in her side, sending waves of pain. 'You fool. I've got a deal with Klein. If I'm not at the fight tonight Tommy won't go in the ring. Klein knows that. He'll kill you Graham, he'll kill you.'

Unease swept through Graham. He moved forward. 'You're lying.'

Her words came now molten soft, fuelled by the heat in her side. 'I swear it. If I am not there, you are dead.'

'Klein wouldn't make a deal with you.'

'Tommy *did* and Klein knows. Tommy knows someone tried to kill me in Venice. He promised me, if I die he doesn't fight. If I'm not at the ringside he'll not fight Lucius. Klein loses the championship, the knighthood my husband can give him, *everything* – and you'll pay.'

Graham was truly frightened of only one man, Lewis Klein. His head reeled with confusion. She knew about Venice. He had to kill her. But if what she said was true, Klein would . . . He shook his head to clear it of the vision. Anxiously he said, 'If . . . if I don't . . . if I take you to the fight . . . then what?' He pointed to the small flower of blood, deeper red on the red dress.

'It's nothing. I'll tell my husband I fell on one of the kitchen knives. I won't tell Klein.' She threw him a weapon. 'Tommy and I have been to bed together, if ever I tell Klein you can tell my husband. We'll both owe something to each other. You'll never come near me again.'

She was at the edge of panic now, gambling desperately for her life; talking with the artificial control of a person on the border of hysteria.

Graham thought, his eyes closed, the stiletto hanging loosely in his hand. Like a child he said, 'You promise?'

She put out a hand and touched him diffidently on the arm. 'Yes,' she said wearily, 'I promise.'

They took a taxi to the garage and drove through the heavy traffic towards north-west London. Despite the warm night Margot pressed the fur tightly to her. The dull pain had subsided now, but she could feel the warm blood on her stomach, soiling her underslip and soaking the fabric of her gown. She was cold and pulled the coat even closer as they neared the stadium.

Klein spoke one sentence before they marched into that cauldron of sound. 'Tonight Tommy you're fighting for your life out there.'

They emerged into the open and the noise of a hundred and four thousand voices hit them like a tidal wave. 'To-mmy, To-mmy.' The noise made Klein flinch but Tommy's face was impassive as he half walked, half ran along the carpeted path to the ring, arms swinging in the red dressing gown. Klein, Maxie and a praetorian guard of uniformed policemen were his escort. He climbed into the ring and acknowledged the crowd, their sound rising and falling like waves on a beach. He looked quickly round the ring and caught sight of Margot in the front row, sitting next to Graham. He shook his glove in greeting and she replied with a jerky, puppet-like wave.

Lucius was already in the ring, the hooded, menacing head impassive and immobile, leaning insolently on the ropes. Tommy spotted Bannerman in his ringside commentary position and winked cheekily. Bannerman, despite himself, found he was winking back. You'd got to agree the kid had guts. At the introduction Tommy found the champion's eyes boring through him, penetrating, disturbing. He mentally switched off and concentrated on the fight ahead.

At the bell a deep, throaty roar went up from the arena and Tommy and the champ circled cautiously. There was a flurry of punches with neither man really connecting, and they spent the whole of the first circling and punching from long range, scouts testing the power of the enemy.

In the second Lucius came through punching hard, and Tommy replied, skipping himself out of trouble to cheers from the crowd. The two men clinched and locked, sending blow after blow to each other from short range. Margot put a hand to her side and it came up wet and sticky with dark blood. It was a bad cut. She thought ironically how wise she had been to choose her red St Laurent tonight. After the fight she would get first aid.

The third was fierce and brutal. Lucius punished an attack by Tommy with clubbing rights to the body, but Tommy managed a long straight left which caught the champion flush on the chin.

Everything Tommy did was cheered, out of hope, desperation and relief. For the fight cynics every blow survived, every punch delivered, every round gone was a plus for the challenger. At least he'd lose with honour, and perhaps there was even a small chance . . . ?

By the eighth both boxers were bruised and sore, and the TV commentators were getting more and more hoarse. They'd almost exhausted their treasure chest of adjectives. It was a great, great fight. Not a classic but a blood and guts encounter, and they beat classics hands down every time.

Supreme champion, magnificent challenger. Two giants locked in mortal combat.

In the ninth Tommy launched an attack and Margot found herself on her feet screaming madly with the rest of the crowd. She was no longer an individual, she was absorbed into the mind of the crowd, responding to its corporate will. Then she was sitting and hushed, biting her lower lip as Lucius contemptuously clubbed Tommy into a corner. Tommy's right eye was bruised, sore and swelling. A trickle of blood was coming from Lucius's nose. Tommy powered in a right hook and blood spurted from the champion, splashing the front row. She felt the blood, warm on her face and brushed it absentmindedly with the back of her hand. The woman on her right, eyes ablaze, had a scarlet trail down her blouse from the champion's blood and sat, oblivious, shouting, shouting.

The champion sat on his stool as Maguire staunched the flow: 'Sonofabitch, ain't bad.'

'Save your breath,' Maguire rapped.

Klein whispered fiercely, 'Keep in there Tommy. Keep surviving. Keep fighting.'

At the bell Lucius came in fast, his feet making no sense of his size. Tommy counterpunched, Lucius replied, then Tommy saw an opening and snaked a left through the champion's guard. Lucius reeled back on the ropes, arms open. The crowd bayed and Tommy moved in.

Tommy never even saw the right that hit him. It felt simply as though someone had tried to wrench his head from his shoulders, and chopped his legs from under him at the same time. He hit the canvas hard and felt a wave of blackness moving in to engulf him like an approaching night. With an effort of will he refused to let it swamp him, beating it back. He rolled up, and clambered to one knee.

'Three.' The voice of the referee seemed a long way away. In a micro-second a million things flashed through Tommy's mind, like the life of a dying man that flashes in front of him. *I'm going to be world champ, Mr Klein! Margot, the shower, Venice. 'Every door will open.' To be somebody. Sylvia, the flats, the school. A new life. He'd tasted a new life. To be world champion.*

'Four.'

Is this how it would end? On one knee beaten by a sucker punch? Remember the Texan, watch for the Brando caper. Suckered.

'Five.'

Klein was on his feet. He screamed, 'Get up Tommy. Get up at eight. Get up at eight.' He'd suckered him, they'd warned him a thousand times and he'd suckered him. The stupid little bastard. It would all go now, everything, down on one knee watched by millions of people. 'Get up. Get up.'

'Six.' Tommy was aware of the figure of Lucius, the hateful eyes, the bullet head, towering, glaring over him. Victor and vanquished. Tommy tried to rise but something in his legs lacked the strength.

'Seven.' Margot was screaming, tears pouring down her face. 'Tommy. Get up, get up.'

'Eight.' Damn you I'll not go out like this.

Quickly and seemingly without effort, Tommy stood up, and a collective sigh of relief rose from millions of throats.

The referee brushed Tommy's gloves and checked the boxer's eyes. It was a hard one, should have k.o.'d him but Booth was still functioning. Lucius rushed in. I've gotta finish this s.o.b. while he's still on automatic pilot. But how the hell did he get up from that?

How Tommy survived that round would be a talking point for boxing fans for decades. He ducked, he weaved, he closed up, he soaked up a barrage of punches as Lucius threw every punch he knew.

Margot was tired now, her head was pounding and she felt dizzy. The whole of the lower part of her body seemed wet. Beneath her chair a pool of blood was forming, unnoticed in the darkness, growing larger by the minute. In the next, Tommy played it careful, boxing, moving, husbanding his strength, caution in every step. In the twelfth he caught the champion with the first good blow since his knockdown, and the crowd bayed its approval. The boxers' bodies glistened as the humidity rose and the sweat streamed from them under the hot TV lights and the pressure cooker atmosphere of the stadium.

At the bell Graham looked at Margot. Her face was deathly pale: 'Maybe we should get that seen to.' The knife had gone in, he knew that. It wasn't meant to be the death blow. He was going to make her suffer. She shook her head. 'After the fight.'

There was only one existence now, only one reality for Tommy. It was to be locked in this private world of pain with Lucius. Tommy no longer heard the crowds, felt the lights, the glare, the heat. His whole mind was concentrated on the figure who clubbed and hurt his body and who was clubbed and hurt in return. Maxie had told him, 'You're way behind on points, work, work.'

But Tommy could sense something happening to Lucius. It was the kind of sixth sense that hunters have, an ability to realise what is not yet evident. Lucius was slowing. The year out of the ring, the booze, the night-clubs, the women, were coming back like vengeful ghosts to cut at his legs. Tommy began to pick his punches and the crowd roared, sensing something though hardly daring to hope. But Lucius took them and battled on. A minute to go in the fourteenth and Tommy slung together a tremendous combination of punches that sent Lucius back on the ropes. Tommy felt stronger than ever before, he dug and found new, hidden reserves of strength. He ploughed into Lucius with everything he could muster.

The stadium was a storm-whipped sea of noise. Everyone was on their feet. The last left took Lucius on the chin and he went down. Pandemonium.

'Five, six, seven.' The spectators were delirious. Three seconds from a British world champion.

'Eight.' The bell cut through the noise and there was a sigh from a hundred and four thousand throats like air escaping from a deflated balloon.

The champion's corner were working frantically on him. Maguire was looking into the glazed eyes of the champion. Another dumb bastard who thought he only had to turn up to win. All the training in the mountains hadn't been enough: 'Just stay on your feet. Three minutes, that's all. Just stay on your feet. You're way out on points, he can't get it back. Stay on your feet and you've won it.'

Klein took Tommy's face in his hands. 'Three minutes Tommy. Three minutes. Go out there and win it lad.'

Tommy looked out at the crowd. He could see the red blur of Margot's dress and imagined her urging him on, her moist lips parted, the dark eyes shining.

Maxie winked. 'You can do it Tommy.'

Margot felt utterly exhausted. She just wanted to lie down. But she must stay awake, cheer Tommy. The pool of blood had formed tiny rivers now which flowed slowly over her fingers as she clutched at her side.

Lucius came out with the fortress gate barred. Two arms, two gloves in a human portcullis. Tommy battered away. Everything he had, all the energy, the anger, the frustration, the desire and the ambition went into his punches. All his love and hate exploded on the body of the man before him. And slowly, agonisingly slowly, the arms were coming down under the onslaught. Tommy saw a glimpse of the chin and unleashed a right. Lucius reeled and opened. Tommy desperately threw in rights and lefts. A right hook now, bone-shaking, exploded on the champion's chin. Lucius went down on one knee, a glove clawing at his chin. How long to the bell? Get up you bastard. You're not finished, you're playing for time. GET UP..

Lucius stood up at eight and Tommy unleashed a right before the champion could cover. It was the last desperate punch of a desperate man, and it contained all that Tommy had left to give. For Margot, it was a punch for Margot. There was nothing more. It had to be the punch that paid for all.

Margot was on her feet cheering hoarsely, waves of nausea sweeping over her. Lucius tottered, checked, tried to right himself, then crumpled face forward onto the canvas. Margot was aware of the man falling, then she was sliding, slowly into a dark welcoming tunnel.

'Ten.' It was exactly six seconds to the bell.

The referee lifted Tommy's arm aloft and the stadium erupted.

No one noticed in the confusion. Margot was cheering with the crowd's one voice. Then her body slumped to the ground to lie in a dark, deep pool of her own blood.

And selected from Sphere's Fiction lists

## GOODBYE

W. H. MANVILLE

IT WAS ONE HELL OF A PARTY.
NOW THE PARTY'S OVER. BUT THE
HELL HAS JUST BEGUN . . .

Nick Blake wakes up after a drink-sodden party to find beside him a young woman, beautiful, naked – and murdered. He knows her. She is his wife, Clair. And it's the first time he's seen her in two years.

Clair's violent death plunges Blake into a living nightmare of suspense and fear as he sets out to untangle the grim mystery. In the process he finds himself forced to face terrifying truths about what men and women can do to each other – truths that could flay the soul of the strongest human being alive . . .

0 7221 0475 8 £1.25

GENERAL FICTION